54994693

PS
3606
A34
D68
2001

The Jewels of Allarion Book One

THE DOUBLE CROWN

By

Theodora Fair

NORMANDALE COMMUNITY COLLEGE
LIBRARY
9700 FRANCE AVENUE SOUTH
BLOOMINGTON, MN 55431-4399

DEC 3 0 2003

Copyright © 2001 by Theodora Fair

All rights reserved. No part of this book shall be reproduced or transmitted in any form or by any means, electronic, mechanical, magnetic, photographic including photocopying, recording or by any information storage and retrieval system, without prior written permission of the publisher. No patent liability is assumed with respect to the use of the information contained herein. Although every precaution has been taken in the preparation of this book, the publisher and author assume no responsibility for errors or omissions. Neither is any liability assumed for damages resulting from the use of the information contained herein.

This is a work of fiction. Names, characters, places, and incidents either are the product of the author's imagination or are used fictitiously. Any resemblance to actual events or locales or persons, living or dead, is entirely coincidental.

ISBN 0-7414-0848-1

Published by:

INFINITY PUBLISHING.COM

Infinity Publishing.com
519 West Lancaster Avenue
Haverford, PA 19041-1413
Info@buybooksontheweb.com
www.buybooksontheweb.com
Toll-free (877) BUY BOOK
Local Phone (610) 520-2500
Fax (610) 519-0261

Printed in the United States of America

Printed on Recycled Paper

Published November, 2001

Dedication

To my daughter Lyssa,
who began as little April,
and grew to become a strong, beautiful woman.
taf

The Prophecy

When the Sun and Moon
Shine double in the sky,
Then shall the cask be opened.
Then shall the Three be Five.

Twice two shall weep
When the eclipse is done.
Magic will die
When the Darkness is chained,
And the Star arches alive.

Chapter 1

The Dark Lord shifted his gaze to Tobar. "Have you found the boy?"

Tobar knelt on the cold stone floor. "No…no, My Lord," he answered, unable to control the tremble in his voice.

"Then what have you discovered on your little outing? Anything useful, or was it just a pleasure trip?"

"I…I think we found what we were looking for but…but I'll need help." Tobar carefully shifted his weight to ease the pain in his knees.

"He needs help! He needs help!" The Dark Lord roared.

"Let him continue, Lord Belar," said the dark-mailed attendant standing behind the throne. "Alright, alright, Borat." The Dark Lord sank back into his chair. "Let's hear whatever the petty princeling has to say."

Tobar shivered. The icy dark of Lord Belar's hall absorbed all human warmth. This was not the knowledge and power the Dark Lord had promised him. He dared a look at his master, then dropped his eyes once more.

"Is he dumb?" said Belar.

"Go on, Tobar," said Borat.

Tobar ran a nervous hand through his thick, dark hair and pushed his spectacles back up onto the bridge of his nose. He sucked in a breath then looked up at Lord Belar. "There is a cottage and…and." He stopped to clear his throat. "A cottage surrounded by five old oaks. The occupants are a woman and two children about the right ages…and...and a frequent visitor is a middle-aged mechanic."

"How quaint!"

"Hear him out, My Lord," Borat intervened again. "Tell him about the spell, Tobar."

"The cottage is set inside the oaks by someone who knows power. Neither Borat nor I were able to penetrate the circle yet the occupants come and go freely. We are certain we have found the children and their guardians are none other than Kyrdthin and his witch."

"So certain," snapped Belar. "Then why have you failed to snare such a small prize? A thirteen-year old whelp shouldn't give much fight to a seasoned warrior and an intelligent scholar."

"I'm no match for Kyrdthin's magic, My Lord." Tobar whimpered. "And …and I wouldn't want to cross with what he has made of my brother's woman either."

"Now he is afraid of witches and wizards." Belar laughed then sobered. "Stand up my dabbler in the dark arts, my ally in vengence. If all is as you say, Tobar, you will have all the help you need and a generous reward if you succeed." He laughed again then turned to Borat. "I want the boy alive and the girl too if you can manage. Dismissed."

Tobar rose stiffly and backed away. He tried to think of Analinne, strong, lovely Analinne, his precious wife. He was doing this for her and for their son. He took a step backward, another and another. And yes, he was also doing this to spite Frebar his twin. He knew he would win. He had seen it all in the Dark Lord's cards. Frebar had the kingdom, but he had Ann. It was twin married to twin just as the prophecy foretold. Tobar's numb legs continued to retreat. Again Belar's laughter shook the room. Frebar had laughed at the magic of twinning, and Tobar had laughed at his brother's ignorance. Now nobody was laughing except the Dark Lord.

Safely back from Belar's gaze, Tobar looked up. Haunches of black ice arched over the dais where his master sat toying with his deck of cards. The chandelier swung above him glittering like dragon's eyes, watching. Tobar shivered again. Columns of stone marched past where he stood, all the way from Lord Belar's massive carved chair to the heavy metal door at the rear of the hall. Tobar clutched his cloak tighter. Lord Belar shuffled then cut the cards. "Borat, Dokkal, Scarms, you three…no it must be five. Ged you too. Help our scrawny princeling here and get me that boy. To the star sign and away. Kyrdthin may well suspect you have found him with your inept meddling."

The four black-mailed warriors stepped onto the mosaic circle of stars set into the floor before the dais. Tobar gingerly took his place among them.

"Join hand to blade," said Belar. "Here they come, Kyrdthin, you white wizard ninny." He waved the card he had drawn. The torches guttered. A gray mist swirled about the five and they vanished.

Janille wiped the crumbs off the counter and put the two coffee cups carefully in the sink. She had used the cups from the good china today. Hawke had been here, large laughing, tipping his chair back against the bookcase, and letting it snap forward again to punctuate his tale. His essence still lingered. The closed kitchen door still promised to frame him for one last anecdote, one last goodbye. Their life was made of partings, but each time the bond grew stronger. Each time the distance grew less important. The home spell she wove between them could not be broken easily, though miles and years separated them time and time again.

She rinsed the baking pan and wedged it into the drainer. Streusel coffeecake, he had eaten the whole thing, washing it down with cup after cup of coffee. She tried everything she knew to keep him, yet every time he left her. Then he would return unexpectedly, hungry and full of stories.

Janille owed Hawke her life and now she patiently served him, guarding the precious children. It seemed only yesterday that he rescued her and infant April and found this alien but comfortable world for them. Then he brought her Willy, trusting her when he could trust no other. Her royal marriage and the dull, luxurious days at court seemed far away. She folded the dishtowel in her lap. Her hands were red and rough. Had they ever worn the rings of Frevaria's queen? Banished, living always in fear of discovery, she existed with only Hawke's infrequent visits to sustain her.

"Mother! Mother!" The screen door flew open. "Willy is gone," April cried. "He just disappeared." She sank down on a kitchen chair and buried her face in her hands. Her thick, dark hair fell down her back in a wild tangle.

Mechanically Janille's fingers began to braid her daughter's hair. "Tell me what happened from the beginning." Her voice came out steady and calm as she twisted the binder around April's braid, but a cold, sick feeling slid all the way down inside her to lodge like a tight knot in her stomach.

"There were these really weird guys at the bus stop, five of them," April began then stopped to catch her breath. "They asked our names and where we live."

"Oh gods! What did you tell them?"

"Nothing, mother. I just grabbed Willy and walked away. Then Willy disappeared. His hand slipped right out of my hand and he was gone just like that. I started to run and the one guy took after me, but the big dark guy said 'Let her go' and I just kept running until I got home. Mom I'm scared."

Janille collapsed into a chair beside her daughter. She had failed. She wept with self pity. In spite of all their precautions the Dark had found Willy. All the years of vigilance and worry were for nothing. So close to victory, but she had failed. They sat a long time without talking. Suddenly April jumped to her feet. "There he is!" she cried.

Will stood statue-like on the porch. His arms hung limp at his side. His eyes stared straight ahead.

"Willy! Willy!" April rushed out and threw her arms around him.

Will did not move.

"Willy what's wrong? What happened?"

Will's eyes were glazed. His lips moved without a sound.

"Let's get him in the house," said Janille. She took his hand. Will walked mechanically into the kitchen and sat down. "He'll be OK, April," she said. "It's only a dream spell." Tears of joy and relief streamed down her face.

"A spell? How do we get him out of it?" April shook Will by the shoulders calling his name, but it had no effect.

"He should come out of it by himself now that he is safe."

"What is all this with spells and people disappearing? Now I'm really getting scared," said April.

"Don't worry...." Janille started to say then glanced out the window.

Hawke's van was swinging into the driveway. "Well, I see you found the little man," he said leaning out of the car window as he came to a stop. He snapped his fingers. "How are you doing, Will?"

"Hi Uncle Hawke," said Will blinking his eyes and giving his head a shake. "Gonna stay for supper?"

"Please stay Hawke," Janille begged.

"You know I can't, Janie, not now. Keep the kids home for a few days. I'll get back to you as soon as I can."

Janille grabbed his hands. "Please, Hawke, please! I'm scared."

"Well, maybe you're right this time. Tell you what, let me go for now and I'll try to get back before night. Don't hold supper. It'll be later than that."

Janille breathed her thanks.

"You kids lay low," he said swinging up into his van. "And listen to your mom."

April watched him drive away. As the van rounded the curve onto the main road she saw a flash of silver and he was gone. A large black bird circled above the road . Then it too was gone.

The evening was quiet. No one was hungry at supper. April and Will had a million questions they didn't know how to ask. They were all afraid. For the children it was a nameless fear, but for Janille it was all too familiar.

Janille reached to draw the curtains. The full moon hung orange and swollen behind the oaks. Big black storm clouds rolled in from the west, rumbling and sparking. A jagged streak cut across the sky. It struck the westernmost oak with a sizzle. Thousands of spidery, blue fingers of fire encircled the dome of the sky. For a moment it looked like they were inside a gigantic cracked egg. Then she saw them, five dark figures crouched against the tree nearest the driveway. Lightening flashed again and they disappeared.

Janille busied herself washing dishes and putting aside an extra dessert for Hawke. April worked silently beside her, drying each dish with extra care. She watched her mother fold and refold the dishcloth staring out the window above the sink.

"Now what do we do?" said Janille when they were done.

"Tell us stories," said April.

"Yeah, tell us stories like when we were little and there was that big storm," said Will.

"I want my golden Princess story," said April.

"Aw, no!" Will objected.

"Shut up, Will."

"You think of what story you want, Willy, while I tell April's" said Janille.

Will folded up his legs Indian style and pretended not to listen. Janille ignored him.

"Once upon a time," she began settling back against the couch cushions. "When the world was young and the kingdoms of men were still touched by magic, there lived a nobleman's daughter. She was bored by her sheltered life in the manor, though her indulgent father supplied her with every luxury. She was a very curious girl who wanted nothing more than to learn about the world beyond her father's lands. Many nights she slipped away from her nurse to crouch on the balcony above the great hall listening to the men tell tales of adventure and intrigue."

Janille stopped. Lightening cracked and struck. The sky shimmered blue for an instant, then the roar was all around them. The windows rattled as the wind drove the torrent against the panes.

She continued a bit louder. "One day the young girl rode her pony into the neighboring forest. Soon she found herself on an unfamiliar road..." April was drawn into the familiar tale. The thrill of adventure changed to fear. She was lost. The tall trees all looked alike, the shadows menacing. Which way? The road turned and forked and forked again. "This way. This way," the birds sang. "This way," the squirrels chattered. "Follow, follow us," the leaves rustled. "Come to me," beckoned a finger of smoke drifting through the trees. The road turned again. The forest opened up into a small clearing. A thatched cottage stood in its center. Smoke curled lazily from the chimney. "Welcome child," said a voice out of nowhere, drawing her inside the cottage. A kindly, gray-robed man welcomed her. He let her explore his many books and ask questions about the curious tools and travel souvenirs that cluttered the tiny place...

"This is boring!"

Will's voice jerked April back to the present. "Shut up, Willy," she said giving him a shove.

"Willy, be patient. Your story is next," said Janille.

"But I know this one. She keeps sneaking off to see the guy until the king sees her when he's out in the woods hunting. He asks the magician for a magic potent to make the girl love him." Will made a vulgar noise. "It works and they get married." Will made the noise again. "And then they have this golden princess kid and..."

"Stop it, Will. That isn't the story at all," April complained.

"It is so. Then they get this other kid. It's dark like Delven. Everybody hates Delven so the king kicks them out and the magician rescues them and spooks them away to a secret place. Right?"

"You sure spoiled that, Will," said April.

"Yes, Willy," said Janille. "We all know the story. It is the telling that gives pleasure not knowing the ending."

The thunder had passed toward the east but the rain increased. It drove in sheets before the wind, shaking the little house.

"I know what we can do. Let's look for funnels," said Will heading for the window.

"No, Willy! Stay away from that window!" Janille yelled. She snatched him back into a fierce hug.

"Gees!" Will exclaimed wriggling free of her grasp.

The wail outside rose with a crescendo, calling, calling their names. The roar surrounded them. The house shuddered and the door flew open.

"Hell of a night!" boomed Hawke's voice.

"Get out of those wet clothes immediately," Janille ordered.

"Take this first," he said drawing a large package out from under his coat. "It's a birthday present for April."

She took the soaked grocery bag. It was heavy. A twitter and frantic rustling came from inside. "It's alive!" she exclaimed.

"You're lucky it didn't drown the way it is out there," said Hawke.

April unwrapped an ornate, golden cage. Inside a tiny blue bird panicked form perch to perch.

"Purrty Trebil, Trebil," said a voice from the cage.

"It talks!" April and Will chorused.

"Of course it talks. It's a mirror bird, something like a parrot only smarter. Come here little fella." Hawke stuck his finger in the cage. "It's OK."

"OK. OK. Purrty Trebil."

"Yes, you're a pretty bird. Now go to April," said Hawke

April cried with delight as the little bird landed on her shoulder.

"Sit down gently with him. That's it. Now everybody relax. Be quiet and just watch the fire. I have a story for you."

"We were telling stories when you came," said Will.

"And Willy messed mine up."

"It was only that boring golden princess thing."

"It was only boring after you messed it up."

"April! Willy!" Janille exclaimed.

"Quiet, kids," said Hawke. "This is a story you'll like." Hawke winked at April and gave Will a good-natured cuff on the ear. Then he sat down on the couch between them. "Horses galloped into the night…," he began.

"Where were they going?"

"Quiet, Will, and you'll find out. Horses galloped into the night," he began again. "The news was the worst. Prince Tobar was still missing…"

The fire flickered orange and gold. The children watched it dance taking on the shapes of the story. Hawke's voice became a drone matching their heartbeats. The orange fire was swept back and caught in a silver circlet. The face that appeared beneath the auburn tresses was wan and weeping. "We'll find him, Annie," said a shadowy gray voice. Another flame shot up and took form. "Don't worry sister. He will come back," said a fire-haired figure, twin to the first. The flames died down. The smoke swirled seeking the light in the corners of the room. Dark figures crept out, searching, questioning, surrounding a sunlit cottage. The glowing coals fell through the grate then winked out one by one until a single red eye throbbed in the depths of the blackness. Hollow laughter echoed, re-echoed, then faded.

Snap!

"…And so two searches converge," Hawke's voice concluded. He snapped his fingers again.

Will yawned.

"It was all so real!" April said dreamily. "I didn't just hear it. I lived it."

They did not notice their mother's worried look or Hawke's reassuring nod.

"OK you little rascals, to bed with you."

"Aw, Uncle Hawke!" said Will.

"To bed I said. Fast. Or the dark Delven will come and freeze off your toes."

Tobar sat apart from his companions. His cloak was soaked. He was still cold. They had tried all through the stormy night to penetrate the spelled circle, trudging the perimeter of the oaken barrier, bombarding it with both weapons and curses but it still held unscathed. They watched dumbfounded as Kyrdthin's vehicle careened down the road dodging the torrent-filled ruts all the way to the house. Tobar rubbed his bruised forehead. He could still feel the blow he received when they rushed after the vehicle only to crash into an invisible barrier. It was almost dawn. Tobar hugged his knees under his drenched cloak whimpering in self-pity. He tried to wipe his spectacles on his sleeve but it was too wet. He looked through the spotted lenses then tucked them into his pocket. He was exhausted, angry and more than a little scared. He tried to think of Analinne.

Queen Marielle crumpled the note. Lady Cellina had not seen the serving girl slip it into her hand. Marielle eyed Cellina's plump bulk across the room and pondered the content of the cryptic note. Kyrdthin was here again and he needed her help. Absently she twisted Arinth's wedding bracelet. The large silver band weighed as heavily on her thin wrist as the queenship of Arindon weighed on her heart. Kyrdthin could not bring the children back here. It was too soon. She unfolded the note and read it again. "The stolen treasure has been discovered. Where shall I rebury it? Meet me in the west tower after tea."

She looked at Cellina squinting over her needlework again. The castle sitting room was bright with early spring sunlight but the windows were closed and the air was stuffy. Lady Cellina always feared taking a chill. Marielle and the other court ladies had stopped arguing with her long ago. Instead they sat daily, devoid of air and freedom, gossiping on trivialities while they sewed. As usual the mood was less than pleasant. The fact that Marielle was queen and Cellina was not had burned with hatred and treachery between their younger selves, but over the years emotions had mellowed to petty daily annoyances. What if the children…? Marielle forced the thought from her mind. She dropped the crumpled note into the remains of her tea, and watched it dissolve in a sprinkle of silver stars. She would just have to wait to see what her brother needed and why.

In the morning April fumbled her way to the kitchen. She drew back the curtain from the window over the sink. Her mother was hanging up laundry on the line behind the house. The sky was still cloudy. There would probably be another storm.

"Purrty April. Purrty Trebil," chirped a small voice.

"Good morning, Birdy Love," April cooed. "Hey, Will, what you want for breakfast?" she called back upstairs. "I'm having toast. Want some?"

"Naw. Just make me some cocoa. I'm not hungry."

April tore open the packets and poured hot water from the teakettle into the cups, then leaned against the counter to wait for the toast to pop. She thought about the strange events of the previous day. There were the men at the bus stop, and then Will's disappearance and the spell and the storm and the stories, especially the stories. They had been so real.

"Will, I've been thinking," she said picking up the hot toast and reaching for the strawberry jam. "Did you feel weird last night when Hawke was telling his story? You know like you were really into it?"

Will made a non-committal noise.

"Will, there's got to be a connection," April continued. "Those stories aren't in any book or movie but Mom and Hawke know them inside out. They're all about the same place too. It's so real. I'm starting to dream about it. Last night I kept waking up every time it thundered and I had always been dreaming of the stories. Then my bird would start singing and I would fall back to sleep."

"Weird! What are you getting at?"

"I think the stories are real."

"Now you are really weird." Will crossed his eyes and crammed his whole second piece of toast into his mouth at once.

"You're disgusting!"

April sat down with her toast. Will idly stirred his cocoa. Suddenly his spoon clanked to the floor as he let out a big yawn.

"Looks as if you didn't get much sleep either last night," said April picking up his spoon.

"Yeah. I kept dreaming and waking up ."

"Dreaming of the stories?"

"Yeah. All kinds of neat stuff, sword fights and..."

"Told you so, Will. I think the stories are real and Trebil proves it. No bird on this earth is as smart as he is."

"Trebil smart bird, tell stories all night," the mirror bird chimed in.

"See, Will. I'm right aren't I Trebil?"

"More stories now?" said the little bird.

"Yes now, Trebil," said April pushing her chair back from the table and standing up.

"Get story box. More stories in box."

April was puzzled. Story box? She thought for a moment then her eyes opened wide. "Mom's box!".

"Get story box," Trebil said again. "Trebil tell more story now."

"Mom's box!" exclaimed Will suddenly coming to the same conclusion. "April don't you dare!"

April glanced out the window. Her mother was standing in the back yard looking up at the sky. Black clouds were boiling in the west. April saw her look up at the sun again then continue to hang up the laundry. "Come on Will. We have to know."

April hesitated at the doorway to their mother's room. They had been told never, never to touch that box. April's feet carried her to the closet. The door slid open. She stood on tiptoe and carefully lifted down the worn, leather hinged box. Her mother's warning screamed in her head, but Trebil said there were stories in the box. She had to know the truth. Click! The lid fell back. Gold and silver light flooded the room.

"April?".

"Yes," she answered slowly. She looked at Will standing beside her, staring into the box. His face was bathed in light. Inside the box lay two crowns, one silver, one gold, alive with rainbows of precious stones. Will lifted out the golden one. "Be my queen, April," he said crowning her long dark hair.

"Oh. Willy," she giggled and placed its silver mate atop his curls. "My kingdom is yours," she vowed.

Time stopped. The two children stood holding hands, mesmerized by the elfin blue of each other's eyes until Janille's shadow fell across the scene. She snatched the crowns back into the box and snapped it shut. Her face was white with terror.

"April, get five candles," she ordered. "Will, get the big salt box from the kitchen. Hurry! And matches too."

She pushed back the furniture. Quickly but with precise care she poured the salt in a large circle on the floor. She lit the candles one by one, dropping a spot of wax on the floor to hold each one upright. "Come to me," she said from the center of the circle. She took their hands. "Now call Hawke. Call him with all your might."

April squeezed her eyes shut, repeating Hawke's name with her heart's rhythm. Her mother's grip hurt her hand. She let the pain carry the need to bring Hawke home. Will's hand was cold and trembling. She let his fear carry the emergency of her summoning. Even with her eyes closed she could see the candles burn higher and higher. She felt a sudden cold, a sudden empty turning in her stomach. Then there was a presence, tenuous at first, questing, acknowledging, then gradually solidifying into a familiar form.

"Jane, I told you never to use the star sign unless..."

"They opened the box, Hawke. They touched the crowns."

Lord Belar set down his goblet. What was this tingling, this pulsing, this growing throb beneath his crown? What was this brilliance? Pain seared his eyes.

"My Lord!" Borat rushed to attend him. Belar groped at the table.

"What is it, my Lord? What ails you?"

"Bring me the bowl, the bowl and water," he roared.

"You want something to drink?"

"The bowl, you idiot! Pour water in it. I need a scrying bowl," said Belar regaining his composure but still shielding his eyes.

Borat set the brimming bowl in front of his master and stepped back.

"Now leave me alone."

"But my Lord, are you sure you are..."

"I said leave me. Now!"

When Borat's footsteps had faded beyond the door, Belar opened his eyes and looked into the bowl. The sparkling gold ripples shot painful darts but he held his gaze until the water calmed and the vision cleared. Three figures stood atop a silver stairs. He growled an oath when he recognized Krydthin's hooded robes. But the others? His eyes ached. He squinted to see them better but the light from the crowns blurred their features. A roar pounded into his skull. Voices, a sea of cheering voices, the thunder of clapping hands... "Hail!...Hail!"

"No! No!" He pounded his fist on the table. "This will not come to pass." He pounded again and again until the plate and crystal rang with his anger. When he looked back into the bowl, the reflection of his own face looked up from the dark water, mocking him.

Chapter 2

That night Will and April stayed awake listening at the top of the stairs. Hawke and Janille argued in the living room below. Hawke's voice was angry and sharp. Janille whined defensively. Her home spell had brought the men to the bus stop looking for Will. The children had seen her weave the spell many times after Hawke left, tracing the star sign on her heart as she spoke his name. Will and April hugged each other, shivering more from fear than from cold. Will finally fell asleep but April kept her vigil through the verbal duel below and the long silence that followed.

Hawke said Janille had failed him. He called her selfish and weak. She said he was cruel and heartless to lay such a vital responsibility on her when he traveled freely without a care. He said guarding two children was a simple task while he had the affairs of two kingdoms to balance, that she was lucky he found time to visit at all. And so they continued until all the words had been said and their hearts were ragged from the hurts they had dealt.

Janille's eyes blurred with tears pride refused to spill. Her jaw ached with tension. Her throat was dry. She stole a quick glance at Hawke. He drew idly on his pipe making little gurgling noises. He flexed his fingers. His liquid blue eyes stared sadly into the fire. Feeling her gaze he turned. His eyes caught hers then suddenly spilled. He slipped to his knees and buried his head in her lap.

"Janie," his muffled words tumbled out. "I do know. I do care how lonely and frightened you are. Believe me. Oh, Janie, forgive me for hurting you so."

She twisted her fingers in his hair, her tears finally falling.

"Forgive me please," he begged. "I don't want to make you cry. We didn't lose Will. We are all safe here together. I had no right to be so sharp with you."

She held firm. "You could have married me here and stayed with us."

He took her hands and pressed them to his cheek, but did not answer.

Now it was her turn to beg. "Stay with us please. You can't leave us now. Belar knows we are here. I can't do it all alone anymore."

"You know why I can't stay, Janie, but now I guess I will have to take you with me."

"With you!"

"Yes, I will take you and the kids back to Arindon with me," he said kissing her fingers then folding them gently into his large hands.

For an unbelieving moment Janille held her breath, then dropped to her knees beside him crying for joy.

"I have a plan, Janie love," he said wrapping his arms around her. "Analinne's confinement is soon, not to mention Elanille's. A peasant woman to be midwife and nurse with a quiet daughter to occupy little Kylie may be just what is needed to serve all our purposes."

"But what about Willy?"

"Perhaps Rogarth would take on a new page. If not we can always hide him in the village or among the kitchen boys.

Janille's heart pounded. "Dare we try it? Surely someone would recognize us."

"It is a bold plan," he admitted. "May its boldness be our safety."

"I trust you in this as in everything ," she said trying to kiss him but he turned away.

"Let's get some sleep," he said standing up.

"Oh Hawke, just hold me," she said trying to pull him down again. "Just this once."

He gently disengaged her arms. "No, Janie, I said sleep. We'll need it. We have lots to do in the morning." He sat down, stretched his long legs out on the couch and shut his eyes. "Good night, Little Bird."

"I love when you call me that," she said as she stood up and smoothed her skirt. "I love you, Hawke," she whispered smiling down at him.

Hawke's eyes remained closed.

"Willy, Willy, wake up," whispered April. "Willy we're going on a trip. We're going into the stories."

"Lemme alone," he mumbled turning his face away.

"Oh forget it. I'll tell you in the morning."

Dell the Bard arrived with a gust of wind. The door of Armon Beck's tavern slammed shut behind him rattling the window panes.

"Save the furniture friend," the innkeeper called from behind the bar.

"Sorry Armon," said Dell untying his wet cloak. "Some wild weather out there and wilder coming if I can predict." He lovingly unwrapped his harp. "My lady love here is all tight and out of tune."

"Then bring her to my hearth," said the innkeeper as he poured the bard a pint of ale. "Shall I warm your mug?"

"No need, good man. Give it to me now while I tune," Dell said caressing the harp strings, ear pressed close. He sipped the ale as he hummed and gently turned the pegs until the chords rang sweet and true. Then he drained the mug, cleared his throat and sang.

"Child of Time,
And Child of Night,
Born to bring Love
Into the Light…"

The patrons turned their chairs to face him and leaned back to listen. Armon Beck drew another round of pints, wiped his fat hands on a dish towel, then joined them. His rich baritone hummed beneath Dell's clear tenor.

"…lost between worlds,
Hidden from sight,
The Jewels of Allarion,
Shine bright with Light…"

The wind wailed outside. The men wept in their ale as the bard's harp sang with a voice of her own. At a table in the corner Jareth the gamekeeper and Rogarth captain of the king's guard, leaned close together, whispering. Their second round of ale was untouched.

"Don't let your pride make a fool of you," said Jareth. Delven are no match for a trained warrior in a fair fight but when has a Delven fought fair? What they lack in height and muscle they make up with treachery."

"I still don't see what they want," said Rogarth. If we knew…"

"But we don't, so we take no chances while we find out. I say post sentries with backups in the perimeters, and a force disguised as an honor guard in the hall. You man, wear armor and keep your eyes open no matter how distracting certain ladies may be that night."

"Since when does the gamekeeper plan strategy and give orders to the captain of the king's guard?' Rogarth said laughing but with an undertone of seriousness.

"Since the captain of the king's guard has the intelligence to listen to a man with knowledge and experience."

"Well said man," Rogarth answered not quite meeting Jareth's eye.

"Then if we agree, let's drink to the upcoming event and our lady Maralinne's happiness."

They raised their mugs and let Armon Beck's rich brew slide down. Relaxing they turned their attention to the bard's song.

"…in anger the Darkness
The spider webs weave,
While the gods scurry blindly
The jewels to retrieve…"

The men swayed with the rhythm, mesmerized by Dell's music. Armon Beck leaned on his bar with his eyes closed, humming a counter melody, dishtowel in hand forgotten.

"Will, April, time to get up," Hawke called. "Up and at 'em. Will wear your jeans and a long sleeved shirt. April do you have a night gown on or pajamas?"

"My blue gown."

"OK, leave that on and come down. Now, both of you."

"Don't you want me to get dressed?" said April.

"No. Girls wear long things where we're going," said Hawke.

The box was open on the kitchen table. Hawke lifted the golden crown. "April you're going to wear this for a while. Duck your head. Will you're next."

The silver crown was a bit big but Will wrinkled his brow and it stayed up.

He led them outside. It was almost light. A huge star sign was drawn in the stones of the driveway.

"Wait!" April cried then ran back into the house, and grabbed her new friend's cage. When she returned Hawke, Janille, and Will were standing inside the circle of stars. They locked her into a foursome embrace, Trebil's cage wedged between them. Just then the sun slid between the easternmost oaks. The star sign came to life. Hawke began the chant and they all joined in.

"Five for One,
One for Five,
Hie thee home.
Home to Love."

The world was golden for a moment, then it was gone. April fell into an empty void. She was all alone and cold. She opened her mouth but she could not scream. Then warm arms surrounded her. She felt the bars of Trebil's cage against her chest. Her feet were on solid ground. She took a deep breath and opened her eyes.

"Where are we?'

"Arindon kids."

"Even the rain here feels good ,"said Janille lifting her face to drink in the drops.

"Glad to be home again, Janie?"

"Glad to be near you again, Hawke."

Dawn of the second day of their siege caught Tobar unaware. Rough hands shook him awake.

"Something is going on. Wake up," growled Borat.

Tobar rolled over and sat up. His head throbbed. His body ached. In spite of the early morning chill he felt hot. He blinked his eyes to focus on the scene in the cottage driveway. He sniffled, trying to hold back a sneeze as he reached into his pocket for his spectacles. Then he saw what had caused the alarm. Kyrdthin, Janille and the children were standing there in a circle of light. "Stop them…" he started to say as he recognized the spell but it was too late. The air shimmered silver and the little tableau in the driveway vanished.

"Look out!" shouted Borat . The earth trembled, the ancient oaks swayed. "It's down! The barrier is down!"

Tobar struggled to his feet. He sniffled and wiped his nose on his sleeve. Too late. He was too sick to care."

"Let's go have a look," said Borat, not understanding what had taken place.

Tobar's hoarse reply masked the shame of his failure.

Hawke led them into the forest. The gnarled trees towered above them. The road was no more than two muddy ruts winding among the gigantic trees. It was dark and miserable. The rain began to fall faster. Thunder rumbled off to their right. "Let's get a move on and get you kids in the dry," he said.

April's feet were soaked. Her toes cramped with cold as they sloshed through the mud. Janille hung on Hawke's arm, slipping and sliding but too light-hearted to complain. At last they entered a clearing. A thatched cottage leaned against a large tree heavy with white blossoms.

"Who's place is that?"

"Yours for the moment, Will," said Hawke.

"Is Jareth…?" Janille began.

"No, but he should be here sometime tomorrow, Janie. I'll make sure you and the kids are comfortable then see about getting you into Arindon."

It was dark and the place stank. Hawke lit the fire while Janille rummaged through the shelves looking for candles.

"You kids get out of your wet things and wrap up in whatever you can find," said Hawke.

Janille lit the two bent yellow candles she had found and set them on the table.

Will looked around the room. "This place is a dump."

"This is only a hunting cabin," explained Janille. "Jareth has fine quarters in Arindon".

When their eyes were fully adjusted to the candlelight they inspected the meager furnishings. There was a small wooden table covered with half-fletched arrows. Two chairs were pulled up close to the hearth. A dusty hutch leaned against one wall and a sagging quilt-covered bed was pushed up against the other. The floor was wide wooden planking carpeted by a bearskin rug. A ladder led up to a dark loft above. Janille spied a broom behind the door. Soon dust was flying everywhere.

"Gods Janie, Jareth will never forgive you for disturbing his filth."

"Who knows how long you will be leaving us this time," she said without pausing. "April, Willy, shake out that bed," she ordered. "Then hang your wet things on those chairs by the fire. Help her Willy! Take the other end of the quilt."

"Enjoy yourself," Hawke chuckled. "I'll be back as soon as I can." Before they could say good bye he was gone.

Tobar was glad to be away from the terrifying alien world. The tea Borat brewed for him was beginning to ease his tight chest and sore throat but he still had the sniffles. His eyes watered so much his spectacles were useless. There was nothing to look at anyway. He knew every word of every text that lined his musty library corner. He knew history, poetry, geography, alchemy and spells. He had dedicated his lonely life to the quest for knowledge, satisfied to let Frebar have the kingdom and all the power. Then he met Analinne. He let is mind drift back to that first evening. There were guests in the castle. That meant noise and confusion. He avoided dinner and retreated to the library. He was immersed in a text on the properties of solid matter verses the fluidity of time when he realized he was not alone. Tobar let his eyes rest on the place he first saw her looking through a volume of poetry. The fire of her hair in the lamplight, the creamy purity of her skin, the soft curves of her body beneath the folds of her green velvet gown had awakened long-repressed feelings in him. Books suddenly were no longer adequate. He summoned all the courage he could muster and made his presence known. Unaccustomed to speaking much to anyone much less to young women, he startled her at first, then amused her. He could tell by her eyes, those blue-green pools where a man could lose himself.

At first he did not tell her who he was. Instead he quietly courted her. When she came to the library he read poetry to her. He walked the secluded paths of the garden with her. He taught her how to solve mathematical riddles and she taught him how to count stitches of embroidery. Finally on the last night of Analinne's visit Tobar came down to dinner. He took his place beside his brother the king. Frevarian obsession with tradition and protocol would allow no variance in seating in the great hall.

Tobar had known that his brother betrothed the girl to him when she was but an infant, a political maneuver advantageous to the kingdoms at the time. He had agreed, then promptly forgot the arrangement. Years passed. Analinne came of age but her ailing father did nothing to insure her future, and Frebar no longer thought about consummation of the match until Tobar asked for Analinne's hand at dinner that night.

Tobar rubbed his watery eyes. So much had happened since that day and he was ashamed of what he had let himself become.

The steady rain seeped through the thatched roof, falling into the bowls and jars Janille had set to catch the drops. Hawke had promised to be back by sunset but now it was almost morning. The children were hungry and afraid.

"How long do we have to stay in this dump?" Will asked again.

"Only until Hawke makes arrangements for us and brings us new clothes and supplies," Janille answered with measured patience.

"Why did we have to come here anyway?"

"We were only staying in the world you knew until this one could be made safe for us," said Janille pulling Will's head against her shoulder. Her fingers traced a calming spell as she stroked his dark curls.

"Well I don't like it," he mumbled into her damp sleeve.

April sat defiantly on the bed wrapped in Jareth's blanket, Trebil's cage was in her lap. Her dark hair was unbraided and tangled. She had said little since their arrival. Janille sensed rebellion beyond her daughter's fear and confusion. Willy had never fit in with other children but April had left friends behind.

"I know I owe you an explanation April, but I don't know where to begin," she said.

"Well where are we?" said April. "Answer me that for starters."

"We are in Arindon wood, in another world, but you belong here. You were born here."

"The world from the stories, right?"

"Yes the world of the stories and the dreams Trebil told you." Janille looked down at Will. He was finally asleep. She laid him back on the bed and stood up. "This is our home but we are in great danger here. That is why we will be playing different roles for a little while until you are grown."

"Who are we really?" asked April.

For an answer Janille took a worn deck of cards down from the mantel. As she shuffled the cards began to glow. "Draw five for the future," she said. "The first one will be for Willy." She looked at her foster son. "What will he become?" she asked turning over the card.

"This is so cool," April exclaimed as the white knight on the card came to life. He raised his sword high above the moon-silvered landscape. Beneath him boiled dark angry clouds.

"It looks like Will only grown up," said April. "Is it really him"

"The cards tell only possibilities, not promises, daughter. Now turn another one over for yourself. Ask it what you will become."

April's card glowed bright. The young woman looking up at her from the card's face was definitely herself gowned in white and seated in a large wooded chair. She wore the golden crown from the box. "I hope this comes true," she said not quite believing. "Now you draw one Mom."

"No not yet. The seeker's card is drawn last." Janille felt a welcome tingle of power as she touched the cards. How long had it been? How many years of feeling helpless and afraid?

"Mom?" said April leaning anxiously over the back of her mother's chair. "What next?"

Janille laid the next two cards on the table. "The first will be the place we must begin and the other the place were it all will end. Turn them both April"

The moon shone full over a silver city. April stared at the card. Nothing moved but she sensed life in the sleeping scene.

"That's Arindon, the place we are headed. Then we are right," said Janille more to herself than to April. She sat a while without speaking. The fire crackled and Will sighed in his sleep. April hugged her frayed blanket tighter.

"What about this other card mom? I think it's me too but…?"

Janille did not have to look twice. The same young woman looked up from the card only this time she wore black. Janille's face drained of color.

"What's wrong Mom?"

"I…I don't know."

"Well there is one more card. Can I turn it?"

"No." said Janille, her voice seemed far away. "This is what I seek." She turned the last card. "Time," she said as she looked at the glass on the card. The sands ran side to side rather than top to bottom. Silver sand flowed to gold and gold to silver. In the apex where they mingled a rainbow of stars fell into the night.

Suddenly the room was filled with cold gray mist. Trebil screeched. The candle flames leaped and Will sat up with a start. Hawke's presence slowly materialized. He was dressed in gray flowing robes. His hair and beard were wilder than ever.

"I thought you would never come," said Janille throwing herself into his arms.

"Janie, Janie, calm down," he said stroking her hair.

"It's so good to see you like this again in your rightful glory," she babbled.

"Rightful glory! Oh Janie," he laughed. "I thought you loved me in my old flannel shirt and blue jeans."

"Yes, we almost had a life there together," she said suddenly wistful.

"Don't start that again, Jane, not now," he said gently pushing her away.

"What did you bring us Uncle Hawke?" said April spying his sack.

"Will first,' he said pulling out a shirt and breeches of unbleached muslin, some brown hose, a leather jerkin and boots. "Put these on Will," he ordered.

"No way!"

"Put them on I said.".

"Do what Hawke says, Willy," Janille coaxed.

"The shirt is OK but I am not wearing no tights," Will declared. "I'm keepin' my jeans."

Will screamed and kicked but Hawke easily overpowered him. With a little help from Janille, Will put on the new clothes. "Let's see what we got," Hawke said when they were done.

Will blushed and looked down at his new clothes. "These are just temporary, right Hawke?" he said.

"Sure Will, just temporary," Hawke laughed . "Soon you will be dressed like a king and giving orders but until then you will do as I say. OK?"

"OK," Will promised.

Hawke reached into his sack again. "Now it's your turn April."

The dress was green, a coarse weave but somehow shimmering like dew on new leaves. The skirt was long and full. The bodice laced. The blouse was rose with sleeves and a neckline that could be slipped off the shoulder. The petticoats were also rose and long and full and ruffled. April was speechless. She held the dress a moment then with no thought for modesty dropped her blanket robe and slipped on the dress. "It's beautiful, so beautiful!" she chanted twirling the skirt.

"A lusty little wench."

"Hawke!"

"You think I haven't noticed our little bud was opening?'

"She's only fourteen."

"The dress my dear Janie, belonged to Lady Elanille when she was younger than that."

"Who's lady what's her name?" asked Will.

"One of the fine ladies who wait on the queen," Janille explained. "April can be proud to wear her dress."

"Why can't April have a new dress? How come she's gotta wear somebody else's clothes?"

"I told you Willy, we must play different roles here. April, I mean Avrille as we must pronounce it now will be a maidservant and it is the custom for court ladies to hand down their unwanted dresses to their maids."

"Why wouldn't she want this beautiful one?" April said still twirling the skirt.

"From the look of Elanille these days she couldn't fit her belly into two dresses that size." Hawke laughed .

"Hawke don't be so crude!" Janille exclaimed. "Lady Elanille is expecting her second child soon, April. That's what Hawke means."

"What did you bring for Mom?" April asked trying to change the subject.

"Nothing fit for a queen but a dress I think she will remember with pleasure," said Hawke digging into his sack one more time.

"Don't tell me, Hawke," said Janille. "It's my blue."

"Right you are.."

"But what if I can't fit into it anymore?"

"You'd better or I will have to just squeeze you until you do fit." He made a grab for her waist.

She dodged his reach. "I wore this on the day Hawke rescued us," she mused as she held up the dress. "How can it be thirteen years ago?"

"Try it on Janie. I want to see you in all your glory."

Tonight they were a family. Janille and Hawke sat by the fire long after the children had been tucked beneath their blankets in the loft. They talked very little. He smoked his pipe and stared into the flames. She dozed, her head on his shoulder. For the moment all was content.

The Dark Lord drummed his fingers on the arm of his chair. What was taking Tobar so long? He shuffled his deck of cards on the table. He cut and turned them one by one willing a horoscope for Tobar's son. It would be a son if the cards told true. He rushed through the first cards until only the three cards of power remained. Slowly he turned over the first. The Sun! Yes, Frevaria, beautiful, golden Frevaria was playing so smoothly into his hands. Tobar was such an easy tool. He turned over the second card. The Moon. Pretty, pregnant Analinne and her silver dower. Soon, so soon he thought. And the next card ...it should be the Black Dragon, his card. His hand hesitated. His eyes remembered the searing pain and the scene in the scrying bowl. He left the card unturned.

Janille woke to pounding on the door. Hawke was gone. Fear kept her silent.

"Open up good lady. It's Jareth," called a deep friendly voice.

She jumped out of bed, grabbed her shawl and ran to unbolt the door.

"Who is it, mama?" Will called from the loft.

"Get dressed both of you and come down. We've got company."

Jareth the gamekeeper entered the cottage. Sunlight poured in the open door, rich and warm with spring. "Greetings." He gave an awkward bow. "I don't know how to address you given the circumstances but I mean no disrespect."

"Just Janille will do for now, Jareth. I will be called Aunt Jane when we are in Arindon ."

Jareth set down and began to open his leather pouch. He pulled out bread and cheese. "There are apples in the bottom here somewhere and some tea," he said rummaging through the bulging pouch.

Janille set water on to boil while Jareth sliced the bread and cheese. Will soon climbed down the ladder but April hung back. Janille introduced their guest as King Arinth's gamekeeper and owner of the cottage. Will's eyes took in the tall, dark stranger. "Glad to meet you Jareth, sir."

"Just Jareth, my young friend. It is I who should be calling you sir, or doesn't he know yet, Janille?"

"Not completely," she said. "And this is my daughter Avrille," Janille continued helping April down the last rung of the ladder.

"My lady," Jareth said taking her hand. April stood speechless. Jareth was the most fascinating man she had ever seen. His dark deep-set eyes and high cheekbones were framed by thick, dark hair and a full beard. His voice was low and sincere but with a playful note to match the twinkle in his eyes. She liked him immediately.

"A fine brood you have here, Janille," he said.

"Sit down now and eat, everyone," said Janille. "You must have ridden all night, Jareth. Is Kyrdthin coming soon?"

"I saw a hawk fly out as I left. He shouldn't be far behind me."

By mid morning Kyrdthin, joined them. Soon the party of four set out walking through the ancient forest. Will walked ahead with large strides trying to keep pace with Jareth. Kyrdthin walked behind them, a smiling Janille on his arm. April had never seen her mother so content, so young looking or so beautiful. She had worn a worried look for as long as April could remember, but today she was radiant.

By noon they had crossed a deep river gorge on high a stone bridge and headed up a steep but well-marked road. The forest was still lush but thinner as they climbed. At last they came to a high, open space.

A breathtaking panorama spread out before them. Kyrdthin was anxious to ride on but he understood their need to stop. Janille stood reverently beside him drinking in the view. The twin kingdoms lay like two jewels in the broad fertile valley, silver Arindon and golden Frevaria joined by a bend in the dazzling river. The towered castles were surrounded by thatch-roofed villages. Fields, fence rows and wooded patches made a rustic quilt pattern across the valley between them.

"Are they real?" asked April not yet convinced this was not all a dream or a page from a fairy tale.

"How come they're two colors?" asked Will.

"White gypsum is used to build in Arindon, and yellow sandstone in Frevaria," Kyrdthin explained. "Simple building stones, but there is a bit of mica mixed in the stone so that it catches the sun and gives them their glory when you see them from up here."

"Which place is ours?"

"The silver one is where you were born, Will," said Kyrdthin. "The golden one is April's, but it is really all one, my little man. That is why we are here, to bring them all together.

"What about the kingdom on the other side?" said Will.

"What do you see, Will?" said Kyrdthin , a touch of alarm in his voice.

"I saw…I thought I saw.."

"Saw what Willy?" asked Janille.

"Over there." He pointed to the place where the river swung in a lazy arch. "It looked like another castle."

"There's nothing there except some ruins," said Jareth. "Maybe the light caught the old pool."

"Maybe," said Will not quite sure of himself. "Anyway it's all clouded over now."

"You're weird Will," said April. "The sun is out."

"Forget it ," said Will. "When will I be king Uncle Hawke?"

"Not so fast, Will. Let's just get to Arindon for now."

Chapter 3

Arindon was not at all like the fairy tale castle April had imagined. Up close it was dirty gray stone, not silver. The street outside the gate was filled with a colorful congestion of sights and sounds and smells. People and animals jostled each other between makeshift stalls. Kyrdthin led them through the press. The crowd moved back with a bit of awe when they recognized him. Janille clutched April and Will's hands and huddled deep into her hooded shawl. People regarded them briefly then turned back to their shopping.

The formidable castle gate swung open to Kyrdthin's hail. Inside they were met by a thin, dark-haired serving girl.

"If it isn't lovely Larielle," Kyrdthin greeted her. "These are the guests the princesses are expecting."

The girl nodded with a shy smile.

"I guess this is where we part company," said Kyrdthin.

Janille and April hugged Will goodbye and waved until he and Kyrdthin were out of sight. Then Larielle led them across the inner courtyard, and up a flight of stone stairs to a small ante room.

"Make yourselves comfortable while you wait," she said. "There is water and towels to freshen up on the table and a bite of bread and fruit if you are hungry. I will tell my lady you are here."

Janille thanked her then pulled a comb from her pocket and set to work on April's tangled hair.

Soon they were ushered into a cool drapery hung room. Princess Analinne turned. Her brilliant red hair was drawn back straight and severe. She lifted her head regally. Her features were large but chiseled with classic precision. "Kyrdthin's recommendation is all I need," she said. "Welcome to our household."

"We are honored, Lady Analinne," said Janille with a shallow curtsy. "I am Jane to be midwife to lady Elanille and nurse to the new child. This is my daughter Avrille to be companion to young Master Keilen. "

"Come here child," said Analinne to April. "I see you have a little friend hiding in your curls."

"Trebil good boy, Trebil is."

April approached Analinne trying not to stare. The princess's gown was dark green velvet embroidered with silver flowers. Her hair was bound by a silver circlet and the hand that rested on her abdomen was weighed down with rings.

"Is the bird a gift from Kyrdthin?" Analinne asked.

"Yes My Lady, a birthday gift."

"And how old are you now?"

"I'm fourteen next week...My Lady."

"So is my Lari. You met her when you arrived. She is a sweet girl and you seem so too. They even resemble one another. Don't you think so?"

"It is the dark hair," said Janille.

"That must be it," said Analinne.

"When, if I may ask, My Lady, when will the Lady Elanille see us? Soon?" Janille said with an anxious tremble in her voice.

"Elani is sewing with the Queen. I should be there too but receiving you seem a less dreary task today. Let me take you to her."

Analinne rose slowly. She moved with stately grace but not without some awkwardness, unaccustomed as she was to the changes brought about with first pregnancy. They followed her to a room lit with a golden filigree of late spring sunlight. Queen Marielle and her ladies sat in a quiet tableau by the window. Her highness was pale and inhumanly beautiful. April hung back as Analinne presented them with elegant formality.

When Analinne took a seat on the Queen's right the circle of ladies came to life. Although Queen Marielle was the central figure it was a large outspoken woman who dominated the scene.

"Those two," whispered Janille nodding toward the woman and her quiet, proper counter part beside her. "They are the Ladies Cellina and Liella, the spinster sisters of the late Queen Veralinne."

Lady Cellina was beading a piece of copper satin while her sister rearranged a box of embroidery threads with unsteady, nail-bitten hands. Analinne picked up her needle and began to work the edge of the tiny pillowcase she was tatting. Her sister the Princess Maralinne stared out the window, restlessly drumming her fingers on the sill. The lacy camisole she had been trimming lay half finished in her lap. Smaller than her twin, Maralinne's complexion was like carved ivory. Her hair, untamed and fiery, tumbled over her shoulders. Her brow was knit. Her lips pursed.

April returned her attention to her mother as Janille approached Lady Elanille. The young woman was pretty, blonde and sweetly smiling. She was loosely gowned in blue silk. Janille knelt to receive the lady's hand. When she raised her head again tears streamed down her face.

"Mother are you Ok?" April whispered.

"Yes dear. I'm just happy to be home."

"Your journey has been long I am sure," said Elanille. "Since your duties to us do not really begin until the baby comes, please be free to rest and get settled in until we need you."

"You are kind, My Lady. I would like nothing better than to remain here in my present company and perhaps get acquainted with young Master Keilen. I dearly love little ones."

"Come Kylie," Elanille said to a little boy playing quietly on the floor beside her. April had not noticed him until now. "Come, show Aunt Jane how you play soldiers."

Janille sat on the floor with the boy and soon they were lost in their own world. April knew she should be getting acquainted with him too, but she felt reluctant to intrude. Besides Princess Maralinne was much more fascinating. April watched her. Sunlight streamed in the window, lighting the fire in Maralinne's hair.

"Dreaming of Rogarth won't get that camisole finished," Lady Elanille teased her.

"I wasn't," Maralinne snapped.

"What else could bring on such a distracted expression?"

"Nothing you would understand."

"With no disrespect to my own Lord Keilen," said Elanille. "Rogarth is the handsomest man in Arindon."

"I have better things to think about than which cock struts proudest," Marilinne snapped again.

"Oh sister!" Analinne exclaimed. "You make me sick with your talk. Any other woman would be wild with excitement so close to announcing her betrothal."

"I'm not any other woman," Maralinne fumed. "I don't want to bulge like you and Elani with nothing to do but sit and sew all day. I want to dance and ride and have adventures. I don't want to get married."

Elanille resumed her knitting. She was tired of the useless arguing with Maralinne. The length of pink lace she was making fell rhythmically from her needles, looping across her lap. She so hoped for a daughter this time.

All the while Queen Marielle remained aloof. She had a distant look as if she saw the world in different colors from her companions. Her face, pale as a moonstone, was framed with a silvery halo of hair. He blue-veined hands and delicate fingers fluttered like butterflies as she stitched a silk scarf with silver thread.

"You will have one last Midsummer Ball at least," said Analinne to her sister.

"I'll have this one and many more. You will never see me content to simply breed and sew all my life."

"There is much more to marriage than babies and sewing," Analinne insisted.

"I can do without that too," Maralinne replied, her face reddening.

"You may have to after you have done your duty to the kingdom. I'm sure Rogarth will spend his nights with the serving girls if you are so unwilling."

"What's the difference. Tobar disappears when you get to big to bed."

"Ladies enough!" exclaimed the queen. Everyone looked up startled. Marielle rarely spoke and even more rarely showed emotion. "We three will soon be five," she said. "Just as the prophesies foretold."

The women exchanged puzzled looks then quietly resumed their needlework.

Kyrdthin led Will into an infrequently used alley way. Now that I got you away from your mother, Will, we need to talk man to man."

"Sure Uncle Hawke."

"That's the first thing. I am Kyrdthin here. You never saw me before today when I picked you up at Jareth's place."

"But why?"

"Here I am not uncle to pages and kitchen boys. I am a wizard, a politician, a physician, anything you name it, but not an Uncle Hawke."

Will looked down and dug his toe into the dirt.

"Will look at me, You know I love you. I love your mother and April too but here we are in great danger. One slip and not only our lives but the world as we know it would be in jeopardy."

"I still don't see what's the big deal," said Will.

"The crowns you and April discovered, they are rightfully yours but there are those who would murder or worse to keep you from wearing them. Until you are both come of age, and that is fifteen here, there is little I or anyone on the side of the Light can do to protect you except to keep you hidden,"

"So what are we gonna do? And who are the side of the Light guys we can trust?"

"There are many trustworthy on the side of the Light, Will, but only Jareth, Queen Marielle and Gil the king's advisor can be trusted with your identity. As to what you must do, I'm going to apprentice you out to a friend of mine, a miller by trade. From him you can learn about the kingdom and the people you will rule someday. He's a family man so you will have a good home too."

"Will I ever see Mom and April?"

Kyrdthin laid a hand on Will's shoulder. "Not often but April's mirror bird will keep you in touch."

Will dug his toe back and forth in the dirt. "I'm not so sure I…"

"One more thing," said Kyrdthin. "Something to make it easier to keep you safe, I'm going to …well…Will just look at me…no…no…look into my eyes. Will…Will…Willarinth…"

Will was swept into the swirling gray mist of Kyrdthin's eyes. He sank into nothingness and when he touched bottom he and Kyrdthin were walking along to road on the outskirts of town.

"Geez what did you do to me Uncle, I mean Kyrdthin?"

"Just locked in your memories of outside the kingdoms to keep you from spilling what you shouldn't and gave you a few facts to get you started on your education here."

"Some things are fuzzy, like school and the house and…"

"And they will stay that way for a while. Now just concentrate on learning all you can at my friend Mabry's place and on staying out of trouble. Here you are just another fatherless brat who's mother just got a fortunate situation serving a lady at court."

Ahead of them stood Mabry's mill, an imposing structure perched beside the river. Standing by the front door was a team of horses and a wagon half loaded with flour sacks.

"I'm not so sure..." said Will hanging back.

"You are a king training," Kyrdthin assured him. "You are strong enough, or I wouldn't ask you to do this."

"But..."

"Just remember, you are not alone. All that is good and of the Light is on your side."

April crossed the room to the window seat where Princess Maralinne had retreated. April followed her gaze. Outside a man on a dark horse galloped toward the forest.

"Is that Jareth?" April asked.

"Yes he's off again," answered Maralinne

"Where to?"

"He is my father's eyes and ears, need I say any more?"

April did not understand but she was intrigued with Maralinne's mysterious tone.

"I wish I could ride as free as he," Maralinne said with a sigh.

"Don't ladies ride here?" asked April

"I rode a lot when I was younger," said Maralinne picking up her sewing again. "And Jareth was forever being sent to fetch me home if I went too far. Sometimes I know he turned his head when I rode out then he followed me. He always knew where I was even when I tried to lose him. Eventually it became sort of a game between us. But then I turned fifteen and had to behave like a lady." Her needle work dropped to her lap again.

"You haven't been riding since?"

"Only twice and that was side saddle in a skirt," Maralinne said with disgust.

"You will forget all about riding when you are married and have a belly full of heirs," said Lady Cellina joining in on their conversation.

"Celli!" exclaimed Lady Liella. "You embarrass Maralinne."

"As if she doesn't know what marriage is all about, Liella."

"As if an old spinster like you does," retorted Maralinne.

"I know a man like Rogarth wouldn't let a wedded night go by without teaching you," Cellina continued undaunted.

"Hush, Celli," Lady Liella told her sister. "There are young girls present who can wait a bit longer for their education even if Maralinne is over ready for hers."

All eyes fell on April. She looked away to hide her amusement.

Mabry the miller wiped another white streak across his face as he looked up. "Well Kyrdthin, so this is the boy?" he said with a welcoming smile. "Will, right?"

"Right sir"

"Just Mabry, no sirs here, just Mabry or Mabry Master Miller if you must give me a title."

Will took the floury hand Mabry offered. "I think I'm gonna like it here," he said. "This place is awesome."

"Milling is hard work, not at all awesome, my boy, but you will find me a reasonable master," said Mabry with a grin.

"As I told you," said Kyrdthin. "The boy is quick to learn. A bit scrawny, been sick a lot, but lifting a few flour sacks will muscle him up."

"Don't worry, milling is not all brawn, Will my boy," said Mabry. "A lot is wit too. Kyrdthin tells me you know you numbers and letters. That will help me more than hefting sacks. Come let me show you around." Mabry put a hand on Will's shoulder and steered him away.

"Then I'll be leaving you two," said Kyrdthin

Will flashed a look of panic and stepped back.

"You are in good hands, Will," Kyrdthin assured him. "Mabry and I go back a long way together."

Will looked down at the white handprints on his shirt. "Sure, see ya," he forced with a catch in his voice.

"Milling may be hard work," said Mabry kindly replacing his hand on Will's shoulder. "But learning to be a man is a lot harder. He said you are thirteen, right? Just the age to start new things."

Will looked back to the doorway. Kyrdthin was gone.

They met in King Arinth's study. Kyrdthin and Jareth waited patiently while Gil arranged Arinth's lap robe, set pen and paper on the desk in front of him then carried in the tea tray.

"Now then," said the King when Gil took a seat at his right hand. "Delven is it? Harrying our borders?"

"Yes sire," said Jareth. "And with no apparent reason, pattern or purpose that we can see."

"Have you sent a force to scare the bastards off?" said Arinth.

"That is what we need to decide today, sire," said Gil. "Do we attack while the threat is small and put an end to the matter or watch first to see what they are up to?"

"How many are we talking about Jareth?" asked Kyrdthin.

"Small groups, threes and fives, scouting parties perhaps."

"Scouting! In my kingdom!" Arinth exclaimed his face reddening.

"Yes sire, it is all here in Jareth's report," said Gil pointing to the papers on the desk. Gil's fingers stroked a calming sign as he touched Arinth's gnarled hand. The blue spell drifted then settled. Arinth's face relaxed. His eyes drooped.

"They could be looking for someone," said Kyrdthin. "Yet how could they suspect the obvious?"

"Or they are just looking because we are looking," said Jareth. "We are still looking for Tobar."

"Or they are looking for something not someone," said Gil. "Jewels attract jewels. And now that yours is here Kyrdthin, Belar's ruby would sense it."

"Yes two jewels so close would but I already took the crowns to Allarion to throw him off the kids' trail."

"So your diamond and Marielle's sapphire are together? Are you sure that is wise?' said Gil.

"Why not? Would you rather that Frebar found out that his topaz is more than a family heirloom?"

"It has always worried me that a focus stone is in Frevarian hands." Gil paused to tuck Arinth's lap robe a bit tighter. Arinth stirred but did not wake.

"It doesn't really matter where the jewels are," said Jareth. Carinna's emerald is still missing so the time for the rejoining is not anywhere near. I think we should turn our attention to more immediate concerns."

"Like Delven," said Kyrdthin.

"Delven again!" said Arinth awakening. "Looking for jewels in my kingdom!"

"We don't know what they are looking for, sire."

"Then let's send Jareth to find out," said the king slamming his fist down on the desk so hard the ink well jumped. Gil's quick hand caught the dislodged pen before it splotched the papers spread out on the desk top. "Jareth can leave off chasing little Mari for one day can't he?" Arinth chuckled.

'Yes, sire, Princess Maralinne is safe here in the castle with her ladies," said Gil.

"My little rubies," said Arinth suddenly wistful. "I want to see my little rubies."

"The ladies are all sewing in the morning room, sire. Shall we send for them?"

"Learning to sew already, my little girls? Yes, have them sent for . Let them show me their stitches so I can be proud of them." Arinth leaned back in his chair. Again Gil's fingers wove the calming. Jareth and Kyrdthin waited until Arinth's eyes closed before they resumed their talk.

Tobar closed the musty text. He no longer needed it. Passage to and from the Dark Realm was much easier via Lord Belar's star sign but that was not the real reason. Tobar knew he was being watched both in the Twin Kingdoms and by Belar's minions. His hand still rested on the book. The five puddles of candle wax around it would have to be scraped off later but that was the least of his worries today. No one in Frevaria would venture into his remote corner of the library. "Home to Love," he said the last line of the spell to himself. How ironic! When he thought he had no one to love, the quest for knowledge, this library, these books had become his life, his only love, his home. Frebar ruled Frevaria, all but this tiny corner where Tobar had discovered the awful secrets of power. Frevarians feared magic and distrusted learning. They put their trust in muscle, fast horses and swordsmanship. Tobar was pale and a little stooped. His eyesight was poor. He hated horses and he didn't even own a sword.

He picked at the wax on the table. He thought he had it all until Analinne taught him what it meant to love. And now with the child, the fruit of their love, everything had changed. Idly his finger traced the star sign on the cover of the book. It glowed slightly. The passage to another world, unlimited riches, unlimited power, how wonderful it had all seemed. Coming and going as he pleased using the star sign and the simple home spell that every child knew from the cradle, now that was the real joke. Who but he had ever suspected the true power of those words?

He slipped the book back onto the shelf. He should never have told Lord Belar about that day when the spell changed. He had been curious and more than a little concerned for his own safety when the spell, his only means of returning home to Analinne, glowed bright white instead of its usual red. First Belar had raged then he began to laugh with insane glee as he cunningly devised the plan.

Tobar was terrified to challenge him. Until then it had all been an adventurous game. Even when Belar promised Tobar's son the high kingship over Arindon and Frevaria he had not seen any real danger. After all he and Analinne were both royal heirs themselves. But then according to Belar's plan Tobar and four Delven warriors followed the alternate home spell to discover secrets hidden half a generation ago. Not one but two contenders to the double throne were hidden away with enough magic to assure they ascend when they came of age. Yes, Frebar's refuse, his witch woman and their Delven brat! What a perfect vengence on his pompous brother to bring back his discarded wife and child to haunt him. But there was also the boy, Arinth's Allarian bastard. Tobar still fought the mixed emotions. Together those two Kyrdthin had hidden on another world could breed a dynasty of high kings and Ann's baby would have nothing. He wanted to give his lovely wife this ultimate gift, but he could not eliminate, no say the real words. He could not kill a child.

"Mari, Annie, come my little rubies," said King Arinth holding out his arms. "My how you have grown."

Maralinne and Analinne knelt before their father's chair. He looked frail and lost in his embroidered dressing gown and red plaid lap robe Gil had draped across his knees. Maralinne could not bear to look up at him. Instead she studied his gnarled white ankles protruding above soft leather slippers worn crooked by an uneven gait. Analinne shifted her now awkward body to lay her hand on his.

"Annie my good girl," he said patting her head. "How old are you now?"

"Eighteen, father."

"Eighteen! My how time flies! I must look for a suitable husband for you."

"Father," Analinne's voice held steady but her eyes blurred with tears. "Father you have already found me a good husband. You betrothed me to Prince Tobar. Do you remember now? You betrothed us when I was just a child and now we are married."

Arinth stroked her hair with a puzzled look on his face.

"Do you remember my wedding, father? You looked so fine in you red tunic and you called King Frebar a fat, pompous, old blue jay right in the middle of the ceremony. Do you remember how everyone laughed?"

"I said that? I said it indeed. Fat, pompous, old blue jay, that tells it all." He slapped his knee with a resounding whump. "Yes that was clever wasn't it? Marrying my little Annie to his brother. Prince and princess, silver and gold, sun and moon as the gods foretold."

"Yes father."

"Let's go Ann," Maralinne whispered

"Speak up Mari," said Arinth. "Now that Annie's got a husband next you'll be wanting one too."

"I don't want a husband..."

"Father," Analinne hurried to say. "You have done well by my sister too. Rogarth the captain of the guard has been wooing her ever so long. You will give your consent won't you, at the Midsummer Ball?"

"Rogarth is it?" Arinth clicked his tongue as he leaned forward. Gil reached out a hand to steady him. "Going behind my back again Mari? Sneaking out again? I'll have to send Jareth out again to fetch you back."

"Father stop it," Maralinne exclaimed.

"Always my fiery one. But whatever you want you shall have. I can't say no to my little rubies. You are all I have of my dear, dear Veralinne."

Arinth broke down into sobs. Gil nodded that the princesses should leave. He tucked the lap robe tighter around Arinth's knees, then signaled for a servant to carry him back to bed. "Rest a while, sire," he said gently. "And when you feel up to it we'll all come back to discuss the agenda for today's court." Arinth did not answer.

Chapter 4

Morning brought Kyrdthin knocking at their door. Janille was still in her nightgown. "Shh… April's still asleep," she said letting him in.

"Morning Janie." He swept past her. "Up, up little bird time to fly." He pinched April's toes beneath the quilt.

"Bug off Hawke. I'm asleep."

"I can't stay long." He turned to Janille. "I really shouldn't be seen here, but once won't raise too many royal eyebrows."

"What is it?"

They sat down on April's bed. He pinched her again. "Bug off," she whined.

"Just stay wrapped up bed bug." He patted her quilt wrapped bottom. "We can talk quick here then I must go. The bad truth is that this part of the kingdom is infested with Delven warriors. No real skirmishes, just sightings. We don't know what they are after. Rogarth has doubled the guard, and Gil says we should wait until they make a move before we strike."

"Who is Gil?" said April.

"Gil is the king's advisor. You saw him at dinner. He's the Allarian who sits beside him," said Janille.

"He helped the king stand up. What's wrong with the king anyway?"

"He's just old and sick," said Kyrdthin

"And longs to return to Allarion," added Janille.

"Why?"

"No more questions, April," said Kyrdthin impatiently standing up then sitting down on the bed again. "We must get back to business. Janie, I don't want you and April to be out of sight of each other until I can find out what is afoot. April you are to say nothing, I mean nothing about you past or where you lived until now, understand?"

"But what if someone asks me?"

"There is no time to invent an elaborate story so just say you are from a long way from here and that life in Arindon is so much more interesting you would rather talk of the present."

"But what if…"

"I have done all I can to shield you here but if there is trouble know that Queen Marielle and Gil are the ones to go to for help."

"OK," said April beginning to feel a little scared

"Just mingle with the other girls but be quiet. Make friends. Fit in. And Janie, you must promise to be more careful. Marielle told me about your tears at the first meeting. Remember past and present must be separated if we are to have a future at all for our children."

Janille looked away.

"What did she do?"

"Never mind the details, little bird. Let's just say coming home is just hard for your mother with seeing people she knew and loved years ago. Give her your support now and don't ask questions. You will know everything when the time is right."

April reached for her mother's hand. "OK Uncle Hawke, Mom and I will do whatever you say."

"That's the other thing. I am Kyrdthin here not you Uncle Hawke."

"Kyrdthin…" April let the unfamiliar name roll on her tongue.

"Where's your bird this morning," said Kyrdthin looking around the room. "He sure is quiet."

"Trebil quiet. Trebil good boy," said the mirror bird lighting on his shoulder.

"Trebil has something important to teach you. Remember the stories I told you and the dreams you had the night before we left?"

"Sure." April sat up and hugged her knees under the quilt. "They were so real."

"They were thanks to Trebil. He is called a mirror bird because he can mirror what he sees to someone else. All you have to do is to let your mind concentrate on something bright like the fire or the sky or a mirror and Trebil can project to you."

"That's really weird!"

"Yes but do you understand?"

"Sort of…"

"Come here Trebil." Kyrdthin held out his finger. The little bird hopped on. "Now go to April."

Trebil flew to the quilt right under April's chin. Kyrdthin picked up a small framed mirror from the dresser. "This will do for a focus point," he said handing the mirror to her. "April, look into the mirror. See only the brightness," his voice commanded. "The brightness...the brightness..." The rhythm of the words drew her. April struggled to keep awake. "See only the brightness...the brightness..." his voice droned on.

The mirror clouded then slowly cleared. Inside the glass was a miniature scene. It was the banquet hall just as it had appeared at dinner the night before. The tiny figures moved. The music and the voices rose in volume. April floated into the scene. What happened next April could not remember, but when she awoke she felt different, as if she had always lived in Arindon. Kyrdthin was talking to her mother and Trebil was back in his cage munching nuts.

"Hawke, I'm scared," said Janille reaching for him.

"Kyrdthin, remember," he said keeping just beyond her outstretched arms. "Just make the sign."

"But we need you..."she begged.

"Make the sign. You can do it."

April watched fascinated as her mother's fingers traced a star in the air before her. A faint hint of silver lingered.

"See you can," said Kyrdthin taking her hands. "Practice Janie. Here you have power again. I will need your help before all this is over." He bent down as if to kiss her then thought better of it and straightened up. "Bye Janie love. You too bed bug."

Then he was gone. April could not remember him opening and shutting the door. The sign her mother had drawn shimmered bright then faded.

Queen Marielle's summons came late that afternoon. Janille changed her dress and rebraided her hair. The note said, "To discuss details of your employment as nursemaid for the Royal Children," but she sensed much more behind the delicately written note and large silver seal.

She was ushered into Marielle's private chamber. The tinted windows bathed the small room in pale blue light. Tea was set for three on a low lace covered table. Queen Marielle and Gil reclined on two of the many embroidered cushions scattered about the floor. Janille dropped a deep curtsy.

"In the privacy of our own chambers you need not be formal," said Marielle raising her hand in greeting. "You are ever as much a queen as I. Come sit as our equal."

When Janille was seated and arranged her skirts on the floor around her, Gil poured the tea. They sipped silently, and when they set the delicate silver cups back in their saucers Marielle began. "This is no light occasion, though I wish it were. Soon we may all be in grave danger. You know about the Delven warriors that have been sighted. Gil believes that they are waiting for the upcoming Solstice Ball to strike when we are all gathered in one place. Kyrdthin is doing all he can to ward the castle and we have ordered a double guard to attend in guise of an honor escort for Rogarth. There are two things that we want you to do Janille. That night I want you to take Avrille up to the balcony. Most of the other girls will be watching from up there so it won't attract attention. But don't leave her even for an instant. She still will be exposed if anything happens. Also be prepared to link with us in the fire spell. There will only be four of us, not five but..."

"The mirror bird helped us make the passage," Janille interjected.

"Then we will be five. I hadn't thought of the bird."

Janille let her eyes wander around the room. There were flowers everywhere, woven into the tapestries, painted on the walls. Pots of exotic blooms lined the window sills and dried bouquets filled vases on every table and shelf. Even the quilt on the settee was a floral motif.

She called her attention back to the issue at hand. "I will do as you ask," she promised. "But you must know my powers are weakened since I was away. They are just now starting to return."

"Mine too are weakened for grief in leaving Allarion," said Marielle with a longing look toward Gil. "But we must protect what we love with everything we have left."

"What about Willy?" said Janille with sudden alarm.

"Kyrdthin assures us he will be safe, though he did not explain how."

"Then we will just have to trust him," said Janille with a resigned sigh.

When their business was done Gil poured them a second cup of tea and the conversation turned to more pleasant subjects for a time. When Janille was finally dismissed she stood up, then looked back down to where Marielle was still seated. Janille dropped an awkward curtsy. Marielle laughed and bid her rise. "So it must be for now, sister queen," she said. "Someday we will stand together, and on that day we will step aside to make way for our children."

Marielle rose, took Janille's hands and tenderly kissed her cheek. Then Gil escorted her to the door.

The weeks slipped quickly by. The warm spring days followed an easy pattern. April was lulled into the rhythm of life in Arindon. Breakfast in the morning room followed by studies with Master Dell, then afternoons sewing with the ladies in the solarium until tea. Now it was time to occupy young Keilen while Lady Elanille rested. April set her sewing basket on the table by her bed and picked up her shawl.

"Chirrp!"

"Hello Birdy Love."

"See Will? April want story?"

See Will? She missed her foster brother but found herself sending Trebil to see him less and less. The life she had shared with him was literally worlds away. "Sure Trebil," she said. "And there will be a treat when you come back."

The mirror bird flitted away. April tossed her shawl over her shoulders and knotted the ends behind her waist. Having her hands free to manage Kylie was a must. Today he insisted on going down to the practice yard again to watch his father. She picked up a book from the table then put it down again. There would be no time to read while Kylie played today. Master Dell's history assignment would have to wait. Her petticoats rustled beneath her skirts as she hurried down the corridor to Lady Elanille's apartments. Long dresses were a nuisance at times, especially when she cared for Kylie but feeling like a fairy tale princess more than compensated for the inconvenience. She picked up her skirts a trifle as she turned a corner. She had only two dresses, the green Kyrdthin brought her the day they first arrived and now this blue and cream Lady Elanille gave her just yesterday. She held her skirts up higher and started up the stairs.

"I hear'd her. I hear'd her." An enthusiastic voice chimed above. Kylie rushed to meet her. "Let's go," he said grabbing her hand and pulled her toward the door.

Darilla, Mabry's daughter stood on the rungs of the chair and leaned over Will's shoulder.

"So zero doesn't mean nothing?"

"Sometimes it does," mumbled Will.

"When?"

"When it's by itself." Will laid his slate pencil down then picked it up again.

"And if its not?"

"Look I gotta get this stuff done for your father," said Will pulling the chair forward in hopes of dislodging Darilla. It didn't.

"I didn't mean to bother you," she said sweetly. "I just want to know. I mean I never met someone as smart as you are and..."

"OK, OK. I'll teach you but lemme finish this tally first or your father will be on my case."

Darilla picked up her weaving frame and took it to a bench beside the window where she could work and wait and also watch Will. Her bobbins were threaded with four different colors. Too many for such a little girl her mother had said, but Darilla was nine and she insisted on trying. She knew if she counted the threads just right the pattern would come out even. It had at first, but now...Darilla studied her work. There had to be an easier way. Will's numbers promised to be the answer.

The mill was quiet. Don the journey man had driven off with today's sacks. The daily dusting of white was still over everything but she was told not to sweep until Will finished the tally. Sweeping always made him cough. She laid her weaving down on her lap and said her numbers to herself. Not many girls could count to twenty five, at least not many nine-year-olds. There were twenty five threads on her weaving frame. She counted again, touching each thread as she said the number. She was almost to twenty when Will laid down his slate pencil again and looked over his shoulder.

"You still here?"

Darilla resumed her perch on the back rungs of Will's chair. There on the tally slate were long columns of numbers. Some had little crosses or X's between them. Some were above or below straight lines. Darilla was fascinated.

"I already can say my numbers," she said. "Want to hear me?"

"Not really," said Will wondering why he had agreed to teach anything to a girl.

Darilla looked so disappointed that Will took pity and said, "Do you know what all the numbers mean like say forty nine or sixty five?"

Darilla didn't know what to say so she just nodded.

"Then do you know how to add?" He read her puzzled look. "You don't...well then...give me that weaving thing." She handed him the frame. "OK so you have four reds here then one blue. How many threads are in the border?"

Darilla counted them. "One-two-three-four-five."

"OK," said Will. "Now just remember that four and one are five."

Darilla leaned over Will's shoulder as he studied the pattern of her weaving. Surely he could get it back on track. Maybe he could help her do one with six colors or even ten.

"OK now here on the other side you have one blue and four reds. Don't count just tell me one and four are how many?"

"Five?" Darilla guessed.

"Right. You just gotta remember them. I'll teach you the easy ones first then when you've got them I'll teach you the rest."

Darilla nodded.

"One and one are two. Now you say it."

"One and one are two," Darilla repeated the numbers.

"Two and one are three. Three and one are four."

"Two and one are three. Three and one are four."

"You know the next one already," said Will. "Four and one are...?"

"Five!" Darilla exclaimed.

" Now say the whole sum. Four and one are five..."

Darilla learned quickly. She would have gone on and on, all the way up to twenty five but Will soon tired of the game.

"When will you teach me the rest of the numbers? You will teach them to me, won't you , please." Darilla begged.

"Sometime. Maybe." Will copied the numbers from the bottom of the tally slate into the ledger book, then put the book away. Darilla picked up the broom. Will coughed as he headed toward the door.

"Tell mother I'll be done sweeping shortly," Darilla called after him.

The hawk had been watching him again. He saw it fly away from the mill and vanish into the cluster of birches behind Mill Cot where Will now lived with Mabry and his family. Will pushed open the kitchen door. There were eleven plates set on the table. Little seven-year-old Nancie was putting the forks and spoons beside each plate. Eleven? Will counted again...Mabry, his wife Rosella, their six children, Don the journey man and himself and...? "Who's coming to dinner?"

"The wizard," said little Nancie. "He made me a dolly from a hankie. Wanna see?"

"Not really," Will mumbled and pushed past her, heading to the front room to look for Kyrdthin.

"Der's my Daddy, over der," Kylie pointing his chubby finger toward the archery range. "C'mon Av'lle, let's go."

April grabbed the toddler just in time. "No, Kylie little boys must stay here where it's safe."

"No, no!" said Kylie wriggling and kicking but April held fast.

"We watch from here or not at all."

"No! Kylie can't see Daddy here...Kylie can't see..."

Kylie's protests diminished to a whimper but his little foot still stamped the dust.

"What seems to be the trouble, Master Keilen?" boomed a deep voice behind them.

"Oh Sir Rogarth, Kylie just doesn't understand the danger."

"Kylie can't see Daddy, Av'ille say no," said the boy.

Rogarth picked up the tearful three-year-old. April sighed with relief. Caring for Kylie was not an easy job.

"You must obey Mistress Avrille young sir," said Rogarth. "A good soldier like your father obeys his commanding officer."

Kylie toyed with the metal studs on the shoulder of Rogarth's leather jerkin. "But she always..."

"And a good soldier does not question his orders," Rogarth continued. "He says 'yes sir' or 'yes my lady' and does as he is told."

"Yes sir," said Kylie in a small voice. He scrunched up his face into a pout.

Rogarth held back a smile. "If you want to see what is going on at the archery range what you need is a higher perch." He hoisted the boy to his shoulders and set off across the practice field with giant strides and a jangle of chain mail.

"Thank you," said April breathlessly trying to match Rogarth's gait. He freed a hand and reached back to take hers.

"Anything to help a pretty maid in distress," he said slowing down a bit.

"I know this is the third time this week, I don't mean to keep bothering you," April tried to apologize "But Kylie just won't behave indoors."

Rogarth squeezed her hand. "Lord Keilen is proud that his son takes interest in the soldier's art at such a young age."

The line of bowmen stood with raised weapons. Their arrows were knocked and waiting.

"Release!" Master Rollin commanded.

The volley of arrows whirred and sank into the straw bale targets with a thwump. The men stood motionless with only their bowstrings relaxed.

"Retrieve!" Master Rollin shouted,

The bowmen sprinted to the targets, anxious to see how accurately they had shot.

"My Daddy he shoot best," declared Kylie

" I'm sure he did," said Rogarth

"Can you shoot arrows too?" asked Kylie poking his tiny fingers in the holes of Rogarth's mail.

"I can and do, but the sword is my weapon of choice."

"My Daddy he has a sword too."

"Soldiers train with all weapons, Master Keilen, but we each have our strength. Your father's is the bow and mine is the sword."

Kylie squinted out over the range. "When they gonna shoot again?"

The bowmen stood at ease. Master Rollin was talking to a man in a dark plaid, hooded cloak.

"Is that Jareth?" asked April standing on tiptoe.

"Yes it's Jareth," Rogarth replied. "He's the best bowman in the Twin Kingdoms and beyond."

"He gonna shoot too?" asked Kylie bouncing up and down.

"Sit still young master." Rogarth reached up to quiet him. "Let's watch and see."

Jareth carried his long dark bow to the end of the line of men. He selected a green-fletched arrow from his quiver, tossed his cloak back over his right shoulder, fitted his arrow then nodded to Rollin.

"Ready!" Master Rollin commanded.

The line of bowmen raised their weapons.

"Aim!"

Muscled arms, steeled fingers, set jaws, focused eyes all waited for the signal. Jareth looked small and slight beside them. Twang! Quicker than an eye could follow Jareth's arrow flew diagonally into the brush. Something squealed.

"Release!" Rollin barked a second later.

Thwang! Thwump! Thwump! Thwap! The straw bales were peppered with arrows.

"Retrieve!"

Jareth darted into the brush to emerge a moment later. In his hand a rabbit dangled limply by the ears. A green-fletched arrow jutted from it's neck.

"He shoot a bunny!" Kylie exclaimed. "Why Jareth shoot a bunny? He made it cry. I heared it." His lower lip began to quiver. "Is a li'l bunny dead Av'ille?" he said eyes welling with tears.

"Yes Kylie, the rabbit is dead. Jareth will probably eat him for dinner."

"It's just a li'l bunny," Kylie wept. "How comes he din't shoot the target like my Daddy?"

"Sometimes a soldiers real target is not a straw bale, Master Keilen," said Rogarth kindly. "Jareth was showing them a valuable lesson. Had it been an enemy rather than a rabbit the soldiers would not have seen him. Their eyes were only on the straw bale."

"My Daddy don't shoot bunnies," said Kylie recovering a little from her grief. "But he could if he wanted to I betcha."

"I'm sure he could," said Rogarth. lifting the boy down from his shoulders. "Now run along with Mistress Avrille. I have duties to attend."

"Thank you ever so much, sir," said April grabbing Kylie by the collar to keep him from escaping.

"Thank you, Mistress," said Rogarth lowering his voice. He pressed a small box into her hand. "If you would deliver this token to my lady Maralinne."

"I said uncover them!"

"But Lord Belar..."

"Borat, do as I say, damn it. Uncover the mirrors."

"I'm concerned for you sire," his servant pleaded. "Remember the last time. Remember why you ordered them covered."

Belar ripped the heavy draperies from their hangings. Gray dust swirled specter-like as the protective coverings tore then thudded to the floor. Unshrouded the five mirrors stood naked around Belar's chair. Gray mist swirled within each glassy surface.

"Show me!" Belar roared. "Show me what these fickle cards refuse to tell." He threw the deck at the closest mirror. The cards fluttered lazily to the floor. All but two fell face down. Belar roared again and kicked the cards, but the White Queen still lay beside the White King staring up at him with unblinking mockery.

"Please My Lord," said Borat. He tried to turn Belar back to his chair. "Come sit down and I will..."

"Will what? Fill my goblet until I'm good and drunk. No? Spike my tea then cover the mirrors again?" Belar faced the tall bank of mirrors. "Now! I want to know now."

The mirrors swirled then brightened with color. A panorama of the Twin Kingdoms spread out before him. Arindon rose in silvery splendor in the right hand mirror and Frevaria glowed golden in the left. The river joined them in a lazy arch . The scene was serene, pregnant with spring blossoms.

"See it is peaceful sire," said Borat but Belar's eyes were riveted to the image in the center mirror. A third castle was being built at the edge of the river's bend. As he watched it grew to dazzling heights. Five white jutting turrets in the shape of a star anchored the walls. Belar shook with rage. Tears streamed down his face. "No! No!" he cried. "You lie! I will not lose a second time!" He drew his ruby-hilted sword. The great jewel flared. He slashed at the mirror, but the image remained unscathed. He stabbed the mirror again and again. "Die you bastards die! You cannot rob me of again." The ruby on his sword blazed brighter and brighter. The heat of the weapon seared Belar hand. He threw it from him. The sword skittered across the floor. Belar sucked his burned hand and sank sobbing to the floor. The mirrors grew dark again.

It was early. Don the journeyman had not yet arrived at the mill. Will sketched hastily on his slate, looked across the room, studied the distance, then studied the room again."

"What are you about?" said Mabry coming in with his arms full of clean flour sacks. "Drawing pictures?" He picked up the slate.

"Just an idea," said Will reaching to retrieve the slate.

"No let me see," said Mabry. "A big wheel on the outside? Now that's a new one. All connected to...but what could drive such a big wheel? The river?'

Will nodded.

"What about in late summer when the water's low? You'd be left high and dry."

Will flipped over the slate. "See here, he pointed to lines he had drawn across a rough map. "We could build a race to sluice the water from above the rapids." His finger traced the path. "A wooden trough sealed with pitch would do. And here..." his finger tapped the wheel he had drawn. "It would empty over the top. Call it an over shot wheel. It would turn, see and..." Will's voice rose with excitement. "Inside an axel would connect to the hub and then we'd connect it with belts and cogs to power the stones."

Mabry studied the plan. He turned the slate over and studied the other side. Then he flipped it back again. Finally he said, "Will my boy, you may have something here. Copy it on the back of the ledger book before you start work. I want to take another look at it later."

April returned to her room. Lady Maralinne had accepted Sir Rogarth's token without comment. April wondered about her new friends. Something was not right between them.

"Chirp."

Trebil was back sitting on top of his cage.

"Back so soon, Birdy Love?"

"Will. Will. Story now? Poor Will."

"Poor Will? Show me now," said April anxiously reaching for her mirror."

"Treat?'

"Yes, yes. Show me now Trebil." April sat down. The mirror clouded in her hand and when it cleared she was holding an image of her brother.

Will worked long and hard until late afternoon. There had been three deliveries today. His head ached and his lungs were choked full with flour. He coughed and cleared his throat again and again.

"Will climb up to the loft with these," said Don handing him a pile of extra sacks. "And check how many balls of twine are there before you come down."

Will stood up. The sudden movement sent him into another spasm of coughs.

"You'll never make a miller with those lungs," said Don trying to sympathize. "I'm sure those numbers and letters of yours could get you more than a miller's earnings. There'd be lots who'd be eager to learn and use your knack. No reason to waste it on little girls and their weaving."

Will blushed.

"Darilla showed me how you taught her to say her numbers. Next you'll be…"

"Darilla's a pest." Will said wiping his nose on his sleeve. "I just did it to shut her up." With that he took the sacks and climbed up the ladder to the loft.

It was hot at the top of the ladder…very hot. There was no air. Will coughed and choked. The sacks slipped from his hand. He grabbed for them. His head swam. His hand hit the ladder. The ladder fell. He fell. The mill turned round and round. Pain! Then everything went black.

Will came to beneath a sea of faces. One face moved closer. He thought he knew who it was but he wasn't sure. Something cool touched his forehead. Another smaller face crowded into view.

"Is he gonna die...gonna die...gonna die..."

The face and the voice swam against the current of the pain in his head. All around him the mill creaked and groaned. Faces swirled around him as if they rode on a gigantic wheel. Will closed his eyes but he still saw the wheel...turning turning...The wheel of faces took on another form. Two men hung from a rope turning with the wheel. One turned toward him. The face was vaguely familiar. The rope twisted turning the face away. The wheel continued to turn until the second hanging man faced him. It too was familiar. It wore the same face as the first man. He knew that face! Will gasped for breath. It was his own!

Will tried to sit up but hands pushed him down again.

"Papa, is he gonna die?" said a girl's voice.

"Shut up pest," said Will trying to sit up again. "Your chatter makes my head hurt."

The scene in the mirror flickered and faded. "Trebil tell good story? Treat now?"

April laid the mirror down. "Here, Birdy Love." She uncovered a little bowl of fruit nuts. Trebil swooped down.

"Trebil, good boy. Oh so good boy," he sang as he greedily munched his reward.

April pondered what she had seen. It was more than a story this time. She had not only seen and heard what went on at the mill, she had slipped into Will's thoughts. The vision, the faces and the giant wheel, what did it all mean? Will was so hurt and scared, and she had felt his pain as if it were her own.

Chapter 5

The day of the Summer Solstice ball arrived. All the usual activities stopped to be replaced by such a flurry that April was overwhelmed. Delicious aromas had been wafting up from the kitchen since before dawn. Breakfast seemed bland and tasteless by comparison. All through the day lesser lords and landholders arrived at the castle gate. The chamber maids scurried to ready their rooms. Keeping Kylie out of the way was a full time job. Castle guards were everywhere, silently watching and waiting. The whispers of Dark Delven sightings fueled the excitement even more. The royal ladies had forgone their afternoon sewing circle today to prepare themselves for tonight's event. Lady Elanille asked April to take Kylie earlier than usual so she could have a last minute fitting of her gown.

By tea time the promise of the magnificent dinner to come was almost unbearable. The crescendo of activity reached an exhausting height. Kylie held a cookie in each fist. "Av'ille hold me," he whimpered in a tired voice. She picked him up and carried him back to the nursery. He was asleep before she could lay him in his bed.

April was too excited to eat anything at tea but Janille insisted. Kyrdthin brought them a plate of cakes. "Snitched right out from under the baker's nose," he bragged then rushed off again. April wondered if he had used magic as she slowly savored the delicately spiced cake.

"Be sure to eat it all," said her mother.

"Why? Did Kyrdthin put medicine in it?"

"Yes, and it is important."

April looked at the half eaten cake in her hand. It didn't look quite as appealing now.

"I taste Freebane," said Janille. "That will protect us if something goes amiss tonight."

"But how? What's Freebane? What if...?"

"Calm down. Freebane blocks a seer's probe. So our minds cannot be read or controlled."

April's fear mounted.

"All you need to know is that Kyrdthin sees the need to protect us with it. So eat it all."

As April pinched the last crumbs and licked her fingers her eyes lingered on the silver sign Kyrdthin had traced on her mother's heart before left. She touched her own chest, telling herself that she too was protected by that lovingly drawn sign.

Tobar lifted his tankard of ale and belched. The terrified innkeeper hurried with refills. The ale felt good even in his present company. The Dark Delven warriors on either side of him drank heavily. Tobar pulled the hood of his cloak down further over his face and fingered the rough leather fastenings of the box tucked under his arm. He had not told the Dark Lord about the box. When he was ordered to return home for the Solstice festivities and await further instructions he was glad he had not. It was the perfect opportunity to put his own plan into action. Now all he had to do was give his escorts the slip. But getting two Delven warriors drunk without getting drunk himself was no easy task.

He took another sip, purposely letting the tankard slip from his hand. "Curse the Five," he roared imitating his fellows as he caught the sloshing tankard just in time. "Fill 'er up again inn…hic…keep."

Jareth slipped out the back door from Beck's Tavern. He had seen enough. Wrapping his cloak tightly around himself he looked up and down the dark alley. No one was in sight. He raised his fingers to his lips. The cry of the hunting hawk that has spotted it's prey pierced the night. Then he waited. The clink of dishes, the sizzle of fat dripping into the fire, the frightened whispers of the kitchen maids could be heard from the kitchen window. Murmurs of voices came from the dining room punctuated by the rise and fall of coarse laughter. There was no music.

A sudden wind and a whir of wings blew back Jareth's hood. When he turned around Kyrdthin emerged from the shadows.

"Three Delven and Tobar dead drunk. In there." Jareth jerked his thumb toward the tavern.

"Talking?"

"Not enough to give us answers."

"Just three Delven,?"

"Yes, I followed them here from the Arindon wood," said Jareth.

"So they're using Five Oak Circle then?" said Kyrdthin.

"I didn't see them arrive but I assume so."

A harsh growl demanding more ale reached them from the tavern. Armon Beck's rich baritone responded in short broken phrases. The kitchen girls fell silent.

"We must warn the castle," said Kyrdthin. "I'll go. I'm quicker. You stay with them and if they leave follow them."

"If they try to enter the castle?"

"Let them. We'll be ready by then."

Jareth hesitated then said, "Kyrdthin, I'd rather not go into the castle, not tonight."

Kyrdthin looked at Jareth's half shaded face. His hood hid any meaning an expression would betray. Kyrdthin clapped a hand on Jareth's shoulder. "You serve the Light best in the woods and alley ways my good man. The castle guard can handle the inside. You watch and wait out here as you always have done."

Jareth nodded.

"Now I must go," said Kyrdthin slipping his arms back inside his cloak. "I have wardings to set."

In a sparkle of silver he was gone.

The hour of the ball arrived. April squeezed between a pillar and the railing at the top of the stairs. People were beginning to arrive in the great hall below. Several knights were clustered by the fireplace talking earnestly, their tankards of ale almost forgotten in their hands. The ladies chatted nervously in billowing hoop-skirted circles. Their eyes sparkled then lowered as they discreetly flirted from behind their fans.

Someone was coming! April pulled herself back behind the pillar. Lady Cellina paused on the balcony before descending the stairs. She hung her voluminous bejeweled bosom over the railing to scrutinize the scene below.

"Go Celli" said her sister pausing behind her.

"No, Liella, not yet. I want to time our entrance perfectly."

"Celli, you old crow."

"Crow! Don't underestimate me sister. Tonight I am a full-fledged vulture and no man can escape my clutches."

"Go Celli," said Lady Liella giving her sister a push.

"One more moment." Lady Cellina surveyed the knights by the fire until one looked up. "Now," she announced and swept down the stairs, an erupting mountain of copper satin. In her wake tripped Lady Liella in frail blue. The musicians paused. The knights put down their tankards to offer their arms to their ladies.

"Isn't it beautiful?" said Janille wistfully as she joined her daughter on the stairs.

"I wonder what is it really like waltzing across that floor," said April

"On the right man's arm it is a thrill beyond comparison but with the wrong one it is only a dull duty."

"Now what are they doing?" said April pointing to the movement below.

"They're lining up to be presented to the king and queen."

The heralds trumpeted. King Arinth and Queen Marielle appeared in the doorway. The king wore red and silver, the queen a misty blue. Gil discreetly guided Arinth by the elbow. Slowly they progressed down the corridor of knights and ladies, pausing to greet each courtly pair. When they reached the dais at the head of the hall, the royal princesses joined them. The trumpets sounded again. The king's guard advanced then stood at attention until Rogarth, their captain, entered and took his place to the left of the throne. Then the guard retreated to their assigned places around the perimeter of the room.

The musicians began to play. With polished grace each couple bowed then moved to alternate sides of the room. The music changed. Swaying to a lively waltz tune the ladies exchanged partners then returned, weaving about the room like a garland of flowers.

"It's all so dreamy," April sighed.

"This is only the beginning dear," said Janille putting her arm around April.

"Do the king and queen dance?"

"Arinth's dancing days are over but Marielle dances beautifully. The knights may ask for the honor or perhaps she will dance with Gil."

"Exactly who is Gil, mother?" said April.

"In Allarion he was Queen Marielle's consort. Here is King Arinth's advisor and personal friend."

April saw the small thin man gently adjust the cushions behind the king's seat. Gil moved with the same delicate grace as Marielle. He had opalescent skin, silvery hair, deep sapphire eyes and the same faraway gaze. When he was sure King Arinth was comfortable Gil smiled at the queen. He placed Arinth's hand in hers, then stepped back to his place behind the throne,

"Gil and Queen Marielle are good people. Kyrdthin said to trust them," said April

"Gil is good and wise and compassionate," agreed Janille. "And Marielle was willing to make a supreme personal sacrifice not once but twice. First for the love of her people, then for the love of her son."

"Tell me about her."

"Kyrdthin could tell her story better than I but it is said that only by taking mates from among others can Allarians have children. Marielle forsook everything to marry Arinth and bear his child."

"But she is a queen. You make it seem so awful." April watched Marielle pat Arinth's hand. He whispered something that made her laugh.

"In Allarion she is more than queen," Janille explained. "They worship her as a goddess."

"But King Arinth loves her so much. I can see it. Are they really Will's parents?"

"Shhh…" Janille cautioned, then nodded her answer.

April pressed her face between the rungs of the stairs railing, mesmerized by the scene below. Colors swirled. Jewels sparkled. Her heart beat to the lilting rhythms. The lines of dancers swayed in courteous ceremony, then broke away, weaving in intricate patterns. They circled and opened to form lines again, stepping to sprightly but elegant tunes. April jumped to her feet twirling her skirts across the balcony. "See mother, I can dance it too."

"April, no!" Janille grabbed her and pulled her again into the safety shadows behind the pillar. "You musn't do anything to draw attention to us."

April reluctantly obeyed "Tell me mother," she said when she took her seat again beside Janille. "Did you dance when you were queen? Mother?"

Janille had dropped Aprils hand. Her eyes had found a familiar gray figure talking to one of the guards. April felt a sudden chill. She remembered Kyrdthin's warning. Here her kind and playful Uncle Hawke was a mysterious and powerful magician. She saw her mother relax when he disappeared again, but April was still afraid.

They inched their way down the stairs for a better view of the dances. The music turned slow and stately. Lady Maralinne was dancing with Sir Rogarth. Her green gown shimmered as she balanced and twirled. Rogarth danced lightly but with power, meeting and retreating, circling every step in perfect time with Maralinne. April sighed. Tonight Maralinne and Rogarth would announce their betrothal. It was going to be so romantic!

"Your time will come dear," her mother whispered.

It was too easy, Tobar tried to tell himself but the ale had begun to have an obvious effect. He held the box under his cloak tighter to his side. He had given them the slip, at least he thought he had lost his unwelcome companions. Now he stood alone at Arindon gate. His head began to spin. He leaned against the wall. He would just stand here a moment and then he would… His stomach heaved. Tobar fell to his knees and retched into the gutter. He knelt there a long time, too sick to do anything else. He could hear the guard pacing on the wall above him. Somewhere nearby a dog barked. He did not see a shadow watching him from across the street.

Tobar staggered to his feet. A cool breeze came up from somewhere clearing his head, giving him courage. He raised his fist and pounded on the gate.

"Is the betrothal going to be now," asked April, her voice rising with excitement.

"Let's watch and see," said Janille dabbing her eyes with her handkerchief.

King Arinth rose. Gil reached out to steady him. The room quieted.

"Maralinne my littlest ruby, come to me."

With a rustle of green satin, Maralinne knelt before him. Arinth laid a hand on her head. She looked up at him. "Yes father," she said forcing a smile.

"A good man has asked for you daughter. Your blood is royal but there is no prince worthy of you." Arinth paused to catch his breath, still patting Maralinne's head as if she were a child. "The man Rogarth is royal in virtuous deeds. I give you to him with my blessing."

"Thank you father," said Maralinne with toneless resignation in her voice.

"Rogarth come claim her so I can sit down," said Arinth leaning heavily on Gil.

Rogarth took her hand, kissed it then turned to the king. "Be at ease, My Lord. Do not tire yourself on my account." As Arinth slumped back into his chair, Rogarth fumbled in the pocket of his tunic. "For you my lovely," he said slipping a tiny garnet ring on Maralinne's finger.

Rogarth led Maralinne to the center of the hall. He signaled to the musicians then called to the assembly. "Dance with us. Be merry."

The ladies crowded admiringly around Maralinne.

"I can't wait to see her ring," April whispered when the dancing resumed.

"I'm sure she will show it to us. Now hush," said Janille.

"It's such a small stone," Lady Cellina was saying. "Being a second daughter in this day and age she can't expect more."

April leaned closer to hear more of the ladies' conversation.

"She doesn't look too happy to be halfway to bed with the handsomest gallant at court," said a lady dressed in rose brocade.

"Look at the poor girl," said another lady in blue silk. "She's just frightened of the responsibilities ahead. Remember being the younger child she was left to do her will until now."

"Yes it was Analinne who was groomed to bear the yoke of state," added Lady Liella. "But I am sure Maralinne will settle down in time."

"Let's hope she does," said Lady Cellina. "I still can't see her content even after a few months of good bedding."

"Yes, she is a wild one," said the lady in rose, dropping her voice behind her fan.

"Careful what you say. She is your better," said the lady in blue.

"She's a spoiled, brat princess or no, and I am in a position to say it," declared Lady Cellina with emphasis on 'I'. "My dear sister Veralinne, rest her soul, would have brought her up better. But what can you expect when an Allarian witch is all the mother the poor child has known."

"Celli hush," exclaimed Lady Liella.

"Don't tell me to hush." Cellina flounced her skirts angrily and turned back to the dancing.

"Oh look," said Liella. "Rogarth is approaching the queen."

"You don't think she'd dare usurp the queen mother's dance!" exclaimed Cellina.

"Hush," said Liella. "I can't hear what he is saying."

April strained her ears and leaned out farther over the railing.

"In the absence of my lady's mother the true Queen Veralinne," said Rogarth. "Would it please Your Highness to accept my invitation to dance?"

Marielle looked first to Arinth then to Gil before she extended her hand to Rogarth. The hall was silent. Then the music began. Massive Rogarth and the diminutive queen honored each other in the center of the hall. He led her into a gentle promenade and after a well timed pause they began to turn in precise, delicate spirals. He was strong and skillful. She was ethereally light. The music rang in hollow echoes. No one breathed. When the last chord had been drawn Rogarth escorted her back to a smiling Arinth, but it was Gil who took her hand and seated her again.

The stillness broke. Servants swarmed into the hall with pitchers of wine and trays of sweets. The music resumed. Dell's clear tenor filled the hall.

"The fires that burn in my lady's hair
Will not be quenched by flood or darkness.
Will not be turned to ash by flight nor fear…"

Rogarth reclined on the steps of the dais next to Maralinne's chair.

"The fires my lady's love has kindled
Will burn through time and transformation.
The light of that fire's blaze will blind the sword
And bind the hand that wields it

The heat of that fire's passion will nurture, heal,
And temper kings..."

Maralinne's eyes were fixed on the singer but did not hear the song. Rogarth took her hand.

"We cannot own fire
But fire can own us, consume us.
The fire that burns in my lady's hair
Will not be quenched by years, nor tears.
And with the autumn of her tresses
She will while away the gray of winter
On the hearth rug of her heart..."

Maralinne pulled her hand away to brush back a stray curl. Rogarth smiled, but Maralinne did not notice. Her gaze had returned to the singer.

"No love burns brighter
No man, no woman
No god, no beast
Loves more full
Loves more deep."

"A strange but beautiful song, Dell," said Rogarth when the singer had finished.

"Sometimes it is my lady love who sings," said Dell caressing his harp. "And I am but her instrument."

Suddenly the doors burst open. Rogarth sprang to his feet. "Hold in King Arinth's name!" he challenged. "Are you man or Delven?"

"Man or Delven! Curse the Five! I may be small, but I'm no stinking Delven." The intruder thrust the guards aside. The hood of his cloak fell back. His long, black hair was disheveled, his clothes filthy. "I am Tobar, Prince of Frevaria, Consort to your own king's daughter and you ask if I am man or Delven. Stand aside, soldier. I have a little something to show my father-in-law."

Janille gasped. In his hands Tobar held a small leather-hinged box. Arinth tried to rise but it was Gil who stepped down from the dais to confront the intruder.

"This is out of order, Tobar, but since you are here..."

"Out of order!" Tobar bellowed. "I have more right in this hall than certain Allarian imposters I could name."

"Be that as it may," Gil continued with heroic calm. "By King Arinth's grace kindly bestow your gift and let the festivities continue."

"Gift? Gift!" Tobar laughed and almost lost his balance.

With that Analinne stood tall. Her face first reddened in shame, then whitened with fear. Tobar ignored her and sauntered toward Maralinne and Rogarth. "Pretty, pretty Maralinne," he said. "Neither you nor your bastards will rob my son of his heritage." He staggered backward. "Come here wife," he said gesturing to Analinne."

Analinne stood firm.

"Come here and bring your belly for all to see. This is mine!" He soundly thumped the front of her gown. "This is the High King of the Twin Kingdoms and in this box is his birthright."

Kyrdthin appeared at the door.

"No tricks, jester." Tobar let out a resounding belch. "I hold the power now."

"What does your precious box contain?" said Kyrdthin. "If it is a betrothal gift I am sure Maralinne and Rogarth would like to display it for all to see."

"Betrothal gift!" Tobar first looked puzzled then he began to laugh. "Oh no. I'm not that stupid. You can't trick me into giving this away." He waved the box and laughed again. "Can't your magic tell what is in this box?"

"That box, my dear drunken man, was fashioned by the gods to house the crown jewels of the kingdoms. How may I ask would you be in possession of such treasure?" said Kyrdthin.

Arinth tottered forward.

"Back you senile..."Tobar began.

Gil raised his hand to strike.

"No Gil!" Kyrdthin warned. "Not here. Not now."

"Then open the box," demanded Gil. "Or can't you unlock it?"

"Of course...it's mine...only I should..." Tobar stammered. His hands shook.

"What are you afraid of Tobar?" said Kyrdthin. "Have you had too many mugs of ale to cope with a simple lock?"

Tobar shook uncontrollably.

"Perhaps the box is protected by a spell to ward off thieves." Kyrdthin prodded the box with his finger.

"None of you tricks...I..." Tobar staggered back a step.

"Then let's let Arinth open it," said Gil snatching the box from Tobar's grasp.

"You...you..."

Kyrdthin clamped a firm, restraining hand on Tobar's shoulder. The box was laid in Arinth's lap. He caressed it lovingly. "So long. It has been so long..." he murmured.

"Open it, sire," prompted Gil.

The latch clicked to Arinth's touch. The lid fell back.

"Damn you Kyrdthin!" Tobar wailed. "Damn your...your tricks!"

"Not much of a birthright, Tobar," said Gil. "Is an ugly box all you can give Analinne's son?"

"Damn you robber. Damn it it's mine. I found it."

"We all know you found the box Tobar," said Kyrdthin, not without some amusement. "But who are you to say who wears the crowns it once contained? You couldn't even open the lock."

"But the prophecy..."

"Ah yes, the prophecy. 'When the Sun and Moon shine double in the sky. Then shall the cask be opened'."

"Shines double...the twinning," argued Tobar.

"Twinning is common Tobar, in the royal houses as well as every horse stable and pig sty," said Kyrdthin .

"You can't cheat me twice. No damn you..." Tobar whimpered. The man stumbled to is knees and started to cry.

Analinne put aside her shame. "Husband come to me," she said approaching him with outstretched arms. "You are tired from you journey."

"Get away from me," Tobar yelled. "You're no good to me until after you have dropped my son."

Analinne opened her mouth but before she could utter a response Lady Cellina rushed to her side and whisked her away.

Maralinne sprang to her feet. She looked first in the direction her sister had gone, then at Rogarth. "Never!" she said between her clenched teeth. Her feet pattered swiftly across the floor and out to the garden.

The room hissed with whispers. Gil signaled to the musicians to resume their playing but no one danced. Tobar rose and made a show of brushing off his knees and rearranging his cloak. Then he sauntered to the banquet table loudly demanding food and drink. Servants scurried to attend him. At a nod from Rogarth the guards arrested Tobar and escorted the cursing man away. That done Rogarth left to search for Maralinne.

Chapter 6

Rogarth found Maralinne in the garden. "Please let me join you," he said taking her hand.

"I want to be alone for a while." She pulled her hand away. "I need a breath of fresh air." Maralinne walked away hoping Rogarth would not follow but he did. "It's not appropriate to be in such a secluded spot together," she said over her shoulder.

Rogarth took her hand again and drew her into a vine draped arbor. "You are my betrothed now. Why don't you want me to comfort you? It has been a tedious evening for both of us."

"I don't want anyone to comfort me," Maralinne said firmly, but he would not be dissuaded.

Maralinne tried to walk faster. The heat of Rogarth's touch on her waist as he guided her beneath the arbor roused fear not passion. The warmth from which she had demurely averted her eyes when their hands met in the dance was nothing compared to this. Rogarth stopped. Maralinne waited immobile, anger and terror rising together. His hands encircled her waist. He pulled her toward him.

"Just one kiss, my fiery lovely, and all will be well."

She struggled but his strong arms soon overcame her. She found her own arms pressing his broad back toward her. What was she doing! His beard rasped against her cheek. His lips touched hers, firm and persuasive. She felt her body responding. Frantically she fought the unwanted feelings. He kissed her neck, her shoulder, her bosom. He bent her backwards until his weight crushed her into the rough wood of the arbor. Maralinne panicked. "Enough!" she cried trying to push him away.

"You can't deny me now, Maralinne. You're my betrothed."

"Don't touch me! Get away!" Maralinne fought herself free and ran, knocking him back with an unexpected blow.

"I'll tame you later," he hurled after her. "Lucky for you I am a patient man."

She was cold but no promise of warmth could entice Maralinne to reenter the castle. She paced from the arbor to the wall. She had run from Rogarth. She wanted to keep running, but to where? Without realizing she had made a decision she climbed up onto the low wall that divided the common gardens from the family courtyard. She slipped off her shoes for better balance, then nimbly walked along the wall toward the balcony of the servant's quarters. She and her sister had often slipped in and out this way, until Analinne grew up that is.

When she reached the balcony the clouds broke open. The full moon emerged triumphant, bathing the gardenscape in sudden light. Maralinne stopped. She let the cold white beams play across her skin. The wind whipped at her gown. She felt wild and free. She would not climb back into that dusky window. She would not be confined in her father's castle any longer. "I will not marry Rogarth!" she declared aloud.

A furtive movement below caught her eye. She took a step toward the balcony. Another shadowed shape moved almost imperceptibly. Sure-footed but terrified Maralinne turned to retrace her steps along the wall. The shapes followed her. When she reached the junction with the outer wall she slipped on her shoes again and began to climb up over the ragged vine-covered stones. She did not stop to pause when she reached the top. Maralinne leaped from the wall, caught a branch of the willow tree outside, slid down the smooth trunk and landed on the soft earth below. She ran without stopping until she reached the fringe of trees beyond the last lights of Arindon.

Maralinne sank down among the black boles of the ancient trees. Only then did reality strike. What she had just done? She was alone, dressed in a ball gown and dancing slippers. She had no equipment for survival in the forest. But she was determined not to go back. Being trapped like Analinne and Elanille was more terrifying than shadows in the dark. She tried to get her bearings in the eerie moonlight. The road was familiar. She had often ridden this way as a young girl, but not recently and never at night.

She started out almost jauntily toward where the game warden's cottage had to be. The rut-filled road was easy to follow in the moonlight. Maralinne walked the bright strip of roadway between the tree shadows. Not daring to think much less plan, she wandered deeper and deeper into the forest. The shadows followed quietly. At first she was unaware of them, but gradually small snaps and rustlings surrounded her, moved with her. She quickened her pace. The shadows kept up with her. She began to run. She stubbed her thin-slippered toes on roots and rocks but she kept going. Now the rustling was punctuated with occasional grunts and metallic clinks. A sudden glint of light on steel flashed off to her right and then to her left. Delven! They were trailing her, herding her.

Maralinne ran faster. They grabbed for her but stumbled. She kept running. The under brush thickened tearing at her dress and tangling her hair. One of her pursuers lunged then screeched, falling, dragging her to the ground. The reeking body twitched then lay still. Dare she move? The harsh voices faded back into the forest. Her heart pounded against the cold dirt of the road. Slowly she crawled out from beneath the corpse. A green-fletched arrow protruded from its back. She inched away to a place where the moonlight shone brightest. She was cold and dirty. Her gown was torn, her hair was unbraided. She felt sick and very much afraid. Maralinne sat down in the middle of the road and sobbed.

"Lady Maralinne," whispered a voice.

The darkness revealed no one.

"Who?" she managed to breathe as a tall dark shadow took shape beside her.

"Come quickly, lady. I know a safe place."

"Jareth? Oh Jareth, thank the gods!" She held up her arms. "Just hold me please."

He pulled her to her feet. "Hurry, Lady Maralinne. We cannot stay here."

"I am not going home!" Maralinne cried pulling back with alarm.

Jareth whistled softly. His horse stepped silently onto the road. Without asking Jareth hoisted Maralinne into the saddle then swung up behind her.

"Hold on tight, Lady. There is no time for proprieties. Speed is prime if your life and honor are to be spared."

The pursuit resumed behind them. Maralinne did not dare to look back. Jareth's arm pressed her tight to his chest. She buried her cheek into the rough fabric of Jareth's sleeve and held on with desperate fingers. The horse galloped beneath them. Her heart pounded inside her. Jareth became her only reality. The horrors pursuing them were a storm raging about their dark throbbing island. The dark steed plunged on into the night its frantic pace drove home every jolt. Her whole body ached. Branches tore at her hair. A tumult rose around them. The roar increased. They must have reached the river!

They sped upstream along a narrow, winding road. Pursuit lagged farther and farther behind. Maralinne kept her eyes pinched shut, fearing even a glance at the swollen river. Where was the bridge? Maralinne's imagination went wild. We should have reached it by now if Jareth intends to cross the river. This road only leads to the falls. We can't climb the cliffs, they're too high.

"Aren't we going…to cross…the bridge?" she gasped out of rhythm with the galloping horse.

"No…another way…narrow place," his voice rumbled near her ear. "Jump if we can…not far."

The horse reared. Cross here? Never! The black water frothed and churned, yet it was evident that the feat had been done before. A faint track led to the edge and continued again on the other side. It may have been a ford in late summer but not now. Maralinne dug her nails into Jareth's cloak. His arm crushed her against his chest. She could feel the tense throb of his heartbeat. She tried to scream but no sound came.

Jareth circled the horse back. "Easy, Dark Beauty, easy." He dug his heels into the horse's sides and they flew. The horse's fore feet struck the far bank. The hind feet scrambled against the loose, wet sand, sliding, dragging them back into the current.

"Up girl! Up! Up!" Jareth shouted.

The back right hoof reached the grassy bank but the soft ledge gave way. They toppled backwards. Icy, black water closed over Maralinne's head. She choked for air. Numb with fear and cold she let Jareth drag her through the raging current. The roar increased. Jareth panted against her, fighting for the shallows. Rocks crashed into them. Fear, cold, pain, they were all one.

Jareth's feet finally touched bottom. He stumbled up the eroded bank dragging Maralinne behind him. He made his way toward a cluster of willows. Maralinne collapsed against a bent trunk. Jareth wrung the water from his cloak then wrapped it around her.

"Can you walk, My Lady?"

Maralinne tested her legs. Jareth's soaked cloak weighed her down but her balance held.

"Good. Then let's get moving before they realize we are not drowned and circle back to High Bridge."

She followed up the slippery trail. They picked their way across the rocks. The falls thundered. The spray drenched them anew.

"Just a little farther," Jareth called back over his shoulder

Maralinne could not answer. The wet, mossy rocks demanded all her attention. Slowly they fought their way along the narrow ledge toward the foot of the falls. Behind the tumbling curtain the path widened then ended abruptly. "Where now?" she panted.

Jareth faced the water-smoothed rock. His fingers traced over a worn sign carved into the rock then waited. Slowly, almost imperceptible at first, then with grinding resistance the rock moved back. A blast of cold air rushed out as the passage widened. Maralinne cried out. Jareth picked her up and carried her through. The door crashed shut behind them.

It was pitch black, then as their eyes adjusted a dull green glow beckoned but offered no warmth.

"I'll build us a fire here near the door," said Jareth. "Farther on it won't be safe. We must dry our clothes and get warm or we will never survive what lies ahead."

He took flint and steel from his pouch as he searched the room for anything that could be used for tinder. When the fire had been kindled and fed to a comfortable blaze, Maralinne studied the cavern room. Remains of furnishings littered the floor. Strange carvings gaped from the beams and trusses. A straw and rag nest in one corner may have been a bed. Jareth shook the rags. Nothing scurried. Maralinne breathed a sigh of relief.

"Lady Maralinne, for your health I must dry your clothes," Jareth said with an anxious tremor in his voice. "Robe yourself as best you can with these." He handed her the ragged bedding and turned his back.

Maralinne slipped off her gown and shift, then knotted the bedding over her shoulders. Jareth hung her clothes neatly on the back of a legless chair near the fire. Then he removed his jerkin and shirt and draped them nearby. The steam rose from the wet leather. Maralinne wrinkled her nose at the smell but said nothing.

"If it would not offend my lady, I would like to dry my hose and breeches also," said Jareth. The tremor in his voice was almost panic.

Maralinne smiled. "Jareth you have saved my life. No simple act of drying clothes could offend me." She removed her outermost blanket and offered it to him. He made a makeshift kilt and soon had his boots and remaining clothes drying with the rest.

"Now we must eat and plan our next move," he said pulling some jerky and water-soaked bread from his pouch. "We have escaped one danger but what lies ahead may be worse."

"What could be worse?" said Maralinne biting into the tough meat. It was dry and too salty but she was too hungry to care. The soggy bread was another matter. She gagged and choked on the amorphous chunks.

"Not fit fare for a princess, but it will keep you alive until I can find better," said Jareth.

When they had finished their meal they discussed their situation and tried to plan what to do next. They would not go back to Arindon. Maralinne was adamant on that point. Jareth agreed in part. Maralinne's safety was his prime concern. With Delven bold enough to infiltrate the castle itself there was no safety there. Why they had singled out her was a mystery. They were both worried how affairs were back in Arindon. Had others been attacked or had Maralinne's pursuers worked alone? Jareth worried about his horse. Had it escaped the swollen river? If so, had it returned to Arindon? And then there was his bow. Even with his short blade thrust into his belt Jareth felt naked and vulnerable.

At last they agreed on a plan. Jareth would take Maralinne to Allarion, then he would return to Arindon for news. The catch to the plan was that the only route to Allarion open to them lay through the caves and the Dark Lord's stronghold.

When their clothes were dry Jareth tore some of the ragged bedding into strips. With these he bound Maralinne's feet over her dancing slippers. "Not a dainty riding boot but it's functional," he said when he had finished.

"It was me that was stupid..."

"No time for that kind of talk now," said Jareth. "Here wrap up in my cloak."

"What about you?"

"I'm wearing a bit more than a seductive ball gown," he said then turned to hide a blush. "Now try to get some rest, My Lady. I will stay on guard."

Maralinne curled up in Jareth's cloak. It was still a little damp and smelled of horse and man-sweat. She was cold. She inched a bit closer to Jareth. He did not seem to notice. Her mind jumped from one confusing thought to another. She was afraid to fall asleep but exhaustion soon took over.

Maralinne woke to clash of steel on stone.

"The right passage...Quick!" Jareth ordered. He tossed her his supply pouch. "I'll hold them off."

She caught the pouch and slipped behind him. She felt her way along the dark tunnel. Jareth backed toward her, cursing and jabbing with his blade. She stumbled to keep ahead of him, led only by the faint phosphorescence. The gravel floor of the tunnel slid with them as they descended. Jareth lost his footing. With a yelp his assailant was upon him. Maralinne swung the heavy pouch. The dark warrior screamed then gurgled as Jareth's blade found its mark.

Jareth shoved himself free, withdrew his blade and wiped it on the dead warrior's tunic. He pulled a small dagger from the boot and handed it to Maralinne. "Here, My Lady, you have proven yourself a comrade in arms."

When Maralinne took the dagger she felt stronger. She would fight side by side with Jareth. She would use the dagger she told herself, but she was still very much afraid.

"There were only two of them," said Jareth. "But whether they have sounded and alarm or our fighting was heard we can only guess. We must assume the worst. I know a place where we can stop and catch our breath. Hurry!"

They went down the damp, gravel-paved passage, sliding, skidding, holding onto each other, clawing at the seeping walls until the floor leveled a bit.

"Turn right."

"Where?" Maralinne saw nothing.

"Give me your hand."

Jareth pulled her back. Their heads bumped. Maralinne let out and indignant. "Ouch!"

"Sorry Maralinne. Look up."

A pale light showed overhead. Maralinne could barely make out the source, but it was definitely moonlight up a tall chimney.

"Climb. There are hand and foot holds. Can you feel them?"

"Yes, there and there..."

She climbed. The rock was drier here. Maralinne did not dare think of heights. Trusting blindly that Jareth climbed beneath her she groped upward.

"Now, off to the side," Jareth's voice echoed up to her. "See the ledge?"

"No!"

"Let go with your left. Feel it?"

"Where?" Maralinne panicked. "I can't!"

"More to the left. There. Feel it now?"

"Yes, thanks the gods."

"Now slide over. It's wide enough," said Jareth. "Just roll. That's it."

Jareth heaved himself up and squeezed onto the narrow ledge beside Maralinne. He wrapped his arms around her to keep her from falling. "We're safe for the moment at least," he whispered close to her ear.

"Is there another way out?" Maralinne asked. Jareth's breath on her cheek both soothed and stirred her.

"I don't think so…"

"Then let's go back down there and challenge the devils," she said anxious to get away from the fears and feelings his closeness provoked.

"I admire your courage, Lady Maralinne, but from now on our route will require more than that."

"What could be worse than Delven?"

" Delven are, believe it or not, no more than a race of miners and smiths. They are neither good nor evil. It is the Dark Lord who enslaves them that we must fear. The Dogs that followed you and those we killed in the tunnels are his servants. You are in extreme danger until we find out what he wants with you. But I pledge he will not have you as long as I can fight in your defense," said Jareth.

"You said we are fighting side by side, Jareth."

"As you wish, my courageous princess.'

"You used to call it foolhardiness and guts,"

"I may have used the terms once or twice," Jareth admitted. "You always were a willful and adventurous girl. Being a grown woman hasn't changed you much."

They eased their way back down the chimney. The tunnel below was quiet. Jareth walked briskly while the floor was dry and even, but when they met a sharp angle, the downward slant became slick and treacherous. Maralinne grabbed Jareth's hand for support. The narrow walls seeped with moisture. There was no light. She thought she felt snail shells crunch beneath each step. Jareth was walking too fast. She tried to keep up with him. She stumbled but Jareth dragged her to her feet and kept going.

Then she heard it. Soft, moist padding keeping pace with them. The floor continued to descend but not as sharply as before. Jareth broke into a run. Maralinne had no trouble following him now. The passage rounded a corner and opened up into a large, dimly-lit room.

"Safe here," Jareth said breathing heavily. "It won't come out into the light."

"What was it?"

"You wouldn't want to know."

"Tell me."

"Maralinne you are a strong woman but this is not Arindon wood. I have never seen this thing in the light but I have fought it in the dark and believe me, you wouldn't want to know."

Maralinne looked down at her hand still clutching Jareth's in a death grip. She had no intention of relinquishing that hold just yet. But Jareth also realized he still held her hand. With a formal bow he kissed it. "My Lady" he said and gently released her hold.

Shivering from both fright and cold, Maralinne sank down onto the smooth glassy floor. Cold, green and faintly glowing the cavern vaulted overhead. Icy, intricately carved pillars lined the room, beautiful but frightening. The air was stale. Her breaths came in uneven gasps."

"Slowly...Breathe slowly," said Jareth sitting down beside her. "We can rest a moment here. That was quite a descent."

Maralinne leaned her head on his shoulder. She was so, so tired.

"Maralinne!" Jareth shook her. "Rest yes, but not sleep. You can't let the Dark lull you. You must stay alert. You must question, challenge each sensation, each step or you're lost."

"Now you are scaring me."

"Fear will keep you awake."

"Talking will keep me awake too," said Maralinne. She laid her head back on his shoulder. "Tell me how you know so much about this awful place."

"It was a long time ago," he began. He stretched out his legs and moved his shoulder a little to make a more comfortable pillow for her. "I was about seven or eight." He stopped and waited.

"What happened?"

"My mother was murdered." He stopped again. This time Maralinne waited until he was ready to continue. "I ran from them...Delven warriors...Belar's dogs." Jareth let his breath hiss through his teeth. "The Great Bear came and found me and took me to his cave. This cave."

"The Great Bear!" Maralinne laughed up at him. "I'm not a little girl anymore, Jareth."

"Then let the wise woman in you see that what we believe as children is often closer to the Light of Truth than the narrow logic of adulthood. It was a bear that guided me through these caves and brought me safely to Allarion just as I am doing for you."

Maralinne didn't know whether to believe Jareth or not but she did know him well enough not to press the subject further. On the far side of the room two passages led into the blackness. Which one would he take? Where would it lead? Jareth sat with his eyes closed. He breathed deeply, evenly but Maralinne knew he was not asleep. He seemed to be listening for something. The Delven? The thing that had followed them and must be lurking just at the edge of the light? Maralinne tried to relax. She curled up closer to Jareth. Her head dropped to his chest. She shut her eyes and listened to his heartbeat. Then she felt it. Another pulse, out of sync with Jareth's heart, vibrating through the rocks surrounding them.

"Time to go," he said straightening up. He helped her to her feet and led the way across the glassy, pillared room to the left-hand passage. The archway was carved with intricate designs as if the stones had flowed then froze solid. A cache of torches was stacked in a niche just inside the arch. Jareth lit one and entered the passage. The colors deepened as they traveled. The walls glowed brighter. The torch flame spread out as if there was a draft but their faces felt none. The smoke felt heavy in the pulsing silence. The gravel crunched loud beneath their feet. The sound of their breathing filled the tunnel. The still wind stretched the flame longer and flatter. Jareth held the torch high overhead. It was so cold. Maralinne's feet were numb. Her lungs labored painfully.

"Keep moving, Maralinne. Just a little farther."

Her feet were no longer part of her body. Their rhythm jarred her aching lungs. On and on she followed him, her hand lock-gripped on his belt. She stumbled but Jareth did not stop. She regained her footing and plunged blindly after him again.

"In here," he said and pushed her into a small, dark side passage "We are on the outskirts of Delvia. I'll try to steal us some clothes and hopefully some weapons. Stay here until I get back."

"I'm going with you."

"No, Maralinne," he said with finality. He knelt on the floor to unwind a rag strip from one of her makeshift boots. "I'm going to tie this across the passage. If someone comes pull the strip and when he trips use your knife."

He left her. Pull the strip and use your knife. How simple! She hated Jareth for leaving. She refused to admit she was terrified. It was dark, too dark to see much but not dark enough to hide her completely if someone came.

Chapter 7

The alarms sounded an hour before dawn. All of Arindon castle, royalty, guests and servants alike assembled in the great hall. Some were wrapped in quilts, some hastily dressed.

"I will be quick and to the point," said Gil. "Princess Maralinne is missing. We have searched the castle for the last two hours. Kyrdthin cannot reach her with any of his magic and the stench of Delven is everywhere. We feared the worst and now it has been confirmed. The gamekeeper's horse has just wandered back alone to the stables. The beast has been ridden hard and the trappings are soaked as if he had swum the river. Piece the tale together for yourselves. Our dearest princess is in the Dark Lord's clutches and Jareth who's watchful eye has often saved her from harm has been lost.

"My dearest sister!" exclaimed Analinne, "I saw her walk out to the garden alone but when Rogarth followed I..."

"I am responsible," said Rogarth stepping forward. He knelt to King Arinth. "I was with her in the garden...We quarreled...and...and I left her there."

"Rogarth," said the king. "I have entrusted my daughter to you and before you legally claim her you have failed to protect her. Yet if she lives it is still my will that you wed her. You are a good man, Rogarth, and as for my daughter," Arinth stopped, cleared his throat and smiled. "I know only too well of Mari's willfulness. I am sure you are not entirely to blame."

Rogarth nodded his thanks.

"Therefore, I commission you," Arinth continued. "To find her and deliver her to me."

"Consider it done, sire."

"Go..." said Arinth and slumped back into his chair. It had been a long speech for him, buoyed up by sheer emotion. Gil placed a steadying hand on his shoulder, exchanging a worried look with Marielle. The people whispered, frightened, angry and mournful all at once until Gil again stepped forward to speak.

"Go back to your chambers everyone, dress and prepare for the day. It is early but I for one know that sleep would be impossible. No one is to go outside the walls without orders. Go about your regular duties but keep your eyes open. Report anything unusual, no matter how trivial seeming to myself or Kyrdthin immediately." He turned to Rogarth, dropped his voice and said, "Meet with us in the tower study in one hour."

Voices! Maralinne huddled against the wall. Just pull the strip...She waited. Footsteps came nearer and nearer. She fingered the knotted strip of rag.

"...skewered right through."

"I won't miss him."

"Neither will I but we got to catch whoever is loose in here or we will be next."

"Could be anywhere in this stinking maze."

"What's an Allarian doing down here anyway?"

"Who says it was one?"

"Nobody said but only one of them or one of us could open the falls gate and it sure wasn't one of us."

The pair turned into an adjoining passage. Maralinne tried to relax her grip on the strip but she couldn't. Where was Jareth? What was taking him so long?

Again footsteps. This time a heavy padding as if some beast lumbered toward its lair. She heard its heavy breathing coming closer. Then she saw it. A mountain of golden fur crossed the passage just below her hiding place. Maralinne sat frozen until her cramped legs cried out in pain. Slowly she stretched them out and tried to return her breathing to normal. The air was heavy and stale. She forced herself to breath deep and slow but her heartbeat still raced inside.

She had almost relaxed when sounds again jerked her alert. This time the heavy padding was punctuated by the quicker patter of small feet.

"Wait, wait for me, Mister Bear," said a child's voice. The padding stopped with a low growl. Maralinne shuddered, cringing further back into the shadows. Then curiosity and concern for the child overcame her fear. She leaned forward just a little. What child wandered these dark dangerous corridors alone talking to beasts? The dual footsteps approached. Maralinne watched the intersection of passages until a great, golden bear crossed her view. A dark-haired boy rode on its back, his small fingers twisted into the bear's thick neck fur. "Giddy up, Mister Bear," the child said laughing. The vision faded. Surely they had continued into the adjoining passage Maralinne told herself, but the boy and the bear simply seemed to dissolve.

A long silence followed. Maralinne drifted. For a time she was a little girl again playing in the gardens with her sister, Then she was riding her pony faster, faster into the forest. There were hoof beats behind her. "Whoa, whoa, Little Lady," said Jareth's voice behind her. She saw him reach out. She felt him lift her from the saddle. She saw the mixture of concern and amusement in his eyes as he seated her in front of him and told her to hang on. She felt the sweaty horse's neck and Jareth's strong arm about her waist.

She was alone again. Where was Jareth? Part of her knew she was sitting on the stone floor of the corridor, but she was also standing in the doorway to Jareth's cottage. A deep sadness overwhelmed her as if years were being torn out of her life, as if she would never see Jareth again.

She drifted again. She was almost asleep when something jolted her body alert. Her knuckles whitened on the rag strip Jareth had stretched across the passage. Rough voices! Delven! Behind them something dragged and scraped along the floor. Two Delven guards marched across the intersection and turned straight toward her. The thing they dragged was a man in chains. He had been stripped to the waist. Red welts crisscrossed his back. His dark hair and beard were matted with filth. The man looked up at Maralinne as they passed.

"Jareth!" she screamed. She threw herself at the guards. Her head swam. She was falling, falling.

Then Jareth was holding her, comforting her. His hands stroked her hair. "Maralinne, dearest Lady Maralinne," he said soothingly. His beard brushed her cheek. "Calm down. We are both alright." He released her and stepped back. Maralinne gasped. Jareth was dressed in the dark mail and leather of a Delven guard!

"Oh Jareth, I'm so glad you are alright...but I saw you...or I thought I saw..."

"Everything is alright Lady Maralinne," he said pulling her farther back into the side passage. He thrust something into her hand. "Clothes. Put them on."

"I can't see what I'm doing," she said.

"Then let me help."

Maralinne stood still so that Jareth could unlace her gown. She felt his hands tremble as he fumbled with the hooks and ties. At last the bodice was free. Maralinne turned her back, slipped out of the skirt and kicked it aside. She stood there a long moment wearing only her shift trying to resist the urge to turn around. Jareth was silent behind her. She turned only her head. Eyes averted, Jareth handed her a coarse tunic. Maralinne smiled to herself as she pulled on the tunic then wriggled out of her shift.

There were also some heavy boots and two pair of knitted hose. The boots were too big but with both pairs of hose they were wearable.

"Braid up that hair quick and tie it with this." Jareth handed her the dreadful knotted strip of rag. That done he crowned her with a foul-smelling helmet and thrust a small sword into her hand. "Come here, page, let me look at you in the light."

Maralinne stepped out into the passage.

"You won't fool them for long," he said turning her around. "But if we keep in this half light there's a chance."

They threaded their way through the maze of tunnels, winding ever deeper into the bowels of the dark stronghold. The stench of burning in too little air increased. They did not talk. Maralinne followed mechanically, a pace behind Jareth. The floor sloped sharply downward then leveled again. Jareth made an abrupt stop. Rhythmic clanking echoed through the corridor.

"From now on, Maralinne, we are in extreme danger," he whispered. "Make no noise. Stay with me at all cost and if need be fight to kill. Do you understand?"

Maralinne nodded.

The pounding increased. Metal rang on metal. The dull hiss of steam, the whir of gears and wheels filled the tunnels. The acrid stench seared Maralinne's throat. The red glow ahead began to radiate heat. Jareth slowed their pace a trifle when the passage became bright enough to extinguish their torch. Maralinne choked back a cough.

"Try breathing through a cloth. Your collar or sleeve," said Jareth.

It did not help much. Maralinne's eyes teared. When the passage finally opened up into an enormous smoke-filled room she could hardly see. Jareth dabbed her face with a drop of water from their supply jug. "Now take a sip. Just a sip."

"Where are we?" she managed to croak.

"Delven Forge. All the metals of this world and countless others are wrought here."

Maralinne squinted into the smoky red haze. On the upper levels of the cavern monstrous engines pulled strings of carts onto a towering wooden trestle. One by one the carts tipped over a chute. Their loads of ore rumbled into the gaping maw of the smelter fires below. Dozens of tiny black-clad workers stoked the fires, while others prepared molds pressed into the sandy floor.

Maralinne muffled a startled cry and jumped back. Molten metal erupted from the smelter and flowed hissing into the molds. Jareth turned her by the shoulders. "Over there," he said, lips almost touching her ear so he could be heard above the noise. Maralinne looked across the steaming room. A high-pitched, rhythmic clang assaulted her ears as small but heavily-muscled smiths shaped and tempered new-forged steel. The huge bellows whooshed above and the fires roared. Just to the left of the scene another corridor led back into the darkness. Jareth walked boldly across the intervening space. Maralinne fell in behind him. The workers never paused or looked up.

Inside the corridor the stone was bluish gray. It looked and felt more like dirty ice than stone. Maralinne tried desperately to keep up with Jareth. Her loose boots clumped noisily. Suddenly Jareth stopped. Maralinne crashed into his back. He grabbed her wrist to steady her. Someone was coming. He put a warning finger to his lips, then turned around. Maralinne cringed behind him.

"Better get your boy back to the barracks," said a voice beneath the Delven's dark helmet. "There's an Allarian loose somewhere in here. Cut up Steeds and Helm like holiday roast."

"Thanks I will," answered Jareth.

"There'll probably be a general alarm but me and Sem here are out looking for it on our own. Maybe there'll be a reward for our squad if we find him first. Are you with us.?"

"I'll see the boy safe home first," said Jareth.

"Meet us at the courtyard."

"Right-O."

When they had moved on down the passage Maralinne realized she had held her breath during the entire encounter.

"If I can find a safe place for you," whispered Jareth. "I'm going to go to that meeting."

"What!"

"Hold your tongue, boy," Jareth barked aloud.

"Don't be insolent. I am still your princess."

"No, Lady Maralinne, here we are partners and the role you must play is a boy."

"You don't have to enjoy it so much."

"There are other roles I would rather have you play," Jareth said with a wistful smile. "But enough talking. Let's keep moving."

Maralinne followed two paces behind him. How did he know where he was going? Events raced through her head, superimposed by other events or were they dreams or visions. What had she experienced while she waited for Jareth? She blindly followed this man. She trusted him without question. Jareth had always been there for her. No subject was more loyal to her father. No friend was dearer to her. Why did she now feel so confused, so almost afraid of him?

Just before the passage opened into a torch lit courtyard Jareth found a small storage closet.

"Hide here boy," he ordered as he opened the door. "Keep quiet and don't move until I come back."

"You're not leaving me again!"

"Yes I am." He shoved her inside and shut the door. "If you are discovered, use you knife."

Again Maralinne waited for Jareth, this time she was boiling with anger. It was a long wait in the small stuffy space. Footsteps and gruff voices passed her hideout. She pressed herself against the far wall and held her breath. Time dragged on and on. Her anger subsided and exhaustion started to take over. It was so tempting to lie down and go to sleep. She pushed some dusty boxes aside and slid down to the floor, but it was cold and damp. She pulled herself up again and sat on one of the boxes. Her head drooped. She fought to keep alert, remembering Jareth's warning. But what did Jareth care? He had left her. He said they were partners!. Well when he comes back…If he comes back…I'll….

She must have drifted off in spite of her efforts. She woke with a terrified start. The door latch clicked, lifted, then dropped down again. Soft footsteps padded back and forth outside.

"Mussa be in here. Smells so sweet," hissed a voice.

Maralinne held her breath.

"Mussa be in here. Stoopid lock. Stoopid man lock keepa Spida out. Poor Spida canna reach a pretty. Smells so sweet."

The footsteps shuffled back and forth. The latch lifted and fell once more.

"Canna leave it here. Ugly man come back an' taka pretty 'way from Spida."

Maralinne's legs throbbed to run. Her chest was bursting for breath.

"Somma commin'. Oh no! Poor Spida mussa go. Somma comin'. Quick! Quick! Mussa go."

The footsteps hurried away. The door flew open. Maralinne's breath rushed out with a silent scream. Then she recognized Jareth's silhouette against the light of the corridor.

"It's worse than I feared," Jareth gasped between heavy breaths. "Let's move then talk."

He half dragged her across the corridor and into the now empty courtyard. They threaded their way through the maze of benches and low walls until they came to a gate.

"A chance'?" said Jareth more to himself than to Maralinne.

"Why not?" she challenged

Beyond the iron gate was total blackness. Then as their eyes adjusted Maralinne could make out piles and piles of wooden crates and eerie clusters of draped statuary. They were in a warehouse of some sort. There was a long loading platform to the left of the enormous cavern. Metal rails ran from the platform into the black mouths of stone arched tunnels. Jareth stopped and pulled her into the shadow of a pile of crates.

"Now please tell me what is going on," she demanded.

"It's worse than I feared..."

"You already said that."

"Maralinne, let's not snap at each other. We can be princess and servant again for so we are, but let's be friends above all else. Our lives depend on it."

"Alright, friends," she said trying hard to be strong then she burst into tears. "Jareth, please Jareth just hold me." She threw herself into his arms. Her helmet fell back, spilling out her luxurious hair. "I'm just so tired and so scared."

"So am I, My Lady," he said uneasily trying to comfort her. "Here let's sit down and I will tell you what I learned."

Reluctantly Maralinne disengaged her arms and sat down beside Jareth. The dusty floor vibrated with a rhythmic pulse.

"Well the truth is," Jareth began then stopped, looked around the cavern as if searching for eavesdroppers then he continued but with a lowered voice. "Prince Tobar is in league with the Dark, or so he thinks. Lord Belar is just using him. He has been promised the double crown for Analinne's baby and the regency for himself until the child comes of age. It seems that he bungled a few assignments a while back and Lord Belar decided to take some security measures."

"Security measures?" said Maralinne with whetted curiosity.

"Since you are now involved I think it is necessary to include you in on Kyrdthin's plan, but you must understand that many lives and the welfare of both kingdoms are at stake. This is no game, Maralinne. This is deadly serious."

"My sister and her child are my serious concern, Jareth. Tell me what I need to know." She looked up at him but his face was unreadable in the shadows.

He took her hands. "This involves more than your sister, My Lady. This is about your half brother, Crown Prince Willarinth..."

"But..."

"He did not die as everyone was told. Kyrdthin hid him in another world, but Belar discovered him with Tobar's help.

"My little brother? Where is he?" Maralinne could hardly believe what she was hearing.

"Kyrdthin brought him to Arindon and apprenticed him to Mabry the Miller."

"But that's Avrille's brother!"

"Foster brother," Jareth corrected her. "And that brings us to Avrille. She is King Frebar's younger daughter and her mother, Aunt Jane, is Frebar's banished queen Janille. It is Kyrdthin's plan to wed Avrille and Willarinth. Together they will be High King and Queen if we can keep them alive long enough."

Maralinne was speechless. It was too much to comprehend all at once. Her half brother alive! Her maid servant a princess! But how did all this tie in with her sister and Tobar and....

"The Delven Dogs that trailed you were sent to kidnap Analinne, not you," Jareth continued. "They were sent for the red-haired princess. Lucky for Analinne they found the wrong one. Your stupid flight may have saved your sister's life."

"Analinne's still in danger if they realize their mistake," wailed Maralinne.

Jareth grabbed her shoulders with firm hands. "You are all in danger. You, Analinne, her child and especially Avrille and Will." He squeezed her shoulders to emphasize each name. "Tobar had orders to kill them but he turned soft. If Belar sends someone less scrupulous next time all will be lost."

"What are we going to do?" said Maralinne a lump of fear rising in her throat.

Jareth relaxed his grip on her shoulders but his hands remained, his fingers still entwined in her hair. "First I must get you out of here and safely to Allarion. Then I will return to warn Kyrdthin."

"I'll go back with you. My sister needs me" she said standing up ready to go."

"No Maralinne." Jareth looked at her with intense concern. "You are also a threat to the Dark Lord's plans. He wouldn't hesitate if the wrong red-haired princess fell into his hands. Your betrothal has been announced and as soon as you are wed and bear a child there will be yet one more contender to the double throne."

Maralinne gave her hair a defiant toss. "I ran away from that threat. I may be betrothed but I will never willingly marry Rogarth much less bear him a child."

Confused by her outburst, now it was Jareth's turn to be speechless.

"Take me to Allarion," Maralinne said closing the subject.

No sooner had they resumed their flight than a door opened almost in front of them. The warehouse cavern flooded with light. Two startled warriors shouted, "Who goes there?"

Jareth ran the first one through and leaped to take on his companion. Blades clashed. Jareth parried and thrust again. "Behind you boy!" he shouted.

Maralinne spun around. Two more Delven charged through the doorway. She clutched her small blade and held her ground. They thrust her aside without a second thought and fell upon Jareth.. Maralinne jumped on the back of the closest one. She drove her blade home with both hands and rode him down. Jareth still battled the other two. She rolled off the warrior she had killed just as Jareth's nearer assailant stepped back. Maralinne kicked his boots. He toppled backwards, pinning her beneath him. His blade skittered away as his head crashed to the floor. Maralinne squirmed free picked up his blade and whacked his armored chest.

"Out of the way, boy," shouted Jareth.

Jareth and his remaining assailant skillfully parried each other's moves. Slowly they circled until the Delven warrior's eyes lit on Maralinne.

"What have we here?" he said eyes darting between her and Jareth's blade.

Maralinne took a step back.

"No Delven page has hair like that."

Maralinne looked down. A tell-tale red curl had slipped beneath her helmet. With sudden inspiration she whisked it off. Her fiery hair tumbled down over her shoulders. The amazed warrior let down his guard for only a moment but that was enough for Jareth to deliver his blow.

"Come. No time to lose," Jareth yelled. He grabbed her wrist and dragged her through the nearest doorway. The passage was narrow but Jareth did not slow down. Maralinne stumbled along with her oversized boots trying to keep up with him. The passage ended in a flight of stairs.

The stairs went up and up. Maralinne's heart pounded, counting, counting each step. One, two, three…eleven twelve thirteen, level walk two three, up again two, three…. What was this? Something long and sticky touched Maralinne's cheek. She tried to brush it away but it stuck to her hand. "Help me Jareth!" she screamed. She fought the sticky web but to no avail. The more she tried to free herself the more entangled she became. Jareth slashed at the threads with his blade. Then he too became hopelessly entangled in the web. Maralinne began to feel cold. Her hands and toes tingled. Her mind fought desperately but her body moved slower and slower. Something smelled faintly of honey. She began to drift, lulled by sibilant whispers.

April and her mother returned shivering to their room. They dressed in shocked silence. How could this all have happened to her beautiful new friend Maralinne, April asked herself. And Jareth he was so…. A light impatient knock interupted them. Kyrdthin let himself in before they could respond.

"Janie bring a breakfast tray to my tower study. Gil trusts no one else to enter and maybe you can help."

"What shall I bring?" Janille's voice shook with alarm.

"Who cares? Bread. Tea. We won't be there for a party. Just bring something and be sure you aren't followed."

"What about me Uncle...Kyrdthin?" said April.

"Go to Analinne and stay there," he tossed over his shoulder as he disappeared.

April's hands were still clumsily trying to braid her hair as Janille whisked her down the halls to the royal chambers. The door opened before they could knock. Janille dropped a quick curtsy.

"Go. I know your mission," said Analinne before she could speak. With a quick kiss on April's forehead Janille rushed out and down the stairs to the serving pantry. She grabbed a tray and cups from the shelf. The teapot was almost hot on the warmer. She doubled up the corner of her apron and pulled it onto the tray. There was leftover cake from the ball and a few wedges of cheese on the sideboard. She slid the lot onto a pile of napkins and rushed back up the stairs. The cups clattered and the tea sloshed wildly. Kyrdthin waited in the doorway at the top.

"...they will expect us to storm the entrance," Gil was saying as she entered Kyrdthin's round tower study. "And that is exactly what we will do." Gil stopped for a moment to take the tea tray from Janille.

"I will lead the attack..."said Rogarth

"No, that is not the plan. Keilen can lead them well enough," said Kyrdthin.

"But I must..."Rogarth insisted.

"There is another entrance to the Dark Realm on the east side above Allarion," Gil exclaimed.

"Over the mountains! That will take days!" Rogarth exclaimed with almost dispair.

Gil reached up to lay a hand on the large man's shoulder. "That is exactly why you must use the east entrance. An attack from an unlikely direction at a time when they least suspect just may succeed. Keilen's frontal attack is primarily a diversion."

Rogarth paced the length of the well-worn rug in front of the fireplace. Gil and Kyrdthin let him take time to rein in his emotions and consider the tactical advantages of their plan. Janille poured the tea and tried to arrange the hastily assembled tray of food into some semblance of formality.

Rogarth stopped in front of Gil and waited until the pale Allarion spoke.

"The trail is well marked to the summit and beyond that if you submit to Kyrdthin's skills I am sure he can direct you to the gate," said Gil.

"I will go," Rogarth announced. "But I will go alone. No one else should be endangered. Lady Maralinne is my responsibility. I alone must atone for..."

"Enough personal chastisement," Kyrdthin interrupted. "Arinth wishes that you go alone and that suits our plan as well. So sit down and let me spike your tea. Trust me. It will only be to clear your mind for the information I need to give you."

Kyrdthin handed him a cup of tea. Rogarth took the cup, cautiously peering into the amber liquid. Kyrdthin laughed. "Don't worry friend, you will find it very sweet. Take a sip." Rogarth obeyed. Kyrdthin's voice lowered. "The tea is sweet, very sweet and soothing. Relax Rogarth. The tea is very sweet, very, very sweet."

How long she was cocooned in the sticky thread Maralinne did not know. When she awoke she lay on the floor of a small room. Try as she would she could not move. She could hear voices arguing behind her. A chill shivered her spine as she recognized one of the speakers.

"Wassa poor Spida to do?" it was whining.

"You have done a grave deed," said the other voice.

"Itsa mine. Spida found it. Spida trailed it. It run away from its ugly man mate, straight to poor Spida's web."

"A man? Its mate? Where is it?" the other voice demanded.

"Itsa ugly she donna want it. Nobody donna want it," whimpered the first voice"

"I asked where is it?"

"Itsa sleepin'. Jussa little sleepin'."

Maralinne struggled against her bonds. Jareth!

"Bring the man to me. Now!" the stronger voice commanded.

Footsteps padded away.

"And now my royal child, what brings you to the fortress of the Dark and the Watcher's tower?" said the voice in a kindlier tone.

Maralinne felt a warm breeze. Her numbed limbs tingled back to life. She sat up and tried to focus on the speaker in the dim light. "The Watcher!" she exclaimed.

"You know of the Watcher? That is good," said the voice behind her.

Maralinne tried to turn around.

"Tell me. What do men of this age say of the Watcher?" said the illusive voice now on her right.

"It's a dragon," said Maralinne turning but seeing nothing. "The dragon that guards the end of the world!"

"A dragon? So that is how they see me," said the voice with a touch of amusement. "So be it then."

The room gradually took on a warm yellow glow. There in front of Maralinne, on a rough wood stool perched a small but impressive dragon.

"Tell me your name, royal child. I see your lineage but need a name if we are to converse in a civilized manner."

"I am Maralinne, younger princess of the house of Arindon," she answered with pride.

"Arindon. Arindon," the dragon mused. "Then what is your father's name?"

"Arinth of course!" said Maralinne amazed that the dragon needed to ask. She spied another chair and sat down.

"Yes, yes, all the later kings called themselves Arinth," said the Watcher. "Tell me his full name, child."

"Lee. Le'arinth, son of…"

"None by the name of Allarinth yet?" the Watcher interupted.

Maralinne shook her head.

"No?" the small dragon gave a disappointed sigh. "Allarinth will be the last. All Arinth you see, the first and last High King of the new age."

Maralinne shook her head again, sorry to have brought such disappointing news.

The dragon slowly stretched then refolded his wings. "Then it is not yet time," he said with another sigh. "Tell me. Are there twins in the royal houses yet?"

"Oh yes," said Maralinne glad to say something positive. "My sister Analinne and I are twins and King Frebar and Prince Tobar of Frevaria are twins. Tobar is married to Analinne and...."

"Twins in both houses. Twins married to twins..." the Watcher said more to himself than to her.

They were interrupted by the sound of padded footsteps dragging a heavy load. Maralinne turned around and screamed. A dark hairy creature with thin spidery legs backed away and whimpered. His large mouth glistened with sticky spittle.

"Jareth if I remember," said the Watcher to the motionless bundle on the floor. The binding threads glowed brightly then fell away. Jareth stirred.

"Jareth! Jareth are you alright?" Maralinne flung herself on him.

"Poor, poor Spida," whimpered the cowering creature across the room. "Pretty think Spida screamin' bad. Wanna ugly man instead. Poor Spida. Poor, Poor..."

"Silence!" ordered the Watcher. "You are in enough trouble. Go back to your lair and stay there."

"Donna wanna," Spida mumbled as he padded back into the corridor. "Donna, donna wanna..."

Jareth freed himself of Maralinne's fervent embrace and sat up. "So, our paths cross again, Old One," he said.

The dragon stretched his wings again. "Cross and re-cross, time and again, man and beast but ever friend," he said. "Tell me Jareth, how soon is the world to ending?"

Jareth and the Watcher conversed at length on the state of the kingdoms and current events. Maralinne listened quietly. The small room glowed warm and friendly. The furnishings were sparce but adequate. In spite of her recent ordeal she was neither hungry nor tired. Time seemed to have stopped. Everything but the moment was irrelevant.

At last the Watcher said solemnly, "Then the wait is almost done. The High King almost come."

"Yes, Old One," said Jareth. "But Prince Will is still a child. He is in great danger in spite of all Kyrdthin's efforts."

"Bring him to me," said the Watcher. "There are secrets Willarinth should know."

"I will," Jareth promised.

The dragon rustled his leathery wings. His eyes glittered with a rainbow of colors. "Now what may I do for you?"

"Safe passage for Lady Maralinne and I to Allarion," said Jareth taking Maralinne's hand.

"So be it," said the Watcher. The dragon's shape wavered then faded.

Maralinne blinked her eyes. Everything changed! The sky was bright blue. The breeze was fresh and sweet. All around her tinkling voices caroled. Jareth drew her down a flower-strewn path. "Welcome my dearest lady. Allarion is waiting."

Chapter 8

Armor clanked. Horses whinnied. Before noon a company was assembled and riding through Arindon gates toward the forest. Rogarth, flanked by Lord Keilen and his men led them until the castle was lost from view. When the road forked Rogarth relinquished command to Keilen and took the narrow trail which led to the heights. Keilen and the company continued on to High Bridge.

Rogarth urged his horse to climb as fast as safety allowed. Cold rain began to pelt his face and soak through his cloak. The horse tripped and slid up the rocky mud-slick trail. He climbed higher. A sheer drop gave way on his left. He reined his horse tight and slowly skirted the cliff. Raw winds whipped over the barrier crags threatening to hurl him over the edge. Rogarth held on and continued to climb murmuring words of praise and encouragement to his mount. The rain subsided to a foggy drizzle. The wind-stunted trees stood specter-like along the trail as the fog thickened. At last he reached the pass.

Rogarth searched the rock-strewn summit for the cave Kyrdthin had described. The entrance was so narrow he and his horse could barely squeeze through, but soon the cave opened up into a small room. He let his eyes adjust to the dim light, then fed and rubbed down his horse. The animal sniffed and snorted at their surroundings then settled down content. The cavern room looked as if other travelers had also sought sanctuary there. Tinder and logs were stacked along one wall. The remains of a pine-bow bed was against the opposite wall. In the center was a refuse-littered fire ring. Rogarth sat down. He was almost too tired to eat but he forced himself. The journey rations were dry and hard to chew. He washed them down with a few swallows of water. Then he slept.

What alerted him was certainly not a sound. Yet with a soldier's instinct he knew it was morning and was at once fully awake. Blade in hand he edged toward the cave mouth. The air tingled. The rock passage ended with a vista for which he could never have been prepared. They said Allarion was beautiful but this...! A silver mist rose up from the valley below to vanish into a deep sapphire arch of sky above. Blue-green trees beckoned, offering solace and warmth. A shimmering, moss-carpeted trail wound down the slope welcoming his footsteps. The silence spoke of calm, absorbing all his anxieties. Surely this had not been here the night before.

Hoof beats! Rogarth crouched back in the shadow of the cave mouth and waited. His fingers flexed on the hilt of his sword. A lone rider approached on a swift Allarian pony. His cloak flew behind him as he urged his mount up to the pass. The pattern of the rider's dark plaid cloak looked familiar. Yes, it had to be....

"Jareth! Ho, Jareth!" Rogarth shouted.

Jareth reined back. His little pony reared and pranced sensing Rogarth's horse.

"So Rogarth they sent you after her?" called Jareth.

"We thought you were dead," said Rogarth lowering his blade. "And my dearest lady is she...."

"Safe in Allarion," said Jareth swinging down from his pony.

Rogarth knelt before Jareth. "I am indebted beyond repayment. I can do no more than offer you my service," he said laying his sword at Jareth's feet.

"The captain of the guard kneels to the gamekeeper. Now that's a first." Jareth laughed heartily and offered Rogarth his hand. "I'm used to fetching Maralinne from her little escapades as all of Arindon knows." He handed Rogarth back his sword. "You look as if you just woke up. Why don't we share our tales over a bite of breakfast?"

When they had finished eating and had talked long over tea Jareth stood up. "Then three things are clear. First, Maralinne is safe and no longer in need of rescuing. Second, Keilen is leading his men into a death trap. No one can enter the Dark Realm without spilling blood.

"Kyrdthin was busy with some magic before we left."

"I'm sure that will help, Rogarth, but it won't be enough. The third thing is that Kyrdthin and Gil don't know the extent of Tobar's involvement or that Analinne is in danger. I say we ride to Arindon now."

"I will not go back without my lady," Rogarth insisted.

"She is safe where she is."

"But my life and honor depend on returning her to King Arinth,"

Argue as he would, Jareth could not dissuade him. Finally they agreed to let Maralinne decide. Jareth helped Rogarth break camp. Then they descended into the lush, glowing valley below.

The sloping path was gentle and meandering. The deeper they rode the deeper blue the sky became. The trees, even the grassy path took on a bluish hue. Ahead of them the valley's heart pulsed, beckoning them, teasing the heart and eye.

Rogarth shielded his eyes from the dizzying shifts of color. Jareth stopped to wait for him. "Just a bit farther," he said. "Then we will send for Maralinne. A soldier cannot cross the sapphire veil."

Rogarth shook his head and rubbed his eyes, but all he could see was blue. His horse whinnied then waited patiently.

"Dismount friend," said Jareth noting Rogarth's distress. "It's easier when you can feel the solid ground."

"Can you see in this stuff?" Rogarth squinted but still could not focus.

"This close to the veil the light is pretty intense." Jareth slid off his pony. "I'm not affected as much as you seem to be." He waited until Rogarth dismounted.

Try as he would the big man could not regain his equilibrium. Jareth took the reins of Rogarth's horse. He placed a steadying hand on the man's shoulder and together they approached the shimmering blue light. Jareth sang out with what could only be described as birdsong. From beyond the light an answer sang back with liquid notes. Two silvery figures approached then retreated. Rogarth waited with closed eyes but Jareth drank in the dazzling beauty with unquenchable thirst.

At last Maralinne emerged from the pool of blue light. The heady scent of blossoms followed her as she stepped through. She swayed with uncertainty until her feet touched the blue-green path. Her eyes darted about, searching. Jareth caught her before she fell.

> "All that was before be gone,
> Lost in blue Allarion," Jareth chanted.
> "Now is all you need to know,
> As from this enchanted place you go."

They turned their backs on the bright blue valley, walking in silence until the sights and sounds and smells were again familiar. At the top of the rocky divide, near the cave where Rogarth had camped they were met by a party of Allarians sent to equip them for their journey home.

There was a silver dappled pony for Maralinne, sacks of bread and fruit, jugs of both water and wine, and grain for their mounts. Without delay they said their thanks and farewells. Only Rogarth looked back before they started down the zigzag trail on the eastern side. The cup shaped valley was empty. Only a breeze ruffled the green grassy plain.

"Well Jareth, it seems as if my hard earned freedom didn't last very long," said Maralinne.

"Yes, now I must return My Lady to her father as I have promised," said Rogarth.

"I am going back for Analinne, by my own choice," said Maralinne without as much as a glance at Rogarth.

Jareth rode ahead. Maralinne wished it was he who led her horse. Rogarth talked so little. She stole a look at him. Rogarth's steel gray eyes were fixed ahead. Yes, he was handsome. His heavily bearded chin was held high. He felt her gaze and turned with a smile. She tossed her head angrily and looked away.

Jareth stopped for them to catch up. "Shall we press on for the river or camp here in the pines?" he asked.

"If the Lady Maralinne is tired…" Rogarth began.

"Let's keep going Jareth," said Maralinne. "I just want to get home."

"To the river camp then," Rogarth agreed.

"We can make it before night if we pick up our pace," said Jareth.

They continued their downward trek. The wind-stunted pines gave way to aspen. The trail was steep and rocky but the surface had dried from yesterday's drenching making their descent less treacherous than Rogarth's climb had been. Maralinne was sullen. Every jolt of the trotting pony hurt her hips more. Why did ladies have to ride side saddle? On such a trail it was awkward and dangerous. She felt as if she would slip off her pony and fall to her death at any moment. There was no reason she had to be a lady way up here on the mountain. Let Rogarth see how she really was. Her Allarian dress was wide enough to straddle the pony with more than adequate modesty.

"Rogarth hold a moment."

"Of course, My Lady," he said startled that she had spoken to him.

Maralinne swung her leg easily over the pony's neck and flounced her skirt. "There that's more like it,"

Rogarth's eyes widened. A smile played in the corners of his mouth but he said nothing.

Jareth turned and grinned back at them. "I wondered how long that would take. You have ridden like a lady for four hours. I had guessed at half that time. Maybe they will make a proper royal princess out of you yet."

"Never!"

Jareth laughed then turned to lead once more. Maralinne flounced her skirt then tried to smooth it down to cover her ankles. Rogarth watched without expression. She could care less what Rogarth thought but she found herself embarrassed to have him see her ankles. She didn't want Rogarth to look at her much less touch her. The thought of bedding with him sent a confused mixture of heat and chill, quite unlike the comfort she felt with Jareth, who had held her on a fleeing horse, and swam with her through an icy river. Jareth saw her dressed in ragged blankets and in boy's breeches. He unlaced her gown in the caves with the same warm, gentle hands that had held her as a child....

The roar of the river rose to greet them. Jareth called a halt just before they reached the bank. Without a word he rode on ahead alone.

"Lady Maralinne," Rogarth began when Jareth was out of earshot. "I know you have just been through a nightmare and..."

"Really? I think it was rather fun dressing up like a boy and whacking Delven Dogs."

"I admire My Lady's spirit. Though it will take some getting used to."

"Don't bother. I don't want you or any man getting used to me," Maralinne snapped.

"We all have our roles to play, dearest lady."

"We all have our choices you mean."

Where the conversation would have led if Jareth had not returned just then neither of them would ever know.

"There has been a skirmish at the river campsite," said Jareth. "I cleaned things up a bit. Whatever was there is long gone"

They followed the last half mile in silence. High Bridge arched over the frothy chasm. The little shelter at the edge of the woods had been burned and gear was scattered haphazardly about the site.

"I thought you said you had cleaned up," said Maralinne then she choked wishing she had not spoken so soon. There were several tracks that looked as if heavy objects had been dragged through the dirt to the edged of the thicket. She shuddered and looked away.

"May I help you dismount?" Rogarth offered.

"I can get down off a horse by myself, if you please," she answered curtly. "Even if I'm wearing a skirt."

"You are a sporting little lady I must say," said Rogarth trying to keep his good humor.

"I am your princess, not a child," said Maralinne with a haughty toss of her head. "I command that you speak to me with respect."

"Well sporting you cannot deny," Jareth intervened with a laugh.

"Reluctantly sporting," agreed Maralinnne calmed by Jarcth's teasing. "But I do prefer to ride in breeches."

"I thought grown up ladies liked gowns," said Jareth with a wink at Rogarth.

"Only at balls," said Maralinne. "On a horse they are down right impractical."

Jareth's eyes twinkled with mischief. "Rogarth," he said. "How could you want such an immodest and insubordinate woman?"

Rogarth just smiled weakly and looked away. Maralinne wished he would have said something, anything. It was so hard to be angry with a man who said so little and she really wanted to be angry with Rogarth.

The men set up camp. Maralinne sat on her blanket and sulked. She had been through so much and all for nothing. She would soon be back where she had started. She tried to avoid looking at Rogarth. She tried to not even think of him. Instead she watched Jareth carefully place the warding signs around the campsite. It seemed they had been friends forever. How often had he rescued her from her childhood escapades? He had risked his life for her more than once. And now she was in the most terrible plight of her life and he could do nothing to save her.

The smell of supper cooking brought her back to the present. Rogarth tended the fire under the stew pot while Jareth fried biscuits on a pot lid griddle. Maralinne was hungry. Her seething anger tempted her to refuse to eat but her appetite won out over stubbornness. Talk during supper was sparse. They were all tired and tense. After a cup of soothing tea the cook pots were wiped and put away. The fire was fed and banked for the night. When Jareth and Rogarth unrolled their sleeping blankets Maralinne pulled hers to the opposite side of the fire from Rogarth. Neither man seemed to notice.

"I'll take first watch," said Rogarth.

"Then I'll relieve you at midnight," said Jareth.

"When do I get to watch?" asked Maralinne.

"You just sleep, my dear," said Rogarth.

"Alright," she said. "If you insist on treating me like a weakling, I may as well take advantage of it." She turned her back on him and let exhaustion take over. The night was cool and still except for the occasional chirrup of tree frogs.

Jareth jumped awake, hand on his bow. Winged reptiles screeched and swooped down over the camp. Without pausing to aim he raised his bow and shot into the thick of the attack. Twang! His arrow passed through its target with an electric sizzle. Rogarth whirled his blade two-handed over head but his strokes felled nothing. Again and again the reptilian assailants clawed and bit his head and shoulders. Jareth cast aside his bow, drew his own blade and ran to help Rogarth. He swung and slashed but encountered nothing. Still the airborne horrors swarmed out of the forest. Maralinne screamed.

"Fire, Maralinne, Bring fire!" Jareth shouted. "Grab a torch. These things aren't real."

"Aren't real?" Maralinne grabbed a stick from the fire and raced to Jareth swinging the flaming brand at their attackers.

"Don't help me," Jareth yelled. "Help Rogarth." He grabbed Maralinne's flaming stick. "Into the light, man. Into the light."

Rogarth slashed on but his excellent swordsmanship was no defense against creatures that could not be cut or beaten. Jareth plunged into the thick of the swarm swinging the fire brand. He carved a path toward the struggling man. Maralinne grabbed another stick from the fire and stood guard behind Jareth. The hideous screeching rose to a cacophonous crescendo. Jareth dragged Rogarth exhausted and bleeding into the circle of firelight. Their assailants followed weakly then vanished.

"You can put your stick down now. Maralinne," panted Jareth.

"What were they?" she asked.

"Fear illusions. If you are not afraid of them the light will dispel them," he explained.

"Illusions!" exclaimed Rogarth in disbelief.

"Yes that is all they were but the fear was real so the effects which you unfortunately feel were also real. Belar must have cast a fear spell on this camp, which explains some of the cleaning up I had to do earlier."

Jareth sponged Rogarth's wounds then rubbed them with salves, chanting just above a whisper. When he had finished he drew a star sign on the man's forehead then said, "What I'm wondering is who is afraid of tree frogs, winged tree frogs no less?"

After a long moment of silence Rogarth said, "I am."

"You're afraid of tree frogs!" exclaimed Maralinne. She tried not to laugh.

Avoiding Maralinne's eyes, Rogarth continued in a low voice, "As a boy I was afraid of their sounds in the night. No power on earth could convince me that awful sound was made by the innocent little frogs we caught during the day."

"You will carry the marks of tonight's adventure for a long time I'm afraid," said Jareth helping Rogarth to his feet.

"They may have been illusions but the bites and scratches were enough to make a soldier grateful he has the help of wise and brave companions," he said.

"I suggest we break camp and leave now before any of Maralinne's childhood fears come out of the woods," said Jareth with a laugh.

"Jareth! I command you...."

"Don't worry, Lady Maralinne, you and your secrets are safe with me."

They set out guiding their horses across the moonlit expanse of High Bridge. Far below them the dark waters raged and roared. Maralinne shuddered. She didn't want to look down but the churning current drew her eyes, forcing her to relive the traumatic swim she had survived with Jareth. The forest beyond was dense and forbidding but they pressed on. The road was only a faint ribbon between the black tangled walls of trees. Jareth promised that his cottage was less than an hour's ride but to Maralinne the road was endless. She rode close to Jareth fighting the urge to hang on to him. She tried desperately not to think of any childhood fear that a lingering trace of fear spell could set upon them.

At last they came to a small moon-drenched clearing. There Jareth's cottage welcomed them. Rogarth took the horses to the barn while Jareth and Maralinne unlocked the door and lit the lamps. Soon the place glowed with a friendly fire. Maralinne let Jareth tuck her into the dusty little bed.

"I'll take first watch this time," said Jareth

"As you wish," said Rogarth.

Jareth settled in one chair facing the door. Rogarth took the other, pillowing his scratched and bandaged face in his arms on the table. The room was soon quiet except for the occasional crackle of the fire. The hours slipped by. Jareth stirred the fire and looked around the circle of light. There were no eyes and only a few benign rustles beyond the cottage walls. The fire spat and leaped, mingling red and gold with the waning moon. Maralinne stirred. Her pale face and brilliant hair mirrored the moon and the fire light. Jareth watched her breathe, bosom swelling beneath the quilts. Her breaths came faster and faster. Her fists clenched. Suddenly she sat up. Her eyes were wide with unseen terror.

"Jareth! Jareth!" she called out. Jareth knelt beside her and took her hand. Maralinne slumped back into a more pleasant dream. Rogarth watched silently with half-closed eyes. He too had waked to Maralinne's cry but remained still. It was not his name she called.

Unaware of Rogarth, Jareth stayed by Maralinne's bedside. Moonlight fell full on her cheek. A lock of her red silk hair lay across his hand. Slowly, very slowly he lifted his hand. The lock caught in his fingers. With reverence he lifted it to his lips, then placed it back upon her neck.

Rogarth closed his eyes again but did not sleep.

They arrived through the south gate just before noon. The word spread quickly through Arindon. People shouted in the streets, "Princess Maralinne lives!" At the castle gate all was a rush of hugs and tears of joy. The ladies hustled Maralinne inside shouting orders for a bath to be drawn and food set out. Jareth went immediately to find Kyrdthin while Rogarth took a long time caring for his horse.

Dinner that evening was festive but Maralinne was quiet. "I'm just tired," she pleaded after barely tasting her food. As soon as she had told her tale and had been aptly chided by her father she excused herself and sought the quiet of the courtyard. Rogarth followed. She watched him cross the open space. He was a gallant figure. She had to admit it. She would be proud to call him husband. She would like and respect him always, but love him? Never.

"Maralinne."

She looked away.

"Maralinne, my betrothed."

The reality of the words made her shrink from him. How could she submit her whole life to this man? She had come home because Analinne needed her, but she had come home a different person from the rash, rebellious girl that ran away what seemed like a long time ago. So much had changed through all the dangers and hardships she had shared with Jareth. The events of the past few days stood like milestones between the child she had been and the woman, the princess, she must now become. She needed Jareth's quiet strength, his courage, his loyalty. She even needed his incessant teasing. Rogarth could never....

"I need to talk to you," Rogarth began.

"As you wish, sir," she said without turning toward him.

"Not, sir, Maralinne, but friend. I will never be your master though I have legal claim."

Maralinne shot him a questioning look.

"Please call me friend, dearest Maralinne."

"As you wish," she said a bit intrigued to know where the conversation was heading. "I will call you friend instead of husband. That should vex the castle gossips."

"Maralinne, dearest," he said firmly taking her hands.,

She did not pull away.

"Though I have realized only in losing you how much I love you, I will not force you to marry me against your will."

Maralinne looked up. She studied the sadness in his eyes and the resolve in the set of his jaw.

"I am not blind, nor am I hard-hearted," he continued as he thoughtfully turned the garnet ring she wore. "I have seen where your heart lies, and it is not with me."

"You have seen what?" Maralinne searched her memory. What he could possibly mean?

"Jareth is a good man, Maralinne. He serves you far beyond his duty to Arindon. He serves you from his heart. He loves you, yet keeps his distance respecting your royal station and our pledge. Your station I cannot change but from a pledge that binds your person but not your heart I can release you."

"Friend. Is this what you mean by friend?" she said searching his face for an answer.

Rogarth tried to smile. "Love Jareth with my blessing," he said.

Speechless, she stepped back still holding his hand.

"Our marriage was never meant to be," he said. His words tumbled out a bit too fast. "My first duty to Arindon is that of a soldier. Our world is in danger. I cannot be burdened with domestic affairs." He paused then added with difficulty, "One kiss for what might have been and I will leave you."

She kissed him, joyous, yet saddened for her freedom. "Your token…" she said pulling the garnet from her finger.

"No," he said enfolding her small hand between both of his. "Keep it as a wedding gift to you and Jareth."

"I couldn't…" she stuttered. "I…"

"If you will not wear it, then keep it for your daughters. It was freely given." With that Rogarth released her and walked away.

Chapter 9

That night Maralinne asked April, not her regular maid, to help her ready for bed. April was bursting with excitement. "Tell me more about your trip, Lady Maralinne," she begged as she carefully brushed the princess's long red hair.

"You heard it all at dinner," Maralinne answered with a tired voice.

"Forgive me but it all sounds so wonderfully adventurous, so romantic that..."

"Is it that obvious?" said Maralinne.

"My Lady?" April tugged at a knotted strand of hair with Maralinne's jeweled comb.

"That my betrothal to Rogarth is broken?"

April's jaw dropped.

Maralinne rubbed a soothing, rose scented lotion over her arms and shoulders. "Brush harder Avrille. I want my hair to shine tonight."

April brushed until Maralinne's hair crackled with electricity. "Shall I braid it back now?" she said picking up the side pieces of hair and holding them with a twist. Maralinne's behavior was more than puzzling.

"No, I want it down, like so," said Maralinne separating her tresses and letting them fall front over her breasts. Her sheer, silk gown rose and fell beneath her hair. "Avrille I know you must be wondering why I asked you to attend me tonight."

April nodded.

"It's because we are both keeping secrets. I learned of yours in Allarion so I know I can trust you with mine."

What secret did Maralinne know? April didn't know whether to be afraid or relieved.

"I know we are both princesses," said Maralinne taking the hairbrush April had poised motionless in the air above her head. "We are equals, not mistress and servant, and someday I will need to kneel to you as High Queen."

April's heart beat wildly but she managed to relax a trifle when Maralinne gave her a hug.

"Now for my secret," said Maralinne laying the hair brush on the table and picking up an emery board. "It's Jareth. He is coming here to my room tonight and I need you to see that we are not disturbed."

"Jareth?"

"You still don't understand do you?" Maralinne glanced at her reflection in the mirror. She smoothed her gown over her bosom, smiled at herself then turned back to April. "You see Rogarth has released me from our betrothal because he realized that Jareth and I…"

"Jareth!" April squealed with delight.

"Yes Jareth. I suppose it has always been so between us but we did not know it for what it was until now."

"But who will Rogarth marry?" said April with sudden concern.

Maralinne shrugged her shoulders. "I don't know or much care."

A soft knock interrupted them. April ran to answer the door. Jareth was still dressed in the leather jerkin and dark wool plaid he had worn at dinner.

"Your mistress has sent for me," he said with a smile for April.

"Come in Jareth," Maralinne called from her boudoir chair.

Their eyes met. Maralinne rose slowly. Her gown clung seductively a moment then swirled behind her as she turned. She reached for a ribbon to tie about her waist. Jareth dropped his eyes. The color beneath his tanned cheek deepened.

"I called you here to perform one last duty to your princess," announced Maralinne with a regal toss of her head.

"Last duty?" Jareth looked straight into Maralinne's eyes

"Yes Jareth. Your service to Arindon as gamekeeper will terminate at dawn tomorrow."

"Alright Maralinne what game are you playing now?"

April giggled.

"Princess Maralinne" she corrected him. "We are back to Arindon, remember?"

"Yes My Lady, pardon any…" Jareth became more and more confused.

"Jareth come here," said Maralinne holding out her arms. Her eyes were laughing.

His steps were hesitant, his eyes questioning.

"Rogarth has released me from our betrothal vows with blessing to follow my heart," she said taking his hands.

Jareth fell to his knees. He kissed the hem of her gown and wept for joy.

Maralinne laughed and pulled him to his feet. "Avrille please fetch us some wine. We have a new pledge to make."

April obeyed. In the anteroom she took two goblets from the shelf and placed them on a tray. The decanter on the table was half full. That would be enough. She grabbed two lace napkins and hurried with her tray back to the princess's bedroom. She entered with a quick knock and was somewhat disappointed to see Maralinne and Jareth just sitting casually at the bedside table.

"You brought only two goblets," said Maralinne.

"I thought just you and Jareth…"

"That's alright. Jareth and I can drink from the same."

"Shall I pour?"

"Yes," said Maralinne without taking her eyes from Jareth's.

"For me too?"

"Yes Princess Avrille."

April poured. Maralinne took the heavy goblet. Jareth covered her small white hands with his. "Drink, my dearest lady," he said. "Share this with me as we have shared our trials and as we hope to share our joys."

"After you Jareth," said Maralinne. "From this moment I am no longer your princess. You are the master and I the willing servant."

"I'll drink to that." Jareth laughed heartily. "But where is the sassy independent little girl I am forever rescuing?" He raised the goblet and drank long and deep.

Maralinne pulled the wine away from him. "Must you always tease me?"

"Always," he said with the solemnity of a vow. He retrieved the goblet then held it for her to drink.

Maralinne took a sip of the dark red wine. "Oh, Jareth this is why I love you." She threw her arms around him. "Now I can truly say it. I love you. I have always loved you and my love will not change. No man, nor woman, no god, nor beast loves more full, loves more deep."

"And I love you my princess," he said in a hesitant whisper. Tears sparkled in his eyes as he kissed her fire-bright hair. "I am yours. I will love you and care for you as long as time encircles us both."

April had poured herself a full goblet of wine. Her eyes were wide with delight as she quietly watched and sipped. Maralinne turned to her and smiled.

"Avrille, my sister princess and friend, you have been witness to our pledge. May the man you marry, may he also be your friend."

They raised their goblets together. April thought first of he Willy, then thoughts of Rogarth crowded out her little brother. How disappointed Rogarth must feel...

"...Take your wine with you to bed if you like," Maralinne was saying. "I have made arrangements for you to sleep in the anteroom. I trust that you will see that we are not disturbed."

Reluctantly April carried her goblet out of the room trying not to spill a drop of the wine or the warm feeling that swam in her head. She paused at the door. "Goodnight," she said but no one answered.

The next morning after Jareth had slipped away, April returned to her room. The door was open.

"...I will go to her!" April heard her mother exclaim.

"Sit down, Janie. Get a hold of yourself," Kyrdthin's voice replied. "You can't go and that's it."

"Mom, what's wrong?"

Kyrdthin turned but Janille still sat with her head in her hands. "Come in and close the door, Little Bird," he said. "Your mother is upset because Lady Elanille's husband and all his men were killed at High Bridge. You heard their story last night."

"And now Elani is all alone except for us," wept Janille.

"Jane!" Kyrdthin cautioned.

"It's OK mother," said April. "We can take care of Lady Elanille, and Kylie and the new baby when it comes." She gave her an awkward hug, puzzled by her mother's extreme distress.

"Janie she is with Analinne. Let her foster sister comfort her. She can help her concentrate on the baby and the future. It is best that it be she and not you."

Janille sank back into her chair and covered her eyes. "As you say Hawke," she answered with weak resignation.

Kyrdthin turned to April. "Take care of your mother, Little Bird. She needs you. Comfort her but don't ask her any questions."

"But why is she crying over Lord Keilen?"

"No questions I said. She needs love now. There will be answers later."

Kyrdthin touched Janille's shoulder then vanished. April stared at the sprinkling of silver stars where his hand had lingered.

"Kill 'em Delven Dogs dead, dead, dead,"

April watched Kylie make his toy soldiers push the pine cones off the garden bench. It was almost autumn. All through the long summer he had reenacted his father's valiant stand against the Delven Dark at High Bridge. It upset her that a child of barely three could harbor such violent thoughts. She tried to divert him with gentler games. She tried to reason with him but Kylie continued to wage his fantasy wars against the dark.

Lady Elanille was in her last month of pregnancy. April admired how at first she bravely faced her husband's death. She stood solid and strong holding Kylie's hand by the burning pyre, helping him toss their flower garlands into the flames. But as the summer wore on everyone noticed the changes in Elanille. Her cheerful manner faded. She cried quietly in her room. She ate only when urged to do so for the baby's sake. More and more of Kylie's care was left to April and Janille. Even Analinne, who was her constant companion and confidant, could not lift her spirits. Today April was told to take Kylie to the garden until dinner time.

"Av'lle, gimme da big one. He my daddy."

She handed him the wooden soldier that had fallen off the bench. "Come on Kylie, lets do something else. Let's just throw stones in the pond."

"OK. Da lilies be Delven Dogs. We sink 'em. We dwown 'em dead."

"Oh Kylie!." She tried to hug him but the child pushed her away.

"Yep, we dwown 'em ," he said toddling off to gather up handfuls of pebbles.

April gave up. She swung her feet around to the other side of the bench so she could watch him and picked up her embroidery.

Pain filled the night. Cramping waves spread across April's abdomen. She panted for breath. What was wrong! Fear yanked her toward the surface of sleep. More pain, clenching, pulsing, shuddering then aching release. She struggled awake. The pain stabbed again and again, rolling, pressing in rhythmic agony. She screamed and sat up clutching her stomach. Pain throbbed down into her thighs. Then with a final loin-rending stab it subsided. She fell back into the pillows drenched in sweat and sick with exhaustion. Kylie cried out from his little cot beside her bed. She reached out a hand. "It's OK. It's OK," she murmured as they both drifted back to sleep.

Calling! Calling! Shivering with fear and confusion. It was cold and the light was too bright. Calling! Calling! The voice inside her head needed her help. "Who?" April sat up. This time she was fully awake. The pain was gone. The voice was gone but the need was still there. She did not fully understand what had happened but she knew what she had to do. She picked up Kylie and carried the sleeping child to his mother's room. Janille was standing by Lady Elanille's bed.

"Wake up Kylie," said April with a kiss on the child's forehead. "Wake up and see your new sister."

Janille rushed to meet them at the door. "How did you know?" she said with an anxious whisper.

"I felt it all mother," said April. "And the baby called."

"Oh my poor darling, feeling your sister's pain."

"Sister!" April gasped.

Janille panicked. What had she done! What had she unwittingly revealed! She looked lovingly back to Elanille's bed. Young mother and infant lay content in each other's arms. She had not heard. Janille wiped the tears from her eyes and cleared the lump from her throat. "Yes, you are both my daughters," she whispered.

"The golden princess!" April exclaimed trying to keep her excited voice low.

"Yes, Elani's story was always your favorite as if you knew." Janille glanced back at the bed again. April carried Kylie into his mother's room. She approached the bed and took Princess

Elanille's warm moist hand. Elanille looked up and smiled. April kissed the fuzzy golden head of her little niece.

"Hey mommy," said Kylie squirming to get equal attention.

"Come here big boy. Give mommy a kiss," said Elanille reaching for her first born.

"Can I sleep wift you too?" he said trying to climb into the bed.

"Not now Kylie. You must go back to bed with Avrille."

"No. Wanna sleep here," he whimpered.

"Kylie my sweet, Aunt Jane will put baby in her cradle soon and Avrille will put you in your bed. Mama is very, very tired."

"No. No."

"Kiss me again, then be a good boy. I will see you in the morning."

April held him over the bed once more then carried the struggling toddler back to his cot in her room. Her mind raced...the pain...the baby ...my sister...the golden princess...but soon her exhausted body took over and she slept. Kylie whimpered and sniffled, then he slept too.

For Janille there was no sleep. She hardly had time to gather her midwife's basins and cloths when Princess Analinne's maid came running to find her.

"My lady is having labor. She says come quick."

"I will come shortly. Go back to your mistress and keep her calm," said Janille. Her voice was tired. She stooped to kiss her sleeping daughter and granddaughter. Renewed and happy she made her way to Analinne's room.

King Frebar looked up. "Well, if it isn't my twin brother, the little library mouse."

Tobar swallowed hard. The retort he could have made would have been wasted on Frebar. He ran his hands nervously through his thick dark hair.

"Well?" Frebar leaned his chair back against the wall and folded his arms across his chest. Frebar was nothing like his brother. They had been mirror images as boys but now a more accurate metaphor would describe them as views from opposite ends of a spyglass. Both were dark-haired and fair featured but Frebar was taller and heavier muscled. His hair was cropped short, military style and his clean-shaven jaw was hard and set.

He wore a plain blue tunic in the privacy of his study but his sword of state lay across the desk within easy reach. His clear blue eyes stared straight at his brother.

Tobar looked down. His clothes were dirty. His boots were ragged. "I...I wanted to...to congratulate you brother...that is assuming you already heard the good news."

"What news is ever good?" Frebar swung his up his feet and cocked his heavy, polished boots on the desk.

Tobar took a step back. His drooped shoulders made him seem even smaller beneath his oversized shirt. "You...you are a grandfather again by Elanille," he said, lips barely moving behind his full beard.

"Another son?"

"No a...a daughter this time."

"Why congratulate me on that?" said Frebar swinging his feet back down to the floor.

"She's a pretty little thing," said Tobar. His eyes sparkled as he peered above his spectacles. "She's all golden-haired like Elanille was as a babe."

Frebar's face softened a little.

"I...I thought...maybe it would be nice...to...to give her a little something. The naming is in five days."

"A little something?" Frebar almost smiled. "What did you have in mind, little brother, a dusty old book?"

"No...no something pretty...a woman thing. Maybe a gem from the treasury. After all she...she is a little princess."

"Naming..." Frebar said to himself. "The people would expect me to give a gift."

"Yes, the people would expect the royal gems to...to be passed on to the next generation."

"I never gave a gift when she had the boy," Frebar mused. "She chose to stay in Arindon when she came of age, then she married a common soldier. And on top of that Arinth had the audacity to knight him as a reward for sleeping above his rank and station. But Elanille wanted him. She was stubborn at that age. An Arindian bowman could bend her will but not her father the king." Frebar let out a sigh of regret then looked at his brother. "Perhaps I was too hasty to judge. She loved her bowman didn't she?"

"That she did."

"I heard he was killed by Delven a while back?"

"The massacre at...at High Bridge" answered Tobar fidgeting to return the conversation back to the naming gifts.

"She grieved for him?"

"With only the boy, your...your grandson to console her."

"I haven't seen much of my grandson," said Frebar. "She named him for her bowman not for his grandfather, her king."

"Young Keilen, she calls him Kylie, he...he's a fine boy," said Tobar straightening up a little. "A Frevarian through and through...likes to watch the men in the practice yard....looks right cute waving his little wooden sword."

Frebar stood up. He walked to the window and looked out. "I will have to think about this," he said.

"If I may make a suggestion...about the gift that is?" said Tobar.

Frebar turned around to face his brother.

Tobar pushed his spectacles back up onto the bridge of his nose. "The sapphire tiara would look good on those golden curls...when the girl grows up."

Frebar raised his eyebrows. "What about the boy? I suppose you have a suggestion for him too."

"Well..." Tobar hesitated. This had to be done exactly right for his plan to succeed. "Well," he said again. "There is always the amulet...the big topaz...that should impress old Arinth."

"Yes it would," Frebar agreed. "You are pretty good at this brother. You know I'd do anything to tweak Arinth's nose given the chance, but what's in it for you?"

Tobar forced a laugh. "The gem would not...not only show your wealth and generosity, it would show that Frevaria and not Arindon has...has produced a male heir to the throne." His heart pounded. He could feel the sweat beading on his forehead.

Frebar laughed. Tobar risked a sigh of relief.

"You're clever, I must admit, little brother," said Frebar. "I never thought I'd have the occasion to say that to you." He reached for a decanter on the desk. "Let's have a drink together to celebrate."

Tobar took the glass. The dark wine looked inviting but he knew he had to keep his wits about him. He gestured with his glass but did not drink. "To the future of Frevaria. To your grandson and heir. To your new granddaughter." He paused then added with calculated nonchalance. "And to my son."

"Your son?" Frebar set his glass back down on the desk with a clunk. The wine sloshed over the edge. "Damn!" he roared and grabbed a wad of papers to blot the spill. He tossed the soaked paper into the cold fireplace behind him then turned back to Tobar. "Your son?"

"My...my Analinne gave birth the same night, just...just minutes after Elanille."

"So there's more to your being here than gift giving to my grandchildren?"

"No...no I wasn't...I mean I just thought you would like to know...he is your little nephew after all...just a nephew...no contender of course..." That was the last bait. Tobar held his breath and waited.

"No contender to Frevaria but Analinne is Arinth's eldest and the child is male. I suppose Arinth will name him heir."

"Let him," said Tobar. "Keilen is three years older...he will ascend three years sooner and...and will most likely marry and sire a son and heir three years sooner and...and..."

"Go back to your library and give me time to think." Frebar waved his dismissal.

Tobar practically ran from the room. "Yes! Yes!" he cheered as he closed the heavy door behind him. His plan had worked. Little prince Keilen would wear the topaz amulet and no one would know its dark secret until it was too late.

Five days later King Arinth stood before his throne. His stooped shoulders were weighed down by the jewels and brocades he insisted on wearing. Queen Marielle stood on one side of him and Gil on the other ready to support him. Princess Analinne stood alone at the foot of the dais holding her newborn son. Tobar had disappeared again.

Arinth raised his hands. "When the Sun and Moon shine double in the sky," he said. "Then shall the Three be Five. Arindon's twin and Frevaria's twin united in this child....What's the name again?" he whispered to Gil.

"Jasenth, sire."

"In this child Jasenth," Arinth continued. "Let the Darkness be chained."

Arinth's frail hand rested on his grandson's head and traced the sign of the Star. "Red hair like his mother," he said aside to Gil.

"Yes, sire, and a strong sturdy body."

Analinne beamed with pride. Baby Jasenth kicked a tiny foot free of his blanket. Arinth gave the foot a little squeeze then turned back to Gil. "What else do we have to do today?"

"The girl child," said Gil.

"Whose is she again?"

"Frebar's grandchild by Janille's Elanille and the late Lord Keilen, sire."

"Let's have a look at her then," said Arinth swaying unsteadily. Marielle smiled and slipped an arm around him.

Elanille carried her daughter to the dais. April watched from her place beside little Kylie. She squeezed his hand tight. Was this golden-haired woman standing small and alone in her loosely-fitting blue silk gown really her sister? And the baby dressed in lace embroidered with pearls, was she really her little neice?

"The Light at the End of the World!" Arinth exclaimed when he saw the child. "I feel the mantle of prophecy about my shoulders. I have seen the Light with these tired sore eyes. This child...This child...:

Gil and Marielle exchanged worried glances.

"Ask the name," whispered Gil, trying to redirect Arinth's attention. His fingers busily wove a calming spell.

"Frebar's daughter. What name do you give this child?" said Arinth resuming his former calm demeaner.

"Lizelle, Your Majesty," said Elanille.

"Lizelle, Lizelle, gift of the gods, gift of Light," Arinth proclaimed. He lifted a tiny golden curl and drew the star sign on her forehead. His eyes widened. His voice rose a bit too shrill. He tottered a step forward. Gil's ever ready hand kept him from falling.

"It would be wise to unite the kingdoms now, sire, and betroth these two," said Gil.

"Yes, yes it would," said Arinth . "But couldn't I do it sitting down?"

Gil and Marielle helped him sit back into his chair. April wondered how old the king really was, or silver-haired Marielle for that matter. They were Will's parents, her mother had said so, but Willy didn't seem anything like them.

Arinth sighed. "You tie the hands for me, Gil. They move too fast for me."

Gil wound the gold and silver cords around the babies' wrists.

"Then shall the Three be Five," pronounced Arinth. He leaned toward Gil. "Are we done?"

"Yes, sire. You have assured us the kingdoms will thrive."

Analinne and Elanille turned toward the assembly. The people clapped and cheered. "Hail Prince Jasenth! Hail Princess Lizelle! Hail to the future in the Light!" Both babies cried out, startled by the noise. They waved and tugged at their bound hands but the cords held.

"What a wedded pair they will make," said Analinne laughing as she and Elanille hurried across the hall to their waiting nursemaids.

"Wasn't that lovely," said Lady Liella sitting next to April. "A pity my sister and I weren't betrothed that young."

"A pity we weren't betrothed at any age," said Lady Cellina on Lady Liella's other side.

"Elanille is too a lovely girl to be widowed just as life is beginning, don't you thinks so Avrille?" said Lady Liella.

"Yes, my lady..." said April.

"Where's the cakes?" Kylie interrupted. He was tired of sitting still and listening to the ladies gossip. "Av'ille said there'd be cakes if I be quiet."

"Come to Auntie Cellina," said the big woman offering her hand. "We'll go find you some cakes. These skinny gossips would rather talk than eat."

April gladly handed over her little charge over to Lady Cellina. The two of them made a comic pair as they headed toward the buffet. Cellina was wide and flamboyantly bejeweled, and Kylie small and uncomfortable in his finery.

Marielle stepped down from the dais. Today she wore bright blue but her face was drawn and pale. Arinth was gravely ill. None could hide it now. She had participated very little in today's festivities, wanting the people to focus on the future and the children. Janille and April dropped a deep curtsy as she approached

"Attend me in my chambers when the feasting is over," said Marielle to Janille.

"As you wish, My Lady."

Marielle returned to Gil. He took her hand and together they presided over the feast. Arinth had been carried back to his room to rest.

Chapter 10

They gathered in Marielle's private chambers. The early evening sun slanted low through the blue-tinted windows, bathing the room in pale, cool light. The scent of musty flowers hung heavily. Marielle lit candles and set a silver tea service on the low table, then bid them sit. Frebar's name day gifts to the children lay in an open chest, sparkling in the candlelight. The sapphire tiara he sent for baby Lizelle brought tears of memory to Janille's eyes. Kyrdthin laid his hand on hers.

"I say a grandfather has a right to send a gift to the boy," said Gil holding up the topaz amulet sent for Kylie.

"Frebar is basically a good man," said Janille. "In spite of everything, it wasn't April and I he hated. It was anything Allarian, anything he didn't understand."

"Didn't understand! Then explain this gift." Kyrdthin grabbed the amulet and waved it in front of her. "Look at it Jane. What do you feel?"

"It's the royal topaz, nothing more," she answered careful not to let her eyes be drawn into the stone. "Frebar is only claiming Kylie as his heir. I know him."

Kyrdthin threw the amulet back into the chest. "I will never forgive what he did to you and April."

"Calm down little brother," said Marielle. "Past grievances are not the issue here."

Gil nodded his agreement.

Kyrdthin paced. His long, heavy strides crushed deep footprints into the plush, flower strewn carpet. "It's still a focus stone," he argued unwilling to be pacified.

"I'm sure Frebar has no idea," Janille insisted.

"Frebar perhaps not," said Gil picking up the amulet again. "But what about his brother? We all know Tobar has dealings with Belar." The topaz glowed in his hand with deep golden fire.

"I think we are too busy blaming someone and missing the most important point, Kylie's safety," said Marielle. "If he wears the stone, Belar has direct access to him."

"Let's not question the gift or the giver then," said Gil. "Let's just be glad the stone has fallen into our hands so easily." He lay the jewel back into the box.

"But what do we do with it? We can't let Kylie wear it," said Janille catching Kyrdthin's hand as he paced by her. She pulled him down onto the cushion beside her.

The blue shaft of sunlight slid lower through the lace-draped windows and crept across the tea table. Marielle lit more candles. The calming scent floated in the still air.

"Yes, what do we do with the damn thing?" said Kyrdthin. He reached for the plate of cakes Marielle set out.

"I say we have a glass copy made and let the boy wear it on state occasions," Gil suggested. "The stone itself should be sent to Allarion for safe keeping. We can't afford to lose Frevaria's good will by not accepting the gift. We may need their help and more for the cause of the Light before this is over."

"Three jewels in one place? Are you sure Gil?" said Kyrdthin.

"Why not? Maybe the joining is closer than we think."

Kyrdthin helped himself to another cake. "Perhaps it is, but let's not forget the other reason for this gathering."

"Yes, Tobar. Where is the man?" said Gil. "You would think he'd attend his own son's naming."

Analinne fearing the worst had come to them begging that search parties be sent out for him when he did not come home. They all agreed that he may be in grave danger but they knew he was not dead. If a royal twin died they would all have felt the rent in the pattern. There had to be another reason for his absence. Had he sold out to Belar completely? Had he been duped again into aiding the Dark Lord? Was he being held captive and in need of their help?

"I can't believe Tobar or anyone could give up their own child for money or power," said Janille.

"Money and power no," said Kyrdthin exchanging a quick look with Marielle. "But for the cause of the Light we do what is required of us."

"We must stop this bickering among ourselves and concentrate on our children," said Marielle taking the plate of cakes from Kyrdthin and offering the few remaining to the others.

Gil took a cake and placed it on Marielle's napkin, but she pushed it aside. He laid the cake back on her napkin. "Let's have our tea and take some nourishment before we continue," he said. "We need the strength and calming."

When they had finished they parted, each to their agreed upon task, Kyrdthin to find a trusted smith to copy the amulet and Gil to make arrangements to transport it to Allarion. Janille lingered a few moments more with Marielle then hurried back to April.

Tobar waited in the cold anteroom. Why had Lord Belar summoned him? His fingers nervously combed through his tangled, dark hair. Fear and guilt battled inside of him. Had Belar found out about the topaz? He looked at the guard standing silently by the door. His dark metal armor did not reflect the torchlight. Why did Belar keep him waiting and under guard?

"Enter princeling," a voice rang through his head. Tobar looked at the guard. He had not moved nor spoken.

"Now! Do not keep me waiting," the voice commanded.

Tobar jumped up. The heavy metal door swung open. He walked past the statue-like guard into the dimly-lit hall beyond. The torches lining the walls flared then steadied. Tobar felt the shift, the sudden wrenching of mind and body lost for a moment between worlds. Then the stone floor was beneath his feet again. He let out his breath.

"Little Tobar, my rebel prince, I hear you have been clever. Brothers are so easy to fool aren't they?"

"I...I...thought you would be pleased." Tobar's heart sank. Did Belar know?

"No one would suspect a naming gift. Oh that was clever!" Belar crooked his finger. "Come closer."

Tobar took a few steps. This was too easy. Belar was too pleased.

"That's better," said Belar. "Now tell me all you know about the gems in the Frevarian treasury."

The truth? No he couldn't, not all of it. But what if Belar already knew? "The sapphires they're a...a pretty woman thing. I remember my mother wearing them..."

"How sweet!"

"And...and the topaz it's a stone of power..."

"Power!" Belar's eyes widened. His demeanor changed. "Why would Frebar give a stone of power to a child?" Belar laughed a bit too shrill.

Now Tobar was sure Belar at least suspected his plan, but how much of it? "He is claiming the...the boy as his heir," he decided to say.

"With a stone of power?"

"Frebar doesn't know what the stone is."

"But you do?" Belar clicked his tongue. "Now how would you learn such a thing? One of your dusty old spell books?"

"Yes My Lord," said Tobar. "And...and..." Should he tell the rest? If he did his plan could fail. "Just something I remembered...long ago...I'm not really sure but..." Tobar stopped and twisted the stained edge of his sleeve. He did not look up.

"But what?" Belar prompted, impatience rising in his tone.

Tobar dropped the hem of his sleeve but he still did not look up. He could not face Belar with a lie. "It's about Frebar's woman...Janille..."

"His woman?" Now Belar's interest was caught. He sucked in his lower lip and waited for Tobar to continue.

"She wore the stone once and...and it made her feel dizzy...I heard her say so. I...I forgot about the incident until recently when...when I was reading the history of the five lost jewels. I knew by then that Kyrdthin had most likely had the diamond in the crowns and...and I well...I surmised that your sword had ...had the ruby and..."

The hilt of Belar's sword answered with a bright red throb. Tobar's eyes hurt to look at it.

"So you thought to equip a child with a stone of power in Frevaria?" Belar leaned forward. "Do I smell the stench of fratricide and regencies?"

He did not suspect! Tobar swallowed hard to disguise his relief and looked up. "No, sire. Never that!"

"Well whatever you little plan is I won't be out done by a mere king," said Belar. "I would also like to bestow a naming gift. Not on Frevaria's grandbrats but on you own new son." Belar caressed the hilt of his sword. The ruby responded to his touch. "Perhaps my gift will compensate for my keeping you from attending the naming ceremonies. But you should really be thanking me instead, since if I remember correctly you have a way of disrupting family gatherings."

Tobar remembered Maralinne's betrothal only too well. He had had a plan that time and it failed. This time? This time he was also in danger of failing. "I...I'm not used to drinking so much." Tobar affected a laugh. "Your men bested me that night to be sure."

Belar laid his sword across his knees. "Then let me pour you a glass of my best." He reached for a bottle on a nearby table. "You can practice for the next time here with me." Belar poured the dark red wine. "To the health of your new son," he said. He took a large swallow then wiped his chin with his hand. "Now about my gift."

Tobar took a small sip and looked up. He tried to smile.

"It's such a pity that your Analinne could not have enjoyed the safety and luxury of giving birth here in my court," said Belar taking another large swallow of wine.

"My Lord, they said your men tried to kidnap Annie, her in her condition and all. Lucky for her at least they took after Maralinne instead."

"A stupidity the drunken fools have dearly paid for believe me. But kidnapping! How can you call a royal escort a kidnapping?"

Now Tobar was really confused.

"I had only the well being of your little family at heart." Belar smiled. "Now that we understand each other better we could try again with a more reliable escort."

Tobar went rigid.

Belar continued without noticing Tobar's distress. "And when they arrive I can bestow my gift or shall I say gifts. As you can see I have a sword worthy of a king. What I do not have is an heir to bequeath it to. Two gifts in one. What do you say, proud father?"

"No!" Tobar declared. He shook with fear and anger. He could not bring bright Analinne to this cold sunless world. He could not sell his child to the Dark. Not for all the knowledge and power on five earths. "No!" he said again standing up straight and tall.

"Kneel!" Belar roared.

Tobar's knees buckled. Pain screamed through his brain.

"How dare you defy me? How dare you try to deceive me?"

"It was not in the deal to bring them here," said Tobar.

"Deal? What do I care about deals with vermin?" Belar picked up the half-empty bottle of wine and threw it across the room. The crash exploded behind Tobar. He clutched at his throbbing temples. The pain was unbearable. He gasped for breath. Belar raised his hands. A tremor shook through Tobar's body. He cried out in pain and terror.

"You failed me," Belar raged. "I wanted the boy Will, but you failed. I wanted the girl, but you failed and now you failed again. You played games behind my back with powers you cannot begin to know much less control."

The pain stabbed with each word Belar shouted. Tobar cringed totally helpless.

"I said I want your woman and your brat here with me." The veins in Belar's face bulged with rage. He raised his hands again "You will do as I command."

Tobar's head exploded with pain, then everything went black.

"Now you are mine," said Belar. He wiped his hands on his robes. "Rise puppet. Go back to your little family until I send for you."

Tobar obeyed. His feet moved without his will. All that was Tobar huddled hurt and afraid in a small corner of his mind. The Dark Lord filled the rest with hate and cunning.

Mabry jumped back with a start. A silver mist swirled into his mill.

"Hey that was cool," said Will when Kyrdthin materialized and set the pages of his ledgers fluttering to the floor.

As Will scrambled to put his papers in order Mabry tried to regain his composure. "What can I do for you Kyrdthin, sir," he said still a bit shaken.

"It's Will here I came to see," said Kyrdthin. He pulled up a stool and peered over Will's shoulder . "Showing quite a profit I see, Mabry," he said scanning Will's figures.

"Credit partly to my little bookkeeper here," said Mabry patting Will on the back.

"Then maybe what I have to say will be unwelcome news," said Kyrdthin.

"What news?" said Will searching Kyrdthin's face for a clue.

Kyrdthin took his time. He looked over the piles of flour sacks two workmen were stacking in neat rows by the door. He leaned back and inspected the flour-dusted rafters, and walked to the window overlooking the river. Outside a barge was heading for Frevaria.

"What news?" Will begged leaning out of the window beside Kyrdthin.

"How'd you like to go on a camping trip with Jareth?"

"Would I!"

Kyrdthin turned back to Mabry. "I hate to do this to you on such short notice but I assure you this is important."

Mabry just nodded.

"A trip!" Will danced about the mill.

"Settle down Will," said Kyrdthin. "If Mabry can spare you right away go and get packed."

Mabry looked lost, suddenly aware of how much he had come to depend on the boy. He looked at Don the journeyman and the farmer lad helping him stack the heavy sacks. Kyrdthin's words had more depth than the boy perceived. Mabry knew he was losing Will perhaps for good.

"Ok Mabry?" Will was asking.

"Go pack your things and have a good time," he said mustering a smile.

"What shall I take?" Will said to Kyrdthin.

"The choice is yours.

Will's face sobered. "Is this a test?"

"It very well may be," he said with a friendly swat that sent flour dust flying from Will's breeches. "Pack your sack and sleep with your clothes on. Jareth will wake you when it is time to go."

When Will had gone Mabry turned a concerned face to his visitor. "Is everything alright...for the boy that is?"

"For the moment," said Kyrdthin. Without another word he was gone. The mill was quiet except for the rhythm of the men tossing and piling the sacks. Mabry closed Will's ledgers, called, "Lock up when you're done," to his journeyman, then he headed for home.

It was cold. April snuggled deeper into the quilts. "No, I'm not getting up," she mumbled sleepily to herself. "No, not until it's warmer. Stop calling. Lemme alone." But the voice insisted. "Who?" April sat up with a start. She heard nothing but the sense of urgency remained. She slid her feet over the edge of the bed. The floor was icy cold. She took a step, then another and another, drawn by an invisible hand toward the door. The soundless calling continued inside her head. Her heart beat faster and faster. Each footstep jarred through her yet she felt herself floating helplessly toward the darkness at the end of the hall. Without pausing she opened the door to Princess Analinne's room.

Tobar lay asleep in the canopied bed beside Analinne. The calling filled the room. Tobar's face was contorted with pain. His lips moved in soundless agony. April touched his hand. The calling stopped. For a moment she felt a questing then all was silent. April stood petrified. Time stopped in the dark-filled room.

Suddenly the room exploded with hideous laughter. Tobar lunged. His hands grabbed April's throat. She kicked and clawed at him. They tumbled over and over, thrashing at each other. The bedding wound in a tangle around them. Tobar roared and cursed. Analinne huddled on top of her pillow at the head of the bed and screamed. Tobar tore at April's nightgown. She arched back and kicked. Her fingers dug into the satin comforter beneath them. Everything gave way, sliding them to the floor with a thud.

Lights! Voices! The clatter of arms! Large hands pried her free from Tobar's deadly hold. She was flung over the shoulder of a leather jerkin and carried out of the room. The door slammed shut cutting off Analinne's screams behind them. The bouncing shoulder beneath her dug into April's ribs. Coarse dark hair scratched her face and got into her mouth. Numb in mind and body she let herself be carried by the vice-like arms until gentle hands and familiar gray robes lifted her down. Rogarth let out a breath of relief and stepped back to guard the door.

"Uncle Hawke, Oh Uncle Hawke," she sobbed.

"My dearest Little Bird, you're safe for now at least," said Kyrdthin. "Drink this." He handed her a wine glass.

"What happened?"

"Drink first," he insisted.

The wine was bitter. "Is it medicine?"

"Yes, drink it fast."

April tried to drink it but the acrid taste made her choke. Some of the wine spilled down her front. Kyrdthin took the glass, wiped her face with his sleeve then gave the glass back to her.

"All of it. Bottoms up," he said.

April screwed up her face but obeyed. "Somebody called me," she said handing the empty glass back to Kyrdthin. "I don't know who. What happened?" She buried her head against his chest. He stroked her hair with nervous fingers.

"Calm down, Little Bird. Calm down."

"Did he want to kill me? Did he Uncle Hawke?"

"No April, Tobar did not want to kill you but the Darkness that possess him has declared you its mortal enemy. You are in great danger. You must do exactly as I say. Your life and Will's depend on it.

Janille burst into the room. "Hawke, it's coming!"

"The fire spell, Janie!"

"I can't."

"You can. For the love of our children, use it now!"

Janille stood frozen.

"Now Janie. Back to back with me," Kyrdthin commanded. "Rogarth take Avrille to East Gate. Jareth already has Will."

Shadows slithered toward them, black half-human shapes veined with pulsing red. Janille's numb arms sprang to life. Her hands thrust toward the groping Dark. Strength, power flowed from inside her.

"Burn a path for April. Now Janie! Now!"

Electricity surged through her arms and brazenly spat from her splayed fingers. The shadows leaped back. Rogarth threw April over his shoulder again and ran.

"Again! Keep them burning!" Kyrdthin yelled.

All around them electricity crackled. Janille swelled with renewed confidence stood her ground. Zing! Zap! The dark pulsing shadows receded then bellied back again with doubled force.

"We're holding them but we can't win this way. Strike with me Janie. One. Two. Three!"

The flames leaped, circled then swelled outward in concentric rings of fire.

"More Janie. More!"

Her arms ached. The pulse of the flames beat in time with her galloping heart. She felt the solidity of Kyrdthin's back behind her. She felt herself grow taller and taller. The flames were beneath them now. The shadows howled in agony as they fled.

At last it was quiet. Janille's breath rasped in irregular gulps.

"We did it Janie!" Kyrdthin kissed her cheek. "I couldn't have done it without you. Belar used Tobar as a doorway but we fought him back. Tobar must be guarded day and night from now on."

"How did Rogarth know?"

"Just a hunch on my part. I had him take guard duty tonight. Lucky I did."

"Hunch! Don't tell me about hunches, Hawke," said Janille stepping back from him. "You know much more than you tell me. How will all this end? Tell me. Please tell me."

"Janie dearest, I wish I could. If the vision of the future were clear, then we would try to change it. The prophecies give only glimpses to guide us or perhaps to confuse us, who knows?" He held her tight and rocked her like a frightened child.

"Is April safe? Was it Freebane you gave her?"

"Yes but I don't know how much I got in her," he said loosening his embrace a little. "I hope it's enough to shield her until Rogarth gets her out of here."

"How far can they run? Belar knows who she is! We have lost! We have lost!" Janille wailed. Her face was flushed. Her eyes gushed with tears.

"They will get as far as Allarion I hope. We should have taken them there in the first place, but I thought we could get away with keeping them close. We almost did too."

"What good will it do keeping them in Allarion? They're just children," Janille sobbed. "There won't be a kingdom left for them to rule by the time they are grown."

"Janie calm down. You forgot about the time turn in Allarion. They can stay as long as they need to. They will grow in knowledge and skills as well as body and when they are ready we can bring them back. We need a warrior king and a healer queen. Time and Allarion can give us that. We have the resources of three worlds to cut and polish our jewels."

The time turn, she never did understand how it worked but she knew what Kyrdthin told her was true. Time ran differently in other worlds.

"I must say goodbye to them," she begged.

"Then let's be quick." He took her hand and traced a hurried star sign. Grayness enveloped them. There was a sickening lurch and they abruptly materialized behind the east wall near the gate.

"Warn me when you want to do that."

"Its easier when I don't. Look, here they are."

Rogarth led his horse out from behind a low building. April sat in the saddle clinging to the animal's mane with whitened fingers. Janille reached up and hugged her fiercely.

"Love you Mama," said April without releasing her grasp.

"Be a good girl for Rogarth,"

"I will. I will," April promised. Her voice trembled.

Kyrdthin took Janille's shoulders and pulled her away. "Let her go Jane."

"Kiss me too, Uncle Hawke," April begged.

"Quickly Little Bird," he said brushing her cheek.

Kyrdthin handed Rogarth a small sack. "Take good care of her. She is the future of All Light."

Rogarth raised a hand in silent pledge then swung up onto the saddle behind April. With a snap of the reins they were off.

Janille stood in shock staring into the night after the vanishing riders. Kyrdthin's arms around her felt strong and reassuring as the bottom dropped out of her world again for an instant. Back in the castle Analinne was crying and Tobar was nowhere to be found.

Chapter 11

April and Rogarth started off at a gallop, but as soon as they reached the woods Rogarth reigned the horseback. Ahead of them the dark road wound beneath the ancient trees. They kept a slower but steady pace. It was easy to follow the cart ruts worn into the road. It was the tree roots and low-hanging branches that kept them zig-zagging to avoid disaster. The sky, what they could see of it above the gnarled canopy, was hazy and moonless.

A rustle of wings startled them. Rogarth tightened his hold on the reigns then relaxed. When a dark bird swooped past them, the horse whinnied and took off at a confident trot.

"Kyrdthin promised he would send a bird to guide us," said Rogarth.

April still clung tight to Rogarth's waist. The bird darted from tree to tree just ahead of them. "Mama used to say Uncle...I mean Kyrdthin sent the birds to watch over us when I was little."

"Kyrdthin is a man of many secrets," said Rogarth. "Tonight he sent me to watch over you and your secrets."

"My secrets!" April said with alarm.

"Kyrdthin said you are the future of the Twin Kingdoms. That told me all I need to know to keep you safe."

"Did he say anything about my brother?"

"I know Jareth was sent to get him, and that we will meet them, the gods willing, when we get to Allarion."

Rogarth's leather jerkin squeaked rhythmically. After they had been riding more than an hour, the excitement of their flight changed to misery and boredom. April loosened her grip on Rogarth's belt. Her hands hurt. Her bare feet were cold. She shivered in her thin nightgown. The blanket Rogarth had wrapped around her didn't do much good. Worst of all her bottom hurt. Sitting side-saddle was terribly awkward. She felt that at any minute she was going to slide off. Rogarth took up so much room.

"Tired little lady?" he said.

"How much farther?"

"We have barely started on our journey," he said to April's dismay. "But the next stretch of road is fairly even. You may lean back on my shoulder if you like."

"Why do we have to ride double?"

"Kyrdthin thought it the safest way, Lady Avrille,"

"I'm all squooshed sideways like this."

"Perhaps you would be more comfortable riding as a boy rides."

"Hold me Rogarth," she said as she hitched up her night gown and swung one leg up over the horse's neck.

"You are a practical girl, Lady Avrille, if a bit immodest." Rogarth chuckled remembering an earlier trip on this same road with Princess Maralinne.

"Who cares about modesty way out here in the woods?" said April.

"None but us, my lady. And it will make for a faster and safer trip to have you so."

The leather of Rogarth's jerkin stopped squeaking but it is still smelled awful when she pressed her cheek against it. She pulled her sleeve up to cushion her face. Rogarth's arm encircled her like a vice. She was tired and cramped but she felt secure.

The road went on and on beneath the towering trees. The trotting horse stirred up the dank smell of rotting wood and moist leaves as they traveled along the muddy road. The woods were quiet except for the occasional chatter of a disturbed squirrel. At last they began to climb.

"How far is it now? This is steep," said April sitting up again.

"We're going all the way up to the pass," said Rogarth.

"Is Allarion on the other side of the mountains?"

"That and more."

The smaller rocks on the path rattled back down the mountainside behind them. The horse lurched from side to side to keep its footing. The trail switched back and climbed still steeper. The forest thinned until there were only tiny, gnarled shrubs. They made a sharp turn and Rogarth called a halt. The valley below was obscured by a sea of clouds glowing in the pre-dawn light. A hawk cruised the up drafts like a swinging pendulum. April felt dizzy. Her lungs labored in the cold thin air. Shivering she hugged herself under her blanket wrap.

"We can rest and eat behind those trees," said Rogarth. He helped her dismount. "Horses first, then riders."

"Can I feed him?"

"Here hook the nosebag like so."

April stroked the horse's cheek as it munched. Rogarth rummaged through the saddle bags. Above them the sky was beginning to turn pink. April wrapped her blanket tighter around her shoulders.

"I'm freezing!"

"Here are some clothes Kyrdthin packed for you." Rogarth handed her a small bundle.

There was a dress, a shawl, under things and shoes. She was so cold. Her bare feet felt like ice. She put on the shoes first. Then she put on the dress over top of her nightgown and everything else underneath. The shawl was warm but she still wrapped up in blanket to keep off the wind.

"We have only bread and cheese, My Lady," Rogarth apologized. "I couldn't carry much more with both of us riding."

"It's OK. I'm starving. I'll eat whatever you have."

Rogarth cut large chunks of bread and placed equally large chunks of cheese on top.

"Your breakfast Lady Avrille," he said with a bow and a twinkle in his eye. He poured her a cup of water from the jug.

"Aren't you going to pour yourself some?"

"I have my own drink." Rogarth drew a small flask from his wallet.

"Can I have some?" she said reaching for the dented metal container.

"This is not a drink for ladies, especially not for little ladies," he said holding the flask out of reach.

"I'm not little. I'm fourteen years old."

"Then try a sip if you are so old and wise," he said removing the stopper from the flask.

April took it. It smelled awful. She held her breath and took a quick swallow. "Yuk!" she choked. "This is disgusting! Gimme a drink of water quick."

"I knew my lady would prefer water." Rogarth laughed and poured her another cupful of water.

April gulped it down.

"Easy, easy," said Rogarth still laughing. "Save some for later."

"How can you drink that stuff?"

Rogarth took a swig, replaced the cork then wiped his mustache with his sleeve. "It's an acquired taste," he said putting the flask back into his wallet.

When they finished breakfast they rode on. April was much warmer but her thighs and bottom were extremely sore. As much as she wanted to, she knew it was no use to complain.

"If we are lucky, Lady Avrille, there will be a fine dessert for you in a mile or two. I remember some blackberry bushes near the trail. They should be in season now if the bears did not get to them already."

"Bears!"

"Grrrr…"

"Really Rogarth, I'm not a three-year-old like Kylie."

"Yes there are really bears," said Rogarth.

The morning wore on. They did not meet any bears, but they did find the blackberries. Rogarth picked her a handful. They were tiny and sweet. April ate them one at a time as they rode, savoring each burst of flavor. Suddenly Rogarth's arm tensed around her. His other hand slowly reached for his sword.

"Don't move," he whispered

The horse tossed his head and whinnied. There was an uncanny silence, no birdsong, not even the rustle of wind in the trees. April could feel her heartbeat under Rogarth's steeled grasp. Her back rose and fell with his quickening breaths.

Two Dark Delven ponies leaped out from the underbrush. Rogarth's challenge roared in April's ears. With a single thrust of his blade he sent one assailant yelping and spurting blood.

"One down," Rogarth cheered.

April frantically clutched the horse's mane. She pressed her face into its taunt stretched neck. They galloped hard and fast but their double weight slowed them down. The Delven pony easily kept abreast of them. Rogarth brought his heavy blade clanking down on the black helmet bobbing beside them. April hung on tight. Everything was a blur of glinting steel and heaving horse. Rogarth's mailed chest crushed her shoulder with each swing of his blade. The galloping horse jolted against her face. She choked on the stench of horse sweat and blood.

Falling! Falling! Her fingers gave way clutching horsehair. Sliding! Tearing! Ripping across leather. April screamed and screamed. Rogarth grabbed her flailing arm. She caught hold of his belt. Then they were both falling, suspended in a dusty roaring eternity. Rogarth's war cry rose above the Delven's curses. A great weight slammed April to the ground. Thundering hooves passed over them.

Everything hurt. Her ribs were crushed, her legs twisted under her. Her shoulder was on fire beneath Rogarth's mailed elbow.

"Don't move My Lady," Rogarth grunted. "And don't open your eyes."

He rolled slowly off of her and sat up testing each limb. Relieved of Rogarth's weight, April lay still, grateful to simple breathe. She tried to open her eyes but dust caked her lashes.

Alert! Was it sight or sound or sixth sense? There was no time to question. "Look out!" she screamed.

In one move Rogarth pivoted and stabbed the reviving Delven.

"Two and done," he said. "Turn away Lady…"

April heard him drag the corpse off the road. She looked up to see him wiping his blade on the grass. Then he knelt beside her. He gently flexed her arms and legs.

"Does this hurt My Lady? Does this or this?"

"Sure it hurts but I think I'm OK."

He cradled her shoulders and helped her to sit up.

"Oh my poor bottom!" she cried.

"Are you able to stand ?" he asked lifting under her arms.

"I'm gonna be sore tomorrow," she exclaimed testing her footing.

Rogarth's horse trotted up to them and lowered his head. Rogarth rubbed the animal's neck affectionately. "We're alright, boy. We're alright."

April's eyes fell on Rogarth's arm. A red stain was seeping through his sleeve. "You're bleeding!"

"It's just a scratch," he said turning away.

"Does it hurt?"

"Not much."

"Let me see," she said taking his hand. She rolled back the sleeve. Time stopped. She saw a hawk light on a nearby branch. But why was she watching a bird when Rogarth needed her help? She looked at the wound. The blood had stopped flowing but she could see the gash on his wrist was bone deep. I need antiseptic. I need bandages. This must be sutured. She tried to remember what she had learned about first aid but the bird on the branch dominated her thoughts. She felt the bird reaching deep inside of her. She fought to keep focused. What should she do? Rogarth would never swing a sword again if she didn't help him now. Brave Rogarth wounded defending her. Her young heart opened and rose to meet the bird, to bond with the bird. Her hands felt light and tingly when she touched the injured wrist. The loving familiarity of the bird's presence guided her through the intricacies of blood vessels and bone. She saw how they were twisted and severed. She ran her fingers over the gapping wound willing it to be whole. Fascinated she watched the edges knit. She drew Kyrdthin's star sign as she smoothed the newly-healed flesh. Her heart resumed beating. Her breath began in a gasp. Rogarth's face was turned away. His eyes were fixed on the hawk spiraling away over head.

"I'll wrap it up with the hem of my nightgown just like they do in stories," she said. "Give me your knife." April hacked off the ruffle and carefully bound Rogarth's wrist. "There you are as good as new," she said a bit too loud.

"Neatly done," he said examining the bandage. "Not many soldiers have such a young but skillful nurse."

April trembled. What had happened? Rogarth had not seen. For that she was glad. She was confused but somehow unafraid. Whatever had happened had come from deep inside of her, from part of what she was or was becoming, something beautiful, something good. "What do we do now?" she asked. Her voice was small and unsteady.

"We must move on," said Rogarth lifting her up onto the horse again. "I want to put several hours ride between us and this place before we camp for the night."

The sun climbed the zenith and headed westward. April scanned the sky for the hawk but it was gone. Eventually she lay her head back against Rogarth's shoulder and fell asleep. When he woke her they were on the bank of a small stream.

"We will ford here and set up camp on the far bank," he said. "Running water will be some protection however small."

Sunlight slanted into the tiny window of the loft. For a moment Will forgot where he was. Then the events of the night before crowded out the dusty peace that had awakened him. He could hear Jareth moving around downstairs. "Hey Jareth," he called peeking down the ladder.

"Morning Will. Caught up on your sleep yet?" Jareth answered.

"Guess so." Will yawned.

It had been a short night. Will laid down on his bed at Mill cot with his clothes on and bag packed just as Kyrdthin had told him to, but he could not sleep. Jareth came for him just after midnight, They crept out of the house and waded out into the river, hugging the dark shadows beneath the willows. With some difficulty they picked their way up river. Not until Jareth guided him into the mouth of a small inlet did Will get a chance to look back. Arindon castle was alive with pulsing bursts of white fire. Black clouds writhed about the walls in grotesque shapes.

Jareth grabbed Will and shoved him down into the bottom of a small flat boat then poled them upstream beyond the sight of Arindon. When the waters began to roar and swirl too strong to make headway they abandoned the boat on a shoal and trekked overland. They arrived at Jareth's cottage just before dawn. The last thing Will remembered was stripping off his wet clothes and climbing the ladder to the loft.

".. So we got to hole up here until noon. Then we can make the passage," Jareth was saying.

"Where are we going?"

"Allarion eventually but I want to stop off to have you meet a friend of mine on the way."

Will sensed Jareth's anxiety as he watched him try to fletch a few arrows. He repeatedly stared out the kitchen window. He breathed deeply but a bit too fast and his hands shook. The cool morning air was still and fragrant. Yet something was wrong. Will tried to help clean up after breakfast but he kept getting in Jareth's way. He tried to make conversation but Jareth's answers were guarded. Will gave up. "Some camping trip," he grumbled.

Finally when it was almost noon Jareth led the way into the woods. After a short distance they came to a clearing. The trees were old and tall encircling a grassy space. In the center of the space lay a large flat stone.

"I remember this place," said Will. "This is where we came to first when Uncle Hawke brought us from home."

"Yes this is a place of power Will. On the other side of the passage I will answer your questions," said Jareth. He traced Kyrdthin's star sign on the stone. The pattern blazed warm and bright. "Hold on," he said grabbing Will's hands.

The world wrenched. The next moment Will shivered in a dim damp place. Slowly his eyes adjusted to the light.

Rogarth cut evergreen boughs, wove them loosely and covered them with his saddle blanket.

"You expect me to sleep on that?" April exclaimed.

"My Lady would prefer wet rocks?"

"Funny, funny. Where will you sleep?"

"I'll just curl up in my cloak," said Rogarth.

April looked around at the beginnings of their campsite. "Can I help with something?"

"If you wish Lady Avrille. You may help me make a wind break."

"OK I'll get some big sticks." April headed off toward a nearby thicket.

"Don't go out of sight," Rogarth called after her.

Soon they had wedged a few cut saplings and assorted sticks between two boulders. It helped but the raw wind still cut through. "We could use a boy scout care package," April muttered.

"Use what?"

"Nothing. I was just wishing for better camping gear."

"And you will have it," said Rogarth unrolling a long narrow bundle. "Kyrdthin sent this along. I hope you understand its function."

"A nylon tarp! And telescoping poles! Uncle Hawke you darling!"

"Is it magic?" Rogarth asked cautiously.

"No. Everybody has these things where we used to live," she assured him.

Rogarth still held back. "Kyrdthin's magic is white and practical," he said. "I trust him but I would fear to cross him."

April laughed. "Don't worry. Will and I have crossed him many times and we are still alive. He'd do anything for us. Anything except marry mom that is."

135

"Marry? Kyrdthin marry!" Rogarth exclaimed.

"It's no joke Rogarth," said April taking the tarp from him. "Mom loves him but he won't stay with her. In the other place we lived he would just show up one day then disappear again. Mom would cry every time but he would never stay. Now that we're here it isn't much better."

"Love is not a thing we can control," said Rogarth almost wistfully. "The gods determine whom we mate in spite of where our hearts are bound."

"Yeah, I'm stuck with Willy," April said with a resigned sigh. "Here put these pointy ends through the grommet holes in the tarp." She slid open the telescoping poles and handed them to Rogarth.

"Kyrdthin tells me you two will be High King and Queen when you come of age."

"Really Rogarth, the thought of marrying my little brother is ridiculous. I want to fall in love and well it's not that I don't love Willy, I do, but he's the little kid I've had to take care of almost all my life. I want somebody strong, heroic, romantic. You know what I mean."

"Know what Lady Avrille?" Rogarth ran his hand over the smooth surface of the tarp.

"Oh Rogarth you weren't even listening."

"Yes I was." Rogarth's voice dropped almost to a whisper. "I too looked for love but found it too late."

April reached out to touch his bandaged hand. "I'm sorry things didn't work out for you and Princess Maralinne, but she and Jareth, well they…"

"If she is happy then everything is as it should be," Rogarth said with finality.

They finished setting up camp in silence. Kyrdthin's tarp sheltered them from the chill wind. Soon April was sitting safely beneath it while Rogarth cooked supper. She was so tired. The adventures of the last twenty four hours were finally catching up with her. She was almost asleep when a familiar aroma jostled her senses. "Chocolate! I smell chocolate! Where did you get…?"

"Kyrdthin sent along My Lady's tea."

"Uncle Hawke, you double darling!"

Rogarth picked up the steaming teapot. "Would you like your tea now since it pleases you so much?"

"Oh yes!"

He poured the hot chocolate into a large metal cup. It almost burned her fingers but April cradled the cup like a long lost friend. She had not realized how much she had missed her morning cocoa until now. She took a big swallow letting it fill her mouth then gradually let it slide down her throat."

"Here Rogarth you must taste this." She handed him the cup.

"But it is for you. Kyrdthin said..."

"Try it please."

Rogarth took a small sip. His eyes lit up.

"Good?"

"Yes, very good," he said licking the drops still clinging to the corners of his mouth.

"More?"

"No it is yours."

"You have it," she insisted. "I've had chocolate lots of times. Go on drink it."

April watched him down the sweet, steaming cupful. She felt warm and wonderful, happy to give him such a simple pleasure. Then she found herself wondering if she would ever taste chocolate again. Would life ever be normal again?

After a supper of toasted bread and a soup of dried meat and herbs, they arranged their camp for the night. April curled up in the bed Rogarth made for her. It was almost comfortable. She shut her eyes then opened them again. Rogarth wrapped up in his cloak and lay down at her feet. Above them the light of fading day stretched between two towering pines. Far out over the valley a hawk circled. She shifted her weight on her pine-bough nest and tried to match her breathing to Rogarth's. Time dragged on. Her body ached for sleep but her mind still raced with recent events. The sky darkened and the campfire cracked with a friendly glow.

"Rogarth," she whispered.

He stirred but did not answer. April watched him in the firelight. His eyes moved beneath his lids. His beard ruffled with each breath. She felt so safe with him near. He had fought for her very life. He had been wounded for her. And he had been healed. April relived the sensation, the outpouring of strength she had felt when she touched his injured wrist. The rightness, the goodness of what she had been able to do stirred her heart. She reached to touch his hand. He returned the touch.

"You awake?" she asked.

No answer.

"Rogarth please hold me." She flung herself across his chest.

He gently pushed her back. "My lady we must keep proprieties."

"I don't care. You saved my life. You are so strong and brave. You are my very best friend," she declared with innocent passion.

"You must lie back," he insisted. "Even in this time and place we must remember who we are."

April threw her arms around him. "I love you Rogarth. I will always love you. Even when I love and marry Will."

Again Rogarth gently pushed her away. "I love you too, My Lady," he assured her. "Now as my young friend and someday I will love you as my queen."

A cold blast of wind rattled their makeshift shelter.

"Hold me please, Rogarth," April begged. "I'm so cold and scared."

Rogarth wrapped his cloak about her shoulders. She cuddled up next to him. Soon her head drooped on his chest. Rogarth kept vigil centering his thoughts on April. He did love the blossoming child in his arms. Even more he loved the strong beautiful woman she would soon become. To her he would dedicate his life and service. Maralinne seemed far away.

"Is it he?" said an ancient voice as Will's eyes strained in the faint light. "Come here Willarinth. No need to fear."

"Are you Jareth's friend?"

"Is it friend he calls me? The word rings sweet though truth clamors with a harsher tone. Friend, yes, Willarinth, I am Jareth's friend and more."

"What's your name?" asked Will squinting to see to whom the voice belonged.

"I have many names and many faces," said the voice." But in this place I am known as the Watcher of the Caves. It is for you and yours that I have been waiting. Come closer."

Will stepped into the pale golden mist that surrounded the voice. Immediately he was swept into a vision of Chaos giving birth. A parade of kings and queens marched from her loins. Each one wore the double crown. Each face was clearer than the last. Will felt a flood of strength and power pouring down upon him. At last the long line stopped. The vision focused on the last regal figure. Will recognized Arinth's worn features. The golden mist swirled and parted. A young man stood on a precipice with a gleaming sword raised in defiance. Beneath him seethed dark and terrible clouds.

Chapter 12

The White Queen stood on the dais before the intricately-carved wooden throne. Her head was poised with youthful dignity. Her hands were gracefully clasped but her knuckles were white beneath her many rings. Her gown was a heavy gold Frevarian brocade embroidered with pearls. The sleeves and bodice were gossamer Allarian silk as blue as her eyes. She smiled. Her features were pale contrasting with her dark luxurious hair she wore braided and caught in a pearl-studded net. She was crowned with a simple gold circlet set with a large diamond cut in a blazing sunburst.

The White King stood beside her in silver mail over dark red silk. He was tall and thin like a willow sapling, but his shoulders were squared and his head held high. The silver crown on his sleek dark curls tipped a little but his steel blue eyes held a steady gaze beneath its diamond cusp of a moon.

Cheering throngs thundered like a drum roll. Janille sighed with relief. Five cards lay on the table in front of her. For two long years the cards had been silent. At first she had laid them out daily, her mind full of questions and worry, but the cards mocked her with their mute painted faces. She tried again at the celestial balances of sun and moon. The response was the same negative silence. At last she gave up, letting the months and seasons turn as they will. She was happy to be home in the Twin Kingdoms, reunited with her first-born, Elanille. She thanked the gods each time she played with her grandchildren, but her heart ached to tell them who she really was. She longed to hear their sweet voices call not Aunt Jane, but grandmother.

Today Kylie was five. She had laid out the cards for a birthday horoscope, but the questions that came to her were not for her grandson but for April and Will. Today the cards finally answered. The first two she turned were the White King and Queen wearing the faces of her children. They were grown and ready to return to claim their heritage. The third card answered her even before she could ask of their safety and happiness. The elements of Sky and Air sent clouds billowing across the clear blue face of the card. She watched the colors deepen then change to sunset rose and emerging stars. Finally the card turned midnight blue, swelling, enveloping the White King and Queen into an infinity of sapphire and starlight.

The fourth card glowed bright. When she turned it face up a brilliant flash almost blinded her. She shielded her eyes as the Star card rose in a jeweled rainbow arch above the thrones. For a brief moment there was but one throne, one crown, one ruler for the Light. Then as quickly as it had ascended the star faded into its painted image on the card.

The last card still lay unturned. This one was for herself, the seeker. She let her eyes roam the small room she had shared with April. She still had so many question, so many hopes and yes so many regrets. Her eyes stopped on Kylie. He was almost finished tying his second boot lace but the loop slipped from his chubby fingers. "Dumb boot," he said kicking his foot. The loosely-tied lace flew open again. "You do it Aunt Jane."

"Kylie can do it for himself," she assured him. "See how well you did the right one." She gave the lop-sided bow a tightening tug. "Try again."

The last card waited. She tried to project her thoughts to the future but no one question could give all the answers she sought. Finally she simply asked, "How will it all end?" and turned the card.

Two cards must have stuck together when she dealt. What did this mean? Was the foretelling true or false? There was no way to know. She looked at the cards. Time and Compassion lay overlapped. The sands of Time sparkled as they fell but when the glass was empty the bright sands flickered once, twice then feebly a third time and the card went black. The god of Compassion looked up at her with features that were familiar yet unnamed. Who was he? His lips moved. She tried to listen. She could not hear the words but she knew in her heart he had said, "I love you."

Kylie stood up. Both laces were tied.

"Come here big boy," said Janille. She gave him a hug then tugged at his little blue velvet jerkin. "You are growing out of this."

"Do I must wear it?"

"Yes, you must wear it. It's your birthday. A big boy must look fine on his birthday."

Janille put her cards back in her work basket. "Go back to your mommy now and try to keep clean until dinner time." She leaned back in her chair ready to enjoy a few moments of peace. Kylie marched across the hall chanting, "Ho, two, three, four," out of rhythm with his steps. He was gone only a short time when, "Hey git outa der! Aunt Jane!" sent her running to Lady Elanille's room.

The two-year-olds, Jasenth and Lizelle were playing on the rug with a box of buttons and ribbons. Trebil, April's mirror bird, was perched on the side of the box trying to play with them. Elanille had carried her knitting to the window for more light to correct a mistake. While her back was turned Jasenth had toddled off the rug and discovered Kylie's prize bag of pebbles.

"Mine! Hey Aunt Jane!" Kylie yelled. "Dem is mine."

"Jayjay give the bag back to Kylie," said Elanille without looking up from her yarns. "That's a good boy."

"Kylie it would be nice to share one stone with your cousin," added Janille.

"No!"

"Kylie share just one stone like Aunt Jane said," his mother agreed. "Not your best, just any stone."

Kylie held back a moment then dug in his bag for his least favorite stone.

"Me too stone," said Lizelle.

"No, Lizzie. Girls don't play with stones," said Kylie clutching his precious bag.

Lizelle stamped her tiny foot.

"Lizzie, bring me the prettiest ribbon from the box and I will tie it in your hair," said Elanille.

Trebil picked up a bright red ribbon. Lizelle grabbed it from his beak and threw it on the floor. "Me too stone," she declared.

"I said no, Lizzie. Stones are boys' toys."

"No Lizzie. No Lizzie," echoed Trebil.

Lizelle kicked the box. Buttons and ribbons scattered over the rug. Her lower lip pouted. Her brow knit in a ferocious scowl. Elanille sighed and returned to her knitting. Janille leaned over her shoulder to try to help her pick up and correct a dropped stitch.

"Hey gimmie! Aunt Jane make her gimmie," Kylie yelled. Kylie's pouch of stones hovered in the air just out of his reach. Lizelle's rosebud mouth was pinched in a gloating smile. She held out her hand. The pouch moved toward her until her fist closed upon it.

"Kylie, Kylie, dumb dumb," she chanted then laughed.

"Lizzie, be quiet," said Elanille still engrossed in her knitting.

Janille stood gaping, eyes wide and mouth open. What had she just witnessed? Had Lizelle really moved Kylie's bag of stones? A wave of fear swept down on her. Kyrdthin must know of this right away. "Trebil," she whispered to the little bird. "Go find Kyrdthin. Tell him what Lizzie can do. Tell him to come. Now."

"Treat?"

"Yes, yes. Now hurry."

Kyrdthin arrived so quickly the blue draperies billowed back from the windows. Jasenth started to cry. Janille picked him up and sat down with him on the bed. Kylie rushed to Kyrdthin insisting that he, "Spell Lizzie bad." The little culprit sat defiantly on the rug with Kylie's bag of stones in her lap. Kyrdthin squatted down beside her. He tried to humor her but she declared she did not want to play special magic games with Uncle Kyrdthin. Elanille sat in shocked silence. Her knitting had dropped to her lap. Tears streamed unchecked down her cheeks. Janille tried to comfort her but could find no words. What powers did Lizelle have at her command? How could they protect her until she could learn to control it and use it for the Light?

Janille and Kyrdthin argued while Elanille passively looked from one to another. Marielle and Gil were summoned. The discussion intensified.

"I say we give her Freebane," said Gil.

Reluctantly Marielle agreed.

"But she's so young," Janille objected. "Freebane has never been given to anyone younger than puberty. It could damage a young mind."

"We don't know that, Janie," said Kyrdthin.

"That's right we don't know."

Marielle put out a hand for Trebil to perch. The little blue bird flitted to her. "We must protect her at all costs. Frebane will prevent Belar from probing or controlling her,"

Elanille burst into tears. Gil picked up Lizelle and placed the child in her arms to comfort her.

"Mommy. Mommy don't cry," Lizelle pleaded. The room swirled with colors-red, pink, and yellow. Flowers floated in on a fragrant breeze to fall at Elanille's feet. "Me pick 'em for you," said Lizelle with angelic sweetness.

"Thank you darling," Elanille sobbed.

"Hey where dey all come from," said Kylie sweeping a path through the flowers to his mother's knee.

Janille looked out the window. The garden was bare!

All three of the children were tucked in for a nap. With Kyrdthin's dream spell they would remember nothing of the afternoon's events when they awoke. Janille climbed the winding stairs to the tower study. The worn steps creaked under her weight. She was not in a hurry. Kyrdthin waited in the musty, tome-filled room at the top of the stairs ready to show her how to process Frebane for Lizelle. They had finally agreed to give her diluted daily doses of the drug. Kyrdthin would come each morning to play 'magic games' with her. Afterwards he would put her under a dream spell so she would not remember her lessons until she was old enough to use her gift wisely.

It all sounded so simple. Janille slowed her steps. The problem was that Lizelle was only two years old. How long would she need to take the drug? No one knew the long-term effects. The smell of dust and soot and a heady mixture of herbs in stale air greeted her at the top of the stairs.

"There's my quick thinking good girl," Kyrdthin said smiling at her from the door of his study. "I'm proud of the way you handled things today." He gave her a quick kiss on the cheek and drew her into the room. "Why the glum face? Making Freebane isn't difficult and giving it to Lizzie won't be hard either. She shouldn't balk if we mix it with enough honey."

"I feel that I am either selling my granddaughter if I give it to her or selling the kingdoms if I don't."

No amount of Kyrdthin's cajoling or attempts at humor could lift her mood as she studied the combinations of herbs and spells needed to make the drug to hold back Lizelle's magic until the Light had need of it.

It was still early. The upper halls of the castle were quiet. The door to Maralinne's room opened. Jareth paused in the doorway to readjust the buckle on his quiver strap.

"Jareth, come back here," Maralinne called from the bed. "Don't you dare leave without kissing me goodbye."

Without looking back into the room, Jareth reached for the longbow that was propped against the doorframe.

"Jareth!" Maralinne ran across the room with unslippered feet.

"Go back to bed Maralinne," he said disengaging her shameless embrace. "I'll be back before noon."

"Why must you go at all? Can't someone else play spy for once?"

Jareth carried her back to the bed. He tucked her in with kisses but would not let her dissuade him from leaving.

Armon Beck's tavern was already bustling when Jareth arrived. The smells of baking bread and frying ham were welcoming.

"Your usual, Arinth's Eyes and Ears?" the innkeeper called from behind the bar.

"The usual," said Jareth. "Dell here yet?"

"Just stepped out back to the alley. Said for you to wait if you want to hear a tale worth telling." The innkeeper plunked a plate of fried eggs onto the table in front of Jareth. "I'll bring your bread as soon as it's sliced. Linnie!" he called back into the kitchen. "Jareth wants his bread."

Dell appeared at the kitchen door. His harp was slung over his left shoulder. With him was a small boy of about seven or eight. "Set up another breakfast, Armon," said Dell leading the boy to Jareth's table. "And be sure there's a large pot of blackberry preserves," he added as he pulled up a chair for himself and the boy.

"Will the laddie be wanting a mug of milk?" asked the innkeeper.

The boy nodded. His eyes darted about the room, curiosity juggling with fear.

"Jareth, this is Lonny, Farmer Jular's son," said Dell. "He's been a good lad to tell his elders when he's heard and seen things that look amiss."

The boy looked from Dell to Jareth and back again.

"Lonny, tell Jareth just what you told me."

"The Black Dogs came to our place," said the boy.

"Jular's place is last on the Frevarian road before High Bridge," Dell put in.

"Momma asked them to supper 'cause she was scared. She dint wanna cross them or nothin'. Me and my sister we dint want no Black Dogs eatin' our supper so we run to git Pa. He and the hands was still out in the hay field."

"Did they harm your family?" asked Jareth.

"No. They dint even want our supper and it was chicken and potato pie too. They just told Pa they was takin' over the tool shed."

Armon Beck arrived with a large stack of buttered griddle cakes, two fried eggs, a half dozen slices of bacon and a pot of blackberry preserves. The boy stopped talking to stare at the man-sized breakfast set in front of him.

"This all for me?" he said already reaching for the pot of preserves. He dug a finger into the dark jelly, scooped up a whole berry and popped it into his mouth.

"Use the spoon, Lonny. This is a public place," said Dell holding up the utensil. "Try to tell Jareth the rest of your tale between bites."

Lonny Jularson ate his breakfast and washed it all down with two mugs of milk as he told about the canvas-covered wagon and its mysterious load that arrived last night at his father's farm. There was a big, thick metal pipe mounted on wheels and boxes of iron balls and a barrel of smelly powder. The Dark Delven warriors stashed it all in the tool shed and posted two guards by the door. Then the wagon drove away back down the road toward High Bridge. When they had gone Lonny slipped away and headed straight toward Frevaria to tell the king.

"I met him on the road this morning," said Dell. He patted the boy on the shoulder. "Now tell Jareth one more thing. Tell him about their leader."

"The one who just sat in the wagon?"

"Yes, tell Jareth what he looked like."

The boy picked at the few remaining crumbs on his plate. "I couldn't see him, real good. He had this black cloak over him, but his hair was dark and real long and he had these...these glass...What'd you call 'em, Dell?"

"Spectacles."

"Spectercals on his eyes and he kept pushin' 'em up an' pushin' 'em up."

Dell and Jareth exchanged looks.

"You are a brave and smart thinking lad, Lonny," said Jareth. "You have brought us valuable information that may not only save your family but all of the Twin Kingdoms."

"I thought I'd put him up with Mabry until a Frevarian wagon can take him home," said Dell.

Jareth took the boy by the shoulders. "You must promise to tell no one else what you saw. We will tell King Frebar and King Arinth. This is a military secret. Understand?"

Lonny nodded and Jareth drew a star sign on his heart. "We better have Kyrdthin pay him a visit just as a precaution. What do you think Dell?"

"The wizard!" Lonny exclaimed.

"Don't worry. He's on our side in this," Dell assured him. "Kyrdthin can help keep you safe and make it easier for you to keep our military secret."

"Trusted gamewarden woos princess," Elanille teased. "Your life is like a bard's tale, Maralinne. I don't think you have anything to complain about."

"Jareth is unhappy. I know he is," said Maralinne.

"Then be done with all this secrecy. You two have played at this game for almost two years."

"Father would never know if you two just rode away into the sunset," added Analinne.

"Father loves and trusts Jareth. I will not be the one to shatter that trust," said Maralinne.

"I think His Majesty would not be entirely displeased," said Elanille. "After all he and the Queen..."

"Mother Marielle sides with Jareth. Keep Maralinne locked up in the castle so she doesn't have any fun like getting kidnapped or something. Don't tell father. Don't tell anybody. A royal wedding would call attention to you, make you more vulnerable. And whatever you do don't get pregnant," Maralinne fumed.

The young women were gathered in Lady Analinne's room. Today they had decided to dismiss their maids and help each other dress and arrange their hair just like the had done as girls. A breakfast of muffins and creamed cheese was spread out but untouched on the table. A pot of raspberry leaf tea, once steaming hot was now cold.

The trio of women tried to recapture the joys of their girlhood together, but the bonds of their sisterhood were now forged with grief as well as joy. Analinne's large velvet draped bed had not been slept in. She spent most nights in the nursery with Jasenth. Tobar was rarely home. Elanille's bed had been empty for two years. She had not easily accepted her widowhood. Her devotion to her children had become almost an obsession. And Maralinne, her stolen moments of passion with her soul mate Jareth were tormenting both their spirits.

"We all know father has his lucid moments," said Analinne brushing through the tangles in her twin sister's hair. "Why don't you just tell him and ask his blessing?"

Elanille handed her a pair of Maralinne's barrettes.

"I don't think Jareth wants to marry me," said Maralinne. She grabbed the barrettes before her sister could clip them in and threw them on the table. "I don't want to pin my hair up like a matron."

"How did you think it would be, sister? Would you rather cook and clean for him in that cottage of his out in the woods?"

"That wouldn't be safe," Maralinne snapped with sarcasm. "I hate safe. I'd rather wear a peasant's dust scarf any day than be safe here and have Jareth so unhappy."

"None of us are really safe," said Elanille. "I married a soldier and now there is no one to love me and protect our children."

"No, none of us is safe," Analinne agreed. "Perhaps Jasenth and I least of all. I was so smug to marry a prince and bear his child. But the quiet, gentle man who courted and won me has...has changed so...I hardly know him when he comes to me." Her voice broke. Analinne looked away. "The Light is gone from him," she sobbed. "There are times I wish he were truly dead like your lord Keilen, not lost to the Dark."

Elanille embraced her. Together they wept for lost hopes and dreams. Maralinne tied her hair back with a plain ribbon. She made a face at herself in the mirror then pulled the ribbon out.

"Lizzie!" Elanille exclaimed suddenly. Analinne's jewelry box lay open. Necklaces, tiaras and rings were scattered over the table. Elanille had almost forgotten that her daughter had toddled into the room with them.

"Lizzie don't touch Lady Analinne's things."

The air shimmered between them slightly. Analinne turned around but Elanille looked away, ashamed that her child would misbehave. But when Analinne said nothing Elanille looked back. She gasped in disbelief. All of the jewelry was replaced and the box lid was closed as if it had never been touched. Lizelle stood with her arms folded and a smug smile on her baby face.

"Ann I should really go now. Lizzie is getting restless and I left Kylie alone. Who knows what he may have gotten into if Janille hasn't come yet."

"Yes I should check on Jayjay too," said Analinne. "I'm sure he could not have slept this long."

With that they parted, each to their own separate lives. When Elanille and Lizelle returned to their rooms Lizelle announced. "We fool 'em good dint we mommy?'

"What do you mean honey?"

"We pull a curtain dint we? You help Mommy. It's fun. We fool lotsa people OK?" Lizelle laughed a shrill not at all baby-like laugh.

"You made an illusion?" Elanille said still in shock. "How Lizzie?"

"Just do it."

"Let's go find Uncle Kyrdthin," said Elanille starting to panic. "I want to show him our new game."

"No! No!" Lizelle wailed.

"Yes we will," said her mother turning her around and dragging her by the hand back down the hall. "Uncle Kyrdthin must know all our games. He likes magic games."

Elanille picked up the now screaming, kicking toddler and hurried up the stair to Kyrdthin's tower study. She hesitated only a moment at the door then knocked boldly.

"Well ladies, what occasion brings you here," Kyrdthin's voice boomed in greeting as the door swung back.

Elanille peered beyond him into the cluttered room. He was not alone. Gil sat at the great burl wood table. A steaming tea cup was poised in his hand.

"I...I..." she stuttered, not knowing where to begin.

"Come in. Come in. Gil and I were just planning the future of the world, nothing important." He laughed then turned to Lizelle and wrinkled up his face in mock scowl. "Is the little girl up to new tricks? Are you Lizzie Lou?"

"We have a new game, don't we Lizzie," said Elanile.

"A game is it? Or is it a trick?" said Kyrdthin, a twinkle in his eye belying the ferocity of his face.

"Mommy says must show you," said the child.

"Alright then show me," he said leaning back and folding his arms. "I'm ready."

Lizelle giggled. "Ok lookee. Bye bye, Gil sir, bye bye." The air shimmered with tiny sliver stars. When it cleared Gil's chair was empty. Only his tea cup remained hovering over the table."

"Dumb, dumb me." Lizelle laughed. "Poof da cup too." The cup vanished in a dazzle of silver.

"Nicely done Lizzie," said Kyrdthin. "Now let's pull back your pretty curtain." He snapped his fingers and Gil reappeared.

Lizelle's face contorted with rage. "No! No!" she screamed.

Burning! Pain! Elanille's hands flew to her temples. Blood thundered inside her skull. She choked and screamed. Her chest heaved and she collapsed.

"Mommy!" Lizelle cried.

Kyrdthin traced a quick star sign in the air. Silver bolts shot out and coiled about the child. "Settle down, Lizzie. You are a very bad girl. Stay put while I help your mother."

Gil was already massaging Elanille's forehead with healing fingers. Her breath came fast and shallow. Her skin was cold and wet.

"Mommy! Poor Mommy!" Lizelle screamed fighting her restraints.

"What happened?" Elanille asked weakly.

"She drained you," said Kyrdthin. "Here drink this." He handed her a cup of tea. "And here is a drink for you too, missy misrule." He poured another cup of tea, dropped in two spoonfuls of sugar. He took down a jar from a high shelf, added a pinch of crystals then stirred. Lizelle pouted and pinched her lips.

"Go ahead, honey. Do what Uncle Kyrdthin says," Elanille told her.

Lizelle drank the tea and promptly fell asleep. Kyrdthin picked her up and laid her on her mother's lap. With the child out of the way for the moment the conversation took a serious tone.

"You have birthed a monster," Kyrdthin declared. "She has not only mastered simple illusion with no instruction, a spectacular feat in itself, she has discovered a most dangerous source of power. It's not from within..."

"Tell us exactly what you felt," said Gil.

"It was as if my head was on fire...like I was being sucked dry of...of..."

"Life itself." Kyrdthin concluded for her. "She would have killed you if Gil and I had not been here."

"What can we do?" Elanille sobbed.

"She is too young to learn ethics," said Gil. "We must concentrate on keeping her and everyone else safe until we can teach her to control this gift."

"From now on Freebane won't be enough," said Kyrdthin. "We'll have to use Firerill."

"Firerill could kill a child this young," argued Gil.

"This is no child, Gil," said Kyrdthin.

"She's only two years old, a baby," Elanille pleaded.

"She's a potential murderess," Kyrdthin insisted.

Elanille wept. Gil laid a hand on her shoulder tracing a calming with gentle fingers.

"Everyone's life is in danger until we get her under control," said Kyrdthin. His fist pounded the table. "It's got to be Firerill."

Gil patted Elanille's shoulder. "Take her home for now. Keep her safe. We will get all this sorted out then send for you."

Elanille stood up, a little giddy from her ordeal. She hugged her sleeping child to her breast. "How long will she sleep?"

"Until morning I hope," said Kyrdthin. "That will give us time to plan."

"Will she be alright?"

Gil smiled at her "You have a powerful jewel for the Light but it is still uncut. What we must do is find the right chisel to free it."

Elanille left. When Kyrdthin closed the door behind her he turned to Gil. "Well it looks like our little gentleman's tete a tete has been interrupted with little hope of continuing. Let's summon Marielle and Janie and make it a foursome."

"How can you be so casual, Kyrdthin?"

"To keep from being scared if you must know," said Kyrdthin taking up his pipe and reaching for his tobacco pouch.

"Then we all should be casual," said Gil with a forced laugh.

"Casual it is, Gil. The ladies then?"

They made tea for four and together they discussed the future of the world, in seriousness this time. Where was Tobar? They were all convinced that he was controlled by the Dark and that he should be watched. But they disagreed what to do with Lizelle. Gil and Marielle wanted her totally controlled and kept safe in Allarion. Kyrdthin argued that such a great power could be an invaluable ally for the Light if they could teach Lizelle in time to use it. Janille simply pleaded as a loving grandmother not to hurt the child. What were they to do? None of them knew. Gil suggested they reread the prophecy to try to make sense of recent events. Kyrdthin took down the great leather tome and handed it to Gil.

"When the Sun and Moon shine double in the sky," Gil began. "We have always believed that meant twinning in the royal houses."

"Well we have Frebar and Tobar in Frevaria," said Janille.

"And Analinne and Maralinne here," added Marielle.

"The trouble is they aren't paired properly," said Gil

Gil looked from Janille to Marielle and then to Kyrdthin. "We thought we had twins lined up in both houses a generation back with Frebar and Tobar born in Frevaria and Arinth and his twin born in Arindon the same night. But Arinth's twin turned out to be a girl, and the elder at that..."

"And she disappeared so what do we have left, Cellina and Liella are Frevarian twins too but that didn't turn out like some expected either," said Janille. She smiled at Kyrdthin, reaching for his hand. "Arinth loved Veralinne. You can't fault him for following his heart."

Kyrdthin squeezed her hand then laid it back in her lap. "In this game, love only complicates things."

"And jealously," said Marielle. "Cellina hates me. She lost Arinth twice. Losing him to her younger sister she could finally accept, but she will never forgive me for taking her second chance when Veralinne died." Her voice was sharp and bitter. She reached for Gil's reassuring hand. He folded her delicate fingers in his and smiled.

"Now we have Ann and Mari," he said. "Twins and more twins in both houses. What a mess!"

Kyrdthin took the leather-bound prophecy from Gil and laid it on table. "What's all this have to do with Lizzie? Whatever she is or is becoming is more a topic of concern than pairing up sets of royal twins."

"Yes, she is our wild card in this game," said Gil. "Let's put on another pot of tea and try to sort things out, beginning with Lizzie this time.

Janille picked up the teapot but Kyrdthin took it from her. "Sit down, Janie. This room is my unforgivable clutter. Your housekeeping skills would be wasted here." He dumped the remains of the teapot out the window, wiped the inside with a cloth of questionable cleanliness and refilled the kettle from the cistern spigot. When the kettle was hung on the fire hook and the fire poked and refueled, he climbed onto a wooden stool to survey the top shelf of his bookcase. He moved books and jars and bags of herbs aside. Dust rose and swirled in disturbed eddies then filtered to the floor. Janille raised her eyebrows but said nothing.

What are you looking for, little brother?" said Marielle sharing Janille's disgust with amusement. "There is a canister of tea on the mantel."

"I know but this occasion calls for something special." He answered shoving a whole row of unlabled jars aside and reaching behind them. "Got it," he announced producing a small cardboard box. "Real green tea from China or was it Ceylon?" He looked at the glyphs on the box. "China," he said.

The kettle boiled. Kyrdthin tossed a handful of tea bags in the teapot and when it had steeped he said, "Would you do the honors sister?"

Marielle poured.

"It's been a long time," said Janille sipping the tea with remembered pleasure,

They filled the gap in the conversation with tea. They all were baffled by recent events and unsure of how things fit into the overall scheme of things. At last Marielle said. "Arinth called Lizzie 'the light at the end of the world' on her naming day, remember?"

"Arinth babbled a lot that day," said Kyrdthin,

"Was it a prophecy?" said Gil. "Perhaps we should continue exploring the verses."

"Not until we decide what to do with Lizzie,"

"We already agreed on Firerill," said Gil. "What more do we need?"

Kyrdthin rummaged through the collection of crocks and canisters on his desk. "I have enough dried here I think to last to the end of the summer, and then we can gather a whole year's supply easily in an afternoon. The slopes are full of fireweed then."

"Supply isn't the only problem Kyrdthin," said Marielle. "It's the side effects we are all worried about."

"She can only use fire as a power source. That will keep her from murdering people. What other effects…?"

"You know it affects growth as well as…"

She will grow, just slower. That will give us all the more time to train her."

"You are sure it won't hurt her?" begged Janille.

"We don't know everything, Janie. What we do know is that Firerill delays puberty, perhaps a good thing in Lizzie's case. We don't want to endanger Jasenth until we know what she is."

"You are talking about a two-year-old, not a wanton woman," Janille argued.

"Here, let's read it again," Kyrdthin handed the book of prophecy back to Gil. "I think this issue of Lizzie is decided and we have more than one thing to discuss today."

Gil read the next verse. "Then shall the cask be opened."

"The kids opened the box," said Janille.

"Yeah the little rascals," said Kyrdthin.

"And now both the children and the crowns are safe in Allarion," said Marielle. "Go on Gil."

"Then shall the Three be Five."

"Three kingdoms, Frevaria, Arindon and Allarion united to overcome Belarion and establish a fifth kingdom of men over all," said Marielle,

"Or so we have always believed," said Kyrdthin. "Remember there are other worlds, not to mention other places in this world.

Face it we don't know if the Three means kingdoms or chamber pots."

"Keep reading Gil," said Marielle giving Kyrdthin an exasperated look. She picked up the pot and poured another round of tea.

"Twice two shall weep," read Gil.

"The girls are all in tears, Ann, Ellanille and even Mari. Until this is over we could all be soaking kerchiefs," said Kyrdthin. He pushed aside his teacup then lit the candle in the center of the table.

Janille gave him a questioning look. "Why a candle in bright daylight?"

"Look at this," he said picking up a silver teaspoon. He laid the spoon between the candle and the edge of the table. "Pick up the spoon, Janie."

She picked up the spoon.

"Hold it between your eyes and the candle. What do you see?"

She obeyed then waited for his explanation.

"The silver spoon blocks out the golden candle or the moon blocks out the sun. They shine double in the sky. In other words an eclipse.

"Is that what it means?"

"It could," agreed Gil, "But then…"

"An eclipse darkens the earth," said Marielle. "Certainly that cannot herald the reign of Light." She stacked the empty cups and saucers then looked around the room for a place to set them. Seeing nowhere in the small cluttered room she set them on the table again and sank back into her chair. Kyrdthin's face quivered with a smile.

"Magic will die, when the Darkness is unchained," Gil continued to read.

"We all know that one," said Marielle. "Humankind will have no more need of us once this is done."

"No it only says magic will die," Gil assured her. "We will have no power but we will still have each other."

"Let's not forget dear brother Belar chained in the dark for his misbehavior. He has been rattling those chains quite loudly of late," said Kyrdthin.

The room darkened suddenly and the candle blew out. Janille rushed to the small tower window. "It's only a cloud across the sun," she said. "But it does look as if a storm is coming."

"Let's finish this then," said Gil and read the last verse. "When the Star arches alive. That's a puzzler."

"Maybe not," said Kyrdthin.

They all looked at him. How much did he know? How much was only guesses?

"When all this is done, where are we going to crown our High King and Queen?"

"In Arindon great hall I suppose," said Gil.

"Think of the royal thrones there side by side." Kyrdthin waited for the image of the two large chairs to come to mind. The high back of each was carved with half a rainbow, Frevaria's rose from the right to reach the sun and Arindon's to the left to reach the moon. Put side by side they would fit together, the sun cradled in the cusp of the moon. "All we need," Kyrdthin continued. "Is a star rising above the eclipse to make the sign of All Light."

"The light at the end of the world?" said Marielle.

"Lizzie!" exclaimed Janille.

"We don't know," said Kyrdthin. "But it does make some sense."

"We must think on these things," said Gil. "And we must also discuss the recent battle reports or there won't be a kingdom left for the children to rule."

Kyrdthin and Gil discussed the Delven raids into both kingdoms and the disturbing news Dell and Jareth had received from the Frevarian farmer's boy. Tobar was helping Belar again. This time he was transporting arms from another world, or were Belar's Delven manufacturing them? Either scenario spelled disaster.

"It's time we join the three kingdoms together," said Gil. "Allarion, Arindon and Frevaria must be one if we hope to stop Belar and his Delven Dogs."

"Frevaria would never..."said Janille.

"Delven are hacking up Frebar's borders too and he has no idea that his own brother is helping them. When Frebar finds out he will need and want our help as much as we need and want his."

"He would never treaty with Allarion. I know him," insisted Janille.

"Then let's start with Arindon," said Kyrdthin. "We can send Rogarth…"

"A Master of War!" exclaimed Janille.

"Who then, an Allarian?" Kyrdthin cut in with undisguised sarcasm.

They all fell silent. Outside the clouds thickened. A rain dove mourned the coming storm. A few drops pattered on the windowpane in the distance thunder rumbled and rolled.

"I know!" Janille said suddenly. "Let's send Kylie to visit grandpa. Rogarth can escort him."

"Janie you are a genius!" said Kyrdthin.

"You mean you didn't know it until now."

Chapter 13

They all expected Frebar to arrive in style but he surprised them. He entered Arindon on a large brown horse with plain trappings. Kylie was perched in front of him, bouncing and chattering. His small round face was bright with smiles. Frebar wore hunting gear, not robes of state. He had added only two of his men to the entourage Arinth sent to accompany them. Was this a show of confidence or an insult? The speed with which he had responded suggested neither. He had been hunting when the message arrived and decided to come immediately. He was obviously delighted to see the child. He held him tight with one hand and pointed out the sights with the other. Kylie held the horse's reins and yelled, "Giddy up horsie." But the well-trained mount responded only to the pressure of a knee and occasional word of his master.

Janille watched the procession from a high window. They were almost to the gate. She suppressed a twinge of feelings for what might have been. This beaming boy was their grandchild, but she was no longer Frebar's wife and queen. This older man with silver-streaked hair was almost a stranger. She would of course avoid any encounter today lest Frebar somehow recognize her. Tears of bitterness and regret welled in her eyes but before they could spill Kyrdthin laid a hand on her shoulder.

"The little tyke has done what armies and diplomats have failed to do for generations."

"Do you question the topaz amulet now?" asked Janille.

"Frebar no. Belar always."

"I told you he only wanted to give the boy a gift."

"And what a useful situation for Belar to make fools of us all. I am so glad the original jewel is safe in Allarion," said Kyrdthin drawing her away from the window. "Shall we find a spot in the upper galleries before anyone enters the hall"

Frebar's company entered the castle. With due courtesy but no formality he was ushered into Arinth's audience chamber. His boots clomped down the carpet with heavy, muffled steps. Arinth waited in his chair. Gil stood by his right hand and Rogarth was on his left. Arinth wore a simple red, silk dressing gown. The thick wool lap robe Gil had draped across his knobby knees was embroidered with large white moons and stars. His white shock of hair was disheveled as if he had just been awakened from a nap. And he wore no crown.

"Well Frebar, you can hobble in on your own power so I suppose I must still consider you a threat to my eastern borders."

"Greetings to you too Arinth. Your tongue is still dagger sharp even if your remarks are only hurled from a chair," Frebar replied.

"Well sit down yourself," said Arinth clapping his hands with glee. "Or better yet, you could kneel."

"You old barking dog..."

"Your majesties," Gil quietly interrupted. "May I suggest we get down to business before the barbs in these jests prick too deep."

"Oh why must we treaty?" Arinth clapped his hands again. "This is much more amusing. Perhaps we should war instead." He threw back his head and laughed, then burst into a spasm of coughing. "Give me some wine," he said feebly. "This foolish rival is hard to stomach." He gulped the drink Gil handed him but continued to cough again and again.

"Perhaps you should rest a moment, sire," said Gil lovingly wiping Arinth's mouth with a napkin.

Arinth could not answer nor did he object when Rogarth picked him up like a child and carried him away.

Gil waited in the audience chamber with Frebar, seeing that the visiting king was seated comfortably and offered refreshment. When Rogarth returned alone Gil suggested that they proceed without Arinth.

"Am I expected to treat with Allarian spies and common soldiers?" Frebar barked with indignance.

"You treat not with one man or another but with life itself," said Gil with quiet restraint.

Frebar stopped a moment. At first he had been baffled by the urgency of Arinth's summons and now seeing the obvious decline in his fellow king he prickled with alarm. His eyes darted around the room. The red velvet draperies, the dark wood timbering and the meticulously polished floors spoke of great attention to tradition and form. "Tell me," he said finally. "What seriousness have you brought me here to discuss?"

"The Children of Light," said Gil. His tone was slow and even. "Your second-born daughter and Arinth's son by Marielle. They live."

"I have only one daughter and Arinth has already stolen her away from me, first to foster and then to shame me by bedding her to a common soldier."

Gil ignored the slurs and continued with the subject at hand. "No, if I may humbly correct you sire, Queen Janille bore you two daughters."

Frebar sprang to his feet. "No Allarian brat is a child of mine!"

"Your daughter Avrille and Arinth's son Willarinth are both the children of man and blessed by the gods of Light. It is they and only they who can stay the Dark that is gnawing at our borders," said Gil with uncharacteristic firmness. "We must unite with these children at our head, for the Light to win the world in this age."

Frebar thought a long time. He twisted the signet on his finger as he stared unseeing toward the doorway where Arinth had vanished. "Where are these children if they live?" he said, disbelief and distrust obvious in his voice.

"Safe in Allarion for now."

"So that's where Kyrdthin hid the witch and her brat all these years. I figured as much."

"Janille is also safe and is now our powerful ally."

Frebar threw his shoulders back with indignation. "It was that gray-bearded trickster she loved, not me her king. How do I know the brat is mine?"

"The princess Avrille is yours if you claim her," said Gil. He waited until Frebar's face relaxed then went on. "The future depends on all of us standing together against the Dark. Alone we fall."

"But these kids...?"

"Young Willarinth is being trained in Allarion but he will need an army to lead. He will need combined forces, your cavalry and Arinth's bowmen. Join us for your daughter's sake."

"Where is Arinth? I'll treat with none but a true king, even if he is only an addled fool."

"Will you treat with a queen since Arinth is obviously indisposed?"

"Another Allarian...?"

"But a queen of two worlds none the less."

"Veralinne, rest her soul, is the one true queen of Arindon!" Frebar shouted.

"Janille is the one true queen of Frevaria," Gil countered.

Frebar's face contorted first in rage and then in desperation. Again Gil waited, resisting temptation to glance upward to the gallery where he knew Kyrdthin and Janille were hidden. Sounds of Arinth's coughing in the next room punctuated the tense quiet. At last Frebar sat back down in his chair. "So be it," he said, his voice just above a whisper.

Gil produced the papers he had drawn up. When Frebar had read them they placed their marks together, one silver and one gold. The plans were laid and witnessed to march united against the Dark. Frebar returned home with double escort to proclaim the Twin Kingdoms were one in the Light.

Marielle stayed by Arinth's bedside. Gil soon joined her vigil. When the time came they sounded no alarms. Marille insisted that Arinth's passage should be quiet. She sat with her dying husband and king, holding his hand and wiping his brow with cool cloths. Rogarth had gone to find Kyrdthin. The passage could not be completed without him. Arinth tried to speak but Gil begged him save his strength. Arinth called for "my little rubies" but when Analinne and Maralinne arrived he did not know them. Unsure of whether to go or stay, they looked to Gil. He nodded toward the door. "We will tell you when it is done," he said. "No need to interrupt your lives. There is nothing you can do here."

When the girls left, Marielle and Gil sat down to wait. Marielle's eyes looked around the room filled with regrets. The high canopied bed with its red velvet draperies, the place that kings and queens had bred and birthed and died since Arindon began had never been her place of rest. For fifteen long years she slept in her own blue-tinted room. She had given birth to Will there, and mourned the loss of Allarion and all the hopes and dreams she and Gil and Arinth had shared. She looked down at Arinth. He slept. His breaths came in shallow irregular gasps. Marielle turned away, unable to reconcile the present scene with the memories and the guilt that came flooding back. Arinth had come to them in Allarion, mad with grief. Queen Veralinne's death and the death of their infant son had taken his will to live. Young Jareth found him wandering in the icy crags starved and almost frozen to death. He brought him to Allarion. There she and Gil nursed his body back to health. That was easy. The more difficult task was healing his spirit. That took all the resources of fair Allarion. But at last the flowers and the birdsong, the warm, healing waters and the light, blue breezes woke Arinth's humanity once more. He was able to love again and his heart had opened to her.

"There are so many memories," said Gil. "Some are beautiful and good. Let's dwell on those."

"He loved me." Marielle's voice cracked with the weight of guilt.

"He loved both of us. He loved Allarion. But most of all he loved Arindon."

"He loved me. He called me his Fairy Queen. He didn't know I was a childless tyrant who plotted with her consort to use him to conceive a child. To us Arinth was but a pawn in this cursed celestial game we are playing. But he loved me."

"He loved all of us. He knew and agreed with what we wanted to do. And because of Arinth now we have Will as our 'Hope of All Light'."

"But look at him!" wept Marielle. There was no denying Arinth was old beyond his years as time runs in the Twin Kingdoms. Yet he was only in the thirtieth year of his reign. He should still be strong and virile like his rival King in Frevaria. Instead he was white-haired and frail in mind and body. "I wanted him to remember." Her tears spilled uncontrolled. "I wanted him to remember that one afternoon he thought I loved him…the bower by the pool when Will was conceived. Arinth gave us the son we wanted. I thought the spell wouldn't…I thought I had the power to…Just look at him Gil. I did this. I knew. Just one simple verse to say, but I wouldn't say it and I ruined a great man." Marielle buried her head in her hands. "'All that was before be gone, lost in blue Allarion….' I wouldn't say it because I wanted him to remember that one time…"

"He had a long life of beauty and love with us in Allarion. That his ending seems untimely here does not mean his life was without purpose. We have our Will. There is no time or place for guilt today, Marielle. We…you do love Arinth and your years of care were not unfelt by him."

The room was almost dark. Gil lit the ornate silver sconces on the walls and the little table lamps with crystal globes and pendants, but the room still seemed somber. Death was near. No light could hold it back. Gil and Marielle sat with Arinth counting breaths until Kyrdthin came.

"Dare we risk a gate here?" Kyrdthin asked with concern.

"We can't move him," said Gil.

"Then hold him and guard him with your lives. Belar knows what's going on I'm sure."

Kyrdthin traced the star sign in the air between the door and the foot of the bed. Gil and Marielle held hands across Arinth's faintly rising chest then looked to Kyrdthin. The star sign he had drawn drifted toward them. In its center swirled an empty void.

"Ward it off!" Gil cried. "Belar knows the gate is open. We can't let him through."

Marielle sprang forward thrusting her small body between the darkening sign and Arinth's feet. Gil slid behind her making a double barrier between the gaping gate and the body Belar was reaching to possess. The gate swirled first black then writhed in bloody red. Marielle backed up against Gil. Together they held strong. Kyrdthin walked circling the gate, concentrating all his will until the red tongues slithered back into the void and the circle of stars was again silver. The space inside the sign quivered and solidified. In its center stood Will.

He stepped confidently out of the star sign into the room. He held his head high. A smile played on his lips. His chin was fuzzed with the first touch of a man's beard. His hair hung in loose, dark curls. Only the deep blue of his eyes told them for certain that this was the frail, frightened boy they sent away to grow up in Allarion. Will walked to Arinth's bedside. "Father," he said with a clear low voice. "Do you know me?"

Arinth's eyes fluttered open and tried to focus. They moved questioning up and down the young man before him. "Whose whelp is this Gil?" he asked in a crackling whisper.

"Your own son Willarinth, sire. Yours with Queen Marielle. Kyrdthin has kept him safe these fifteen years."

Arinth's eyes brightened. "Kyrdthin hid my boy? He's not dead?"

"Our enemies would never have let Prince Willarinth live, sire. It had to be done this way. The secret had to be kept even from you."

"My boy's alive....after all these years," said Arinth, his spirits rallying a bit. "Kyrdthin did it...don't know whether to bless or curse the old gray bastard." He tried to clear his throat. The effort left him speechless, gasping for breath but he shook off Gil's calming touch. "Come closer Willarinth. Let me look at you," he was finally able to say.

Will leaned over the bed. "I have come for your blessing, father."

"Ready to steal my kingdom are you?" Arinth tried to laugh but coughed instead. "Now that my eyes have seen the future they can close in peace." He lifted a shaking hand. Gil took the hand and motioned for Will to kneel. Arinth's dry bony finger traced the star sign on Will's forehead. It burned deep into his brain. Will felt himself begin to drift. The room blurred momentarily and when it cleared again his father looked young and strong. His hair and beard were dark again and the moon-silver circlet on his brow shone brilliant in the noonday sun. Will followed his father's gaze to a beautiful woman with auburn hair holding the hands of two little girls. "Come my little rubies. Come to papa," Will heard him say then he drifted again. A sword gleamed. It was bloody. Will could smell the sweat. He could feel the rushing adrenaline. He could hear the cheers, "Arinth, Arinth." Will felt himself merge with the man who was his father. Blackness suddenly descended. Immeasurable, inconsolable grief weighed him down. Queen Veralinne was dead. He drifted in the darkness. The pain was unbearable. Then healing hands, voices like music, sparkling crystals and rainbows of color woke him. Will drank in the peace and contentment. He knew he was reliving his father's sojourn in Allarion.

On and on Arinth's memories floated through Will's consciousness until the whole wealth of his father's life had been shared. Will swelled strong with his new knowledge, but was also wizened with the sadness and loneliness of his new responsibilities.

"Kiss me Willarinth," Arinth whispered.

Will touched the withered cheek and when he straightened up again Arinth's eyes had paled. His chest was still.

The door burst open. Rogarth rushed to Arinth's bedside. When he saw the quiet there he quickly turned his head that they should not see a soldier weep. Marielle reached out a hand to comfort him but he brushed her aside. Kyrdthin set five silver star signs glowing about Arinth's bed. "Will, stand up and put your hand on his heart. Look at him. Think of the peace you have given him. Don't think of anything else." Rogarth bolted for the door. Gill called after him but grief-stricken man could not hear.

Marielle and Gil stood on either side of Arinth's head. They clasped hands not knowing whether to cry for joy or grief. Kyrdthin stood at Arinth's feet chanting the home spell. "Five for one. One for five." The room filled with blue mist. "Hie thee home. Home to love." A faint scent of flowers wafted into the room. Then Kyrdthin was alone. Marielle and Gil would lay Arinth to rest in Allarion. With a heavy heart he left to find Janille.

"Why did you send Willy back before I could see him," Janille wailed.

"We're not ready yet, Janie. There's a lot of work to do before Will can come into his own. We have a war to win first to assure the people they have a new king worthy of their allegiance before they spill their grief for Arinth."

"Will's only a boy, not quite fifteen," said Janille. "He can't be fighting wars."

"You always forget the time turn in Allarion, Janie. While we get ourselves organized here the kid will have grown and learned even more. I've been checking up on him every so often. He's already quite a scholar and a good swordsman, a bit small and light but quick and witty. He will make a good king. You gave him the right start."

"I hope so."

"You know you did, Little Bird, and with Gil and Rogarth on either side he will serve Arindon and the Greater Kingdom well. All he needs now is a queen."

"April, I miss her so. I suppose she is all grown up too. Hawke why did you have to take away both of my children?" she sobbed.

"It's the way of things, Janie dearest. None can change what we are. None can change what we must be."

The days that followed were dark indeed. The castle was draped in black. People spoke in whispers and cast fearful glances over their shoulders. The Delven attacks on the borders of both kingdoms became stronger and bolder. Frebar's troops fought valiantly beside their Arindian cousins. They were united at last to fight the common foe. When steel clashed with steel the tide of the battle was strong in favor of the Light, but when the loud bolts charged from the Delven machines the men of the kingdoms dropped without a prayer. Only Jareth's bowmen could fight at a safe distance. The cavalry never got close enough to charge. The bowmen picked off the dark warriors as they loaded their machines, but once the machines fired it was certain death to any in their path. Where had these machines come from? Where was the factory for this instant death? What dread world had Belar's minions plundered to bring them here? Or was it Delven Forge within their own mountains that birthed these terrors? Wearied messengers arrived at the castle gates daily with casualty counts and orders for supplies. The people grew restless. Where was the young king they had been promised?

"Now is the time to use magic," Gil insisted

"Not yet, Gil," warned Kyrdthin. "Frevaria would still rather die to the last man than fight beside a magic-wielding Allarian. The bond we are forging between Frevaria and Arindon is the strength that will win in the end."

"But they are dying out there!" Gil waved the battle reports in front of him.

"Can you prevent that with a few spells and illusions? Gil, if we use magic so will Belar. What horrors he could loose on us would make us glad he is only using cannon now."

"Cannon?"

"That's what he's hiding in the out lying farms. I've seen them on other worlds. They're mechanical things, not magic."

Gil paced Arinth's cluttered study. Kyrdthin planted his feet firmly, crossed his arms and waited.

"What can we do if we don't use magic?" Gil picked up the argument again. "Shall I call in Allarian bowmen?"

"Gil be sensible," Kyrdthin shuffled through the disarray of reports piled high on Arinth's desk. "What we need is and eye witness account not numbers."

"Then we will go," said Gil. "You and I to the front and…"

"No Gil," Kyrdthin laid a large hand on Gil's shoulder. He started to trace a calming then stopped. "You and I have roles to play here, my friend. We can't take the risk."

"Then what?" Gil moved away. Kyrdthin's hand fell to his side.

"I say we send April's mirror bird."

"So be it," agreed Gil.

Trebil was sent and they sat down to wait. Kyrdthin lit his pipe and Gil made tea. The heavy air in Arinth's study matched their moods. Gil paced. Kyrdthin stared at the smoke curling up from his pipe. Outside the storm clouds continued to gather.

The court ladies were gathered in the sun room for an afternoon of sewing. The mood was tense. Their needles stopped often when their conversation turned from embroidery stitches to the recent tragedies that shook their placid world. Marielle's small shoulders were weighed down with a black, silk sash. The ladies Cellina and Liella also wore black to mourn their brother-in-law's passing. Outside the sky was brilliant one moment then dark the next. Storm clouds boiled, threateningly then moved on. Analinne and Maralinne sat by the window apart from their elders. A quilting hoop was balanced between their knees. Elanille sat next to them with her knitting. Kylie played on the floor beside her.

"Well I just dare any Delven Dog to set foot in my chambers," Cellina was saying.

"If he is male I doubt that you'd mind a bit," said her sister without looking up from her needlework.

"Liella, my requirements are considerably higher than that," said Cellina punching her needle through her work with force. "The one I invite to bed must not only be male but a real human male. I would not settle for anything less. No offense to present company of course," she said with a nod to Marielle.

The queen met her with a cold stare. "Cellina you have spoken out of turn for the last time."

"Pardon. Your most gracious pardon," said Cellina not quite able or willing to disguise her sarcasm.

"Silence!" The rarity of Marielle's use of force silenced them all even Cellina. "You and I have both loved and hoped to gain power through our late king," Marielle continued. "We have both lost. Let this be an end to our rivalry."

Analinne and Maralinne bent over their quilting again. Kylie arranged his toy soldiers on the windowsill.

"My daddy he coulda killed all dem Delven Dogs," he declared. "My daddy coulda gone whomp, whack, whack and chopped 'em all up wift his sword, couldn't he Mommy?"

"Yes, Kylie sweet, your father was King Arinth's bravest bowman," said Elanille. "He gave his life for us at High Bridge just as our men are doing out there now."

"Yeah, my daddy he coulda chopped 'em all dead. Dirty Delven Dogs. Womp, whack, whack." Kylie made his toy soldiers push their dark-painted foes to the floor. Outside it started to rain.

It rained all afternoon. Kyrdthin and Gil waited in Arinth's study for the mirror bird's return. They shuffled papers and stacked them in different piles. They brewed tea, drank it and brewed some more but nothing really got done. At last there was a chirp and a tapping at the window. Kyrdthin unlatched the rain-spattered pane.

"Trebil wet. Trebil sad," said the little bird fluttering his feathers. "Not like story. So, so sad." Trebil flitted to Kyrdthin's shoulder to huddle between his beard and the collar of his robe.

"Now that the bird has returned we can finally know the truth of things out there," said Gil.

"Sad, sad story. Trebil so sad."

"Alright little fella. Let's hear it," said Kyrdthin.

Kyrdthin and Gil sat down and joined hands. They looked into the deep blue of each other's eyes. Their minds opened to receive Trebil's tale. A Frevarian field stretched out before them, muddy and gray beneath a stormy sky. Bodies were strewn among the corn rows. Men of both kingdoms were united in death. The view hovered over each tangled knot of lifeless forms. Tears rolled down Gil's cheeks as he recognized an Arindian bowman here or a Frevarian swordsman there. Kyrdthin's face was stony as he counted the death toll.

"Thank the gods Arinth did not live to see this day," wept Gil.

"Be thankful we have April and Will to set it right," said Kyrdthin.

Janille tried to mend a tear in the elbow of one of Kylie's little shirts but her mind kept wandering. Kyrdthin had been closeted with Gil every day for weeks and all around her the uncertainties of war hung heavy over the black-draped castle. They were leaderless. Everyone was restless and afraid. Why did Kyrdthin delay bringing Will? She gave up on her mending and laid it aside. "April," she said aloud. "How I miss April. When will Kyrdthin bring her back to me?" She was interrupted by an impatient knock on the door. "Come in," she called.

"Brought you a present, Janie."

"Oh Hawke, where have you been?" she cried hugging him.

"Shut the door before you do that," he reminded her. "Can't have the castle wondering about what's none of their business." The door snapped shut behind them. "I've been to Allarion among other places," he said kissing her cheek then releasing her.

"I thought you were with Gil," she said with an accusing tone.

"I was but then I needed to check up on the kids."

Janille's face clouded with concern.

"Calm down, Janie. They're fine. Don't you want to know what I brought you?"

"What did you bring me Uncle Hawke," she said in perfect imitation of April.

He reached under his cloak producing a bouquet of flowers. "I hope they aren't too mangled."

"Starflowers! Oh Hawke, I love you." She grabbed him with a fierce hug.

"Better get them in water right away," he said "They've had a long trip."

Janille scurried around, found an empty goblet and filled it with water. "You must want something if you are bringing me flowers."

Kyrdthin assumed a pose of mock indignation then grinned. "As a matter of fact you're right." He reached under his cloak again, this time to produce a small, plain wooden box. He flipped back the lid. Janille gasped.

"The topaz!"

"Yes, Janie. It's time you learned to use Frebar's gift."

"So much has happened I almost forgot about it,"

"Yes, that is one trick we pulled off rather nicely. Having this safe in Allarion and its duplicate never questioned here." He took out the gem and gave it to her.

The topaz, the royal gem of Frevaria lay in her trembling hands daring her to look at it. Memories came flooding back...the rings she wore as Frebar's wife and queen...the golden circlet she wore on state occasions and this topaz amulet. She remembered the dizzying power she felt when it rested on her bosom. The world had seemed richer, brighter, strangely amplified. She had not understood it then. Kyrdthin tried to warn her and protect her but there was too little time to learn its uses during those five short years. "Had I only known then," she said.

"You would have been dead and the children too."

"But I could have..."

"Innocence protected you then as knowledge will protect you now," he said. "Look into the stone, Janie. Be brave and look into the stone."

She fell, tumbling helplessly into a well of golden fire. Her skin burned. Her paralyzed hands clenched the stone. Pain danced with ice cold jabs up and down her arms. Her brain touched the swirling patterns within the crystal and recoiled. The patterns followed her, taunting her, daring her to yield, to understand the power of their logic.

Snap!

Kyrdthin was holding her. She trembled, too sick and weak to stand on her own.

"School's out for today, Little Bird," he said.

"It was awful," she groaned.

"Of course it was but you did it." He stroked her hair and kissed the top of her head.

"The pain," she groaned against his chest.

He gently set her down into a chair then poured her a glass of wine. "Here drink this."

"What's in it?"

"Now you sound like April again. What's in it Uncle Hawke" he mimicked in a squeaky voice.

Janille gave a weak little laugh. "Well you wouldn't just give me wine."

"No I laced it with a double shot of Freebane. So bottom's up like a good girl."

Janille obeyed.

"Now here's a refill. Just wine this time I promise." He handed her the glass again. "To toast our future."

Each time it got easier. With Kyrdthin's encouragement the topaz began to respond to her command. She learned to channel its power through her body. Her perception widened. Her senses intensified. The simple healing and binding spells, the calmings and forseeings she had once learned by rote now had meaning and structure. And finally she mastered the fire spell on her own. The power terrified her but knowing that now they had the weapon to fight Belar and win, gave her the courage to use it.

"Where do we go from here?" she said on day after a session with the stone.

"Now we wait for the right time and place," said Kyrdthin.

"How will we know?"

"There will be a sign."

Voices were low and subdued at Armon Beck's tavern. He served more ale and less food these days. Men just came and sat. Sometimes they talked about the war, but usually they came to escape the frightened talk in the streets. They needed to sit with familiar companions and the dulling warmth of Armon's brew. The bar and the stairs were draped with black bunting to mourn the loss of the king. The hearth fire burned bright and the sunlight streamed in through the spotless windows, but the room still seemed dark. Dell had given up trying to sing cheerful songs weeks ago. He pushed his mug aside and pulled his chair around to face the room

"Sing 'Arinth's Passing' again," said a man from the next table.

"Aye give us that one," said the man's companion.

The same song over and over, Dell thought but how else were they to deal with their fears and reconcile their loss? He twisted a tuning peg and sighed out of habit before he leaned his beloved harp against his shoulder. These men, he looked around the room at them, these men had feelings they were unable to voice. They needed his words, his melodies to unburden their hearts and fill their souls. He fingered an arpeggio and started to sing.

"Gently in the arms of friends.
He says farewell.
Eyes close, lights fade, darkness follows.

"Gently carried by friends
He makes the final journey,
To rest among flowers and stately yew.

"Gently surrounded by friends
He joins the earth
To wait for birth."

Trebil flew to the window and landed on the sill with a squawk. "Trebil scared. Dark Delven building big, bad thing. Stop good sun. Poor, poor pretty Allarion home. No more home."

Hold on little fella," said Kyrdthin stroking the little bird's breast with his finger.

"Trebil scared. Trebil sad."

They summoned Gil. While they waited for him to arrive Janille offered Trebil some honeyed bread crumbs but the little bird refused to eat. Kyrdthin poured water into a silver bowl and traced a star sign over it. When Gil came then sat down with the shining bowl in front of them.

"Tell us your story Trebil," said Kyrdthin.

"No, no. Story sad, so sad."

"Tell us now. We must know what has upset you so."

They clasped hands. The waters of the scrying bowl swirled then cleared. It was snowing. They could feel the stinging flakes. The whiteness swirled around them masking any landmarks but there was a dizzying sense of great height. The sky gradually lightened. When the vista cleared two ragged mountain peaks jutted up in front of them. Between them where only a narrow trail had once braved the pass, a fury of black smoke boiled. Delven workers swarmed over the site.

"That's East Pass! What the Hell is going on?" Kyrdthin exclaimed.

Huge engines growled and belched black exhaust. Slowly they pushed loads of snow up a zigzag incline. At the top they dumped their loads then lumbered back down to refill. A dozen or more of the engines worked in laborious precision. The dyke they were building between the peaks rose steadily. The scene shifted to a circle of bonfires. Five piles of stumps and other debris smoldered around a faint but precisely stamped out star sign in the snow, telling them how the machinery had arrived at such an isolated spot.

"A few hours on my tail," said Kyrdthin. "And those bastards pick-pocket a whole world! Moved a whole construction sight right off the interstate!"

"Off what!" said Gil.

"They build roads with those things in the place I hid Jane and the kids."

"Look!" Janille pointed to the bonfires.

The flames leaped, guttered then leaped with new vigor. Smoke churned in the center of the crude star sign. Kyrdthin began to laugh.

"What is it?" asked Gil. "What's the jest?"

"What will they send through next, Janie, the port-o-pot?" Kyrdthin burst into a full belly laugh. "The thing's a trailer, Gil. It's used as a foreman's office. See the wheels. One of the engines can pull it from place to place. It's not a jest. The ingenuity of the whole thing just amuses me."

They followed as Trebil's eye zoomed for a closer look. One of the engines detached from the parade up the mound and backed up to the newly-arrived trailer. After much deliberation, rattling of chains and growling curses the trailer was pulled to a spot out of the way of the machines. The fires leaped again. Black smoke churned and boiled. The ground shook. Then the spot cleared.

"That's Tobar!" Gil exclaimed.

Accompanied by Borat, Belar's man-at arms, Tobar stepped out of the burning star circle. All the noise of the machines clattered to halt. The workers stood watching as Tobar summoned the foreman. They picked their way through the snow to the office trailer.

"It is time," said Janille.

"Certainly it is time, but what do we do first," said Gil.

"I say we take a quick trip to Allarion," said Kyrdthin.

"All three of us," begged Janille.

"Yes, from now on we must work together. We need to summon our new king and queen."

Janille was ecstatic. She was going to Allarion. How she had wished for a glimpsed of its fabled beauty! And to see April and Will! How she had missed them! Oh to see the flowers and the birds! It was a dream come true...

"...Don't you think so, Janie?" Kyrdthin was saying.

"What?"

"What do you mean, what?"

"I'm sorry," she said. "I am just so excited about going I..."

"This is no holiday, Jane..."

"I'm sorry."

"Pay attention then," Kyrdthin said and went on. "We will meet in Arinth's arbor then..."

"But can't I see..." Janille begged.

"Yes, you can see the children and the flowers. I promise," he said pinching her cheek.

"Do you think that's wise," asked Gil.

"Just a glimpse, Gil. I won't let her interfere."

Chapter 14

Analinne stood by the window. The moon was almost full. Her face was pale and weary. She had grown thin in the past months. Her large once majestic frame was angular and awkward beneath her loose nightgown. Her bright hair looked dull in the moonlight. A silver pendant hung about her neck on a chain, Tobar's wedding gift. The tiny cluster of diamonds caught the light like a twinkling star. Baby Jasenth whimpered from his little cot in the corner.

Analinne stepped away from the window and sat down by the hearth. She looked at the empty cradle still in its place by the fire. She tried to remember all her beautiful hopes and dreams but she couldn't. Jasenth was almost two years old. He hardly knew his father. Idly she rocked the cradle with her foot. The rhythmic sound of wood on wood lulled her tired body but her thoughts refused to rest. Behind her the door banged open.

"Tobar!"

"Well, wife, who else would it be?"

"Oh Tobar, where have you been all this time?" She turned to look at him. Her foot still rocked the cradle.

"I don't have to account for my time to you or anyone else," he bellowed. Tobar lurched into the room. His hair was wild. His clothes were filthy. Mud caked his boots and his breath reeked of liquor.

"We missed you so much," she said trying to smile.

"Now did you?" He gave a loud belch.

Analinne reached into the cradle and unfolded the blanket. She whispered, "Hush, hush," to the emptiness.

"Give me my boy," Tobar demanded.

Analinne did not move.

"I want my boy," he said again louder.

Analinne stood. She positioned herself between him and the cradle. Her knees shook with fright but she willed them to hold firm. Who was this madman? Certainly he was not her gentle husband.

"I said I want my boy." Tobar lurched toward her. "Let me see my boy."

"Tobar you'll wake him with all your loud talking. Our boy is fine. Just let him sleep. It's the middle of the night."

"Get out of my way, cow." He swung to push her aside but missed.

"Let me pour you some tea, husband," she said trying to distract him.

Tobar grabbed a wine carafe from the table and gulped greedily. Wine dribbled out the corners of his mouth and down his beard .

"I wouldn't be good for our son to wake and see you so drunken," Analinne chided.

"I'm not drunk," he belched. "Not yet."

Analinne stayed between Tobar and the cradle. Every sense was alert. Her heart pounded wildly inside but her face wore a façade of pleasantness and calm. She kept her eyes away from the corner where Jasenth slept on his little cot. She prayed he would not waken.

"Would you like me to send for fresh clothes and water to bathe?" she said with an even tone.

"Aren't I good enough for you this way? Are you so accustomed to perfumed court dandies that a real man disgusts you?"

"I was just thinking of your comfort," she answered backing toward the cradle.

"Give me my boy." Tobar reeled toward her.

"No. You're too drunk."

Tobar lunged and tripped, crashing into the table. The wine carafe teetered but did not fall.

"You will not touch my son," Analinne said standing strong and tall. "You are a drunken beast. You will not touch either of us until morning when you are sober and hopefully penitent."

Tobar dropped to his knees. "Annie, Annie, please help me," he said in a small frightened voice. He kissed the hem of her gown and wept.

"Tobar?" said Analinne now more puzzled than afraid. She reached down to him.

He pounced like a wild thing, snatching her wrist and tumbling her roughly to the floor. Analinne fought. She kicked and dug her nails into his face. He tore at her clothes and pinned her to the floor with his knees. She bit at his pawing hands, twisting beneath his weight until at last she could roll free. Tobar lay in a panting heap on the floor. Baby Jasenth screamed.

Tobar jerked to his feet. He looked from the silent cradle to the corner where the wailing child sat up in his cot. Analinne froze. Tobar raised his hand to strike. "You lying royal whore!" he roared. He tried to take a step toward her but his knees buckled. He collapsed to the floor and huddled like a cornered animal. "Annie, Annie, help me," he pleaded. "I'm here…inside," he choked. "I…Lord Belar…he said he'd give the kingdoms to our son," he choked again. "It's me inside…Help me." Tobar convulsed with jerking spasms.

"Tobar, dearest husband you are ill," said Analinne with concern. "Come, let me help you to bed." She reached out a hand to help him. His face contorted. His eyes flashed then stared blank.

"Give me the boy," he said in a voice not his own. He seized her wrist.

"No!" she screamed wrenching free. She grabbed the child from the cot and backed away. He stalked her. "Tobar, where is the kind, patient man I married? Where is the man whose love gave me this child?"

Tobar took a step and another step. Analinne dodged him. "Mommy, Mommy," Baby Jasenth wailed. Around the room they danced, Tobar's lumbering countered by Analinne's darts and pirouettes. She backed past the window. The moonlight stuck the silver pendant on her breast. Tobar cried out in pain. He clutched his eyes. "You're blinding me! You witch!"

Analinne held the pendant high. On impulse she chanted the solstice ritual, "Come to the Light, in this our time of darkness. Come to the Light, as a moth to a flame." Tobar backed away, crashing into the cradle behind him. He roared a mighty oath and fell to the floor. "Come to the Light, darkness is our undoing, our desire run cold," Analinne continued to chant, "Come to the Light, there is freedom in the flame."

Tobar lay still. Analinne took one last look and fled. She ran with the wailing child bouncing on her hip, down the castle corridors, past the sleepy, puzzled guards. "My Lady?" they called after her looking for her pursuer but saw no one. She ran up the tower stairs two steps at a time. When she reached the top the door opened before she could knock.

"Come in child." Kyrdthin's voice embraced her. Analinne leaned against the doorframe panting. Kyrdthin and Janille sat by the fire drinking tea.

"Come in. Sit with us, Lady Analinne," said Janille, holding out her arms to Jasenth. The child stopped crying but was reluctant to relinquish his hold on his mother. "Come to Aunt Jane, Jayjay. Your mother is tired."

Analinne handed the boy to her. "Keep him safe," she said then collapsed into a chair. Janille carried Jasenth to the far corner of the room, whispering softly to him.

Between sobs Analinne told Krydthin her tale. "So what am I to do?" she said when she was done. "I can't live with what Tobar has become."

"First, Annie dear," said Kyrdthin putting a comforting arm around her. "First you must understand that it is not Tobar your husband that behaves like such a beast. Belar the Dark Lord has possessed him. You heard the real Tobar fighting beneath the weight of darkness."

Analinne dabbed at her eyes.

"You must also understand that Belar is stronger than Tobar. This is a battle no mortal can win and live. Your Tobar is lost."

"What can I do. Please tell me what to do," Analinne begged.

"Dear, dear Annie," Kyrdthin said as gently as he could. "What I am going to ask of you will be the hardest thing you will ever have to do."

"I don't care. I'll do anything. Anything. Just tell me what to do."

"You must lure the Dark to it's undoing," Kyrdthin began. He cupped her chin in his large hand. Analinne looked up at him. She had stopped crying. There were no more tears left to fall. "Tobar the man cannot be saved," Kyrdthin continued. "Not in this life, not ever. He is Belar's now." He stopped for a moment, then knowing he could not postpone the inevitable he went on. "I am asking you to do one ultimate act of love for your husband, Analinne. You must take his life to free him. That is the only thing that can save your son and the world we know."

"You mean...?" Analinne gasped in disbelief.

Janille began singing Jasenth's favorite nursery song as she rocked him in a chair by the window.

"Yes Annie. You must lure him to his death. The part of him that is still Tobar Prince of Frevaria and your loving husband is the only weak spot in the monster Belar has made of him," Kyrdthin carefully explained. "Belar is using Tobar to escape from his chains and wreak havoc in this world. He already controls his body. Were he to completely control his mind..." Kyrdthin stopped and shook his head. "You must stop him no matter what the cost. Belar cannot be unleashed. Not now."

Analinne sat in false calm as her world crumbled around her. Inside she shivered. The unthinkable enormity of what Kyrdthin had just said shut out all the reality she knew. She fought the invisible walls closing in on her. Her stomach twisted in agony. Then she broke. "I can't. I can't," she sobbed out of control. "I still love him, even now. What he has done was for Jasenth and me. He told me so...." She threw herself into Kyrdthin's arms.

"You do not love the beast Belar has made of him, Annie," said Kyrdthin stroking her disheveled hair.

"But I heard him inside. He needs me. He begged me."

Jasenth broke free from Janille's loving restraint. "Mommy. Mommy, don't cry."

Kyrdthin picked him up and sat him on Analinne's lap. "If you love your husband, Ann, if you love his child, then you must free him in the only way..."

"I can't. I can't," she wailed. Jasenth wailed with her.

Kyrdthin shook her by the shoulders. "Then the kingdoms are doomed. Your son is doomed. Do you want Jasenth to be the next monster lord of Belarion?"

Something inside of Analinne snapped. She floated into a sun-filled vision of the past. It was sunny the day she first met Tobar. She had gone to the library to find a book to take out into the garden. She found a book of love poems on a high, dusty shelf....Tobar's voice trembled as he read to her the day they took a picnic to the riverbank...His hand was warm seeking hers beneath the table at tea....

"Annie?" Kyrdthin's voice seemed far away.

She drifted again. The rain pattered a merry rhythm on the roof of the garden gazebo the first time they made love. She was surprised by the strength of the shy, erudite man's ardor...It was also raining on their wedding day. After that she couldn't remember if the long lonely days were sunny or rainy. Tobar was absent more and more. Sometimes the days after his homecoming were spent in idyllic bliss. But other times he was drunk and his lovemaking was rough and dispassionate. The voice that had whispered poetry became harsh and abusive. Analinne began to cry. Time shifted again. She heard Tobar's voice crying, full of pain and remorse, "Annie, Annie, help me. She heard cruel laughter behind her. When she tried to see who it was the scene changed again. It was the night of Jasenth's birth. She was alone and afraid. The pain was unimportant, only the child, the child...The midwife held the infant high. He wore a dark diadem on his brow. All around her the dark cavernous room filled with hideous laughter.

Jasenth's cries awoke her. Summoning what strength she had left she stood up. The child almost slipped from her grasp. She held him with whitened fingers, steeled by will alone. Her whole body shook. "I'll do it," she declared.

Kyrdthin eased her back into her chair.

"You are a brave woman, a good mother...and wife," said Janille embracing her.

"Yes, you made the right choice, Annie," said Kyrdthin. He gave Jasenth a pat. "Your mother loves you very much, little fella. You sit here and take care of her while I put on some more tea. We have some important plans to make."

Janille joined hands with Gil and Kyrthin for the passage. The air shimmered silver for a moment. She held on tight as the bottom dropped out of the world. A moment of bitter cold, then blue light and the scent of flowers welcomed them.

King Arinth lay in state in a grassy dale. Living garlands of flowers wove around his bier. Sighing willows alive with birdsong arched overhead. Nearby a crystal stream tumbled over sparkling stones, singing a sweet lay for the sleeping king. Arinth's hair was pale beneath his silver circlet. His still features were soft and waxen. His tunic and lacquered armor were as white as the lilies placed in his hands. His silver sword of state rested upon his breast. Beside him two Allarian bowmen kept vigil.

"The White King of the cards," said Janille taking in the scene.

"He waits until all two's become one," said one of the bowmen.

"He waits until the son and daughter of the gods bring forth children in the Light," said the other.

Gil reverently approached the bier. "Arinth my friend," he said. "I honored you in life. I honor you in death. I have come to take your sword that I may arm your son Willarinth for the battle against the Dark." He released the stiffened fingers from the hilt of the sword. He hesitated a moment. Looking lovingly at Arinth he removed his own cloak and covered him. "May my cloak forever warm and protect you as it did when you first came to Allarion."

They left the dale in peace behind them. When they had walked a respectful distance away Gil handed the sword to Kyrdthin.

"Can the kid wield this, do you think?" said Kyrdthin brandishing the weapon with an unskilled thrust and parry.

"He is strong and quick," said Gil. "But it's the fire spell he wields best as you know."

Kyrdthin laughed. "You should have seen him, Janie. He almost set all Allarion on fire but that's a story for another day."

"I don't want to know," said Janille.

"Alright," said Gil impatience rising in his voice. "We have the sword for Will. Our plans are set for full moon at East Pass."

"Agreed," they all said together.

Gil left them then, anxious to return to Arindon and Marielle. Kyrdthin turned to Janille with a mischievous twinkle in his eye.

"Now what?" she asked.

"Come let me hold you," he said reaching out his arms. There was a flash of silver. When she opened her eyes they were standing on a rocky outcropping. Above them the sky was an intense, sapphire blue. Beneath them stretched a sea of pearl-white star flowers.

"I wish you would warn me when you…" Janille began then gasped.

"I wanted it to be a surprise. Like it?"

"I never saw so many star flowers!" she exclaimed. Her head spun with the intoxicating scent. All around them bees hummed and birds sang. Nearby a stream danced merrily in a rainbow of colors. Janille stood enthralled, drinking in the beauty, luxuriating in the perfect moment. Kyrdthin waited patiently enjoying her happiness.

"There is one more thing I want to show you, Janie love," he said after a long while. "But you must promise on your most sacred oath, on your love for the children that you will do nothing to interfere."

"I promise..." she answered dreamily.

He led her into the blue moss-covered forest toward the sound of a waterfall. He stopped just as they caught a glimpse of a deep pool beneath the lacy falls. There, sporting in the misty, warm blue waters were two elfin youths. The girl was dark-haired and pale-skinned, clothed only in flowers. She jumped from mossy rock to rock, laughing and splashing her companion. The slender boy plunged into the current in playful pursuit. With strong, agile strokes he soon caught up with her and tumbled her into the pool. Their laughter rang like tinkling bells as they dunked and splashed each other. At last they climbed out onto a rock to sun themselves dry.

"Are they truly our children?" whispered Janille.

"As true as our love for them," he whispered back, his lips brushing her hair. "Look."

The boy kissed the girl. She responded eagerly. Their bodies entwined in a lover's embrace. The warmth of their passion rose and fell like the rippling stream rushing beside them, carrying away their cries and sighs.

Kyrdthin gently turned Janille away. "You have seen the beginning of the future, Janie love. Now we must go."

Before her vision blurred in silver Janille took one long, last look at the flowers and the two youths asleep in each other's arms.

The thing that was Tobar huddled against the cold stone. Deep inside a throbbing pain cried out for release while the outer husk waited oblivious to the dampness and cold. The body twitched and groaned then lay still. Armor clanked. The door opened. Feet trampled by him. Harsh voices rose and fell in the room beyond.

"Bring it to me."

"Yes, my Lord," said Borat.

The boot steps stopped beside Tobar. "Get up."

He tried to move but his aching body refused to respond.

"Get up," Borat repeated. "Lord Belar commands your presence."

Tobar struggled to obey but all he could do was roll over and collapse.

"You and you," Borat pointed to the guards. "Carry him in."

They hoisted him up, one taking his shoulders and one his legs, carried him into the audience chamber and dumped him on the floor at the foot of the dais.

"Failed again, Tobar." Belar's thumb nail rifled through his deck of cards.

Tobar did not move.

"Sit up and look at me when I am talking to you, puppet."

Tobar rolled over. He tried to raise his head but it flopped to the floor with a painful crack.

"You failed me twice, puppet. I was merciful when you could not catch a scrawny teenage boy, but this time I sent you to fetch a two-year-old infant and you crawl back blubbering and empty-handed."

Tobar retched on the marble mosaic floor.

"Useless! Disgusting! Pathetic!"

Tobar moaned.

"Shut up, you puking weakling," Belar raved. "I want the boy Willarinth. I want your bawling brat too." He pounded his fists on the arm of his chair. The guards snapped to attention. "Do I have to do it myself?"

"No, no, my Lord," Borat cautioned. "The danger...We discussed this...You know you..."

"Stand aside!" the Dark Lord commanded. Borat obeyed. Fire shot from Belar's fingertips. Tobar's body jerked and sat up. The room swirled with blood-colored smoke. When it cleared Tobar's body stood smiling. He flexed his arms and tested his legs. Belar slumped motionless on his throne. The hand of cards he had been holding fluttered to the floor.

"My Lord!" Borat gasped.

"Idiot. I had to do it this way," said Tobar's voice.

"My Lord!" said Borat again looking from one body to the other.

"Get me some clean clothes and order me a bath," said Belar with Tobar's voice. "If I must wear this foul shape I at least want it clean."

"Yes, yes, my Lord."

"And find me some armor, Frevarian ceremonial armor. I am going to a wedding and a coronation!" He laughed and laughed again.

An unseen wind stirred the fallen cards. All were face down except one. Belar did not notice the White Dragon glowing slightly before it turned.

They made camp a mile from the summit. Janille shivered in spite of the furs she wore and Kyrdthin's silver blanket. Tomorrow they would finish the ascent before dawn. She looked across the icy mountainscape to the next peak. Somewhere on that frozen, moonlit finger Will was waiting. Between them, obscured by lesser peaks was East Pass and the dyke Belar's minions had built to stay the dawn light from Allarion. Without the light the gate to that fair place would remain forever closed.

Exhausted as she was Janille could not sleep. Kyrdthin made his rounds of their campsite a second time, checking the wardings he had set to shield them. Then he curled up next to her. She tried to feel joy in having him close but fear of tomorrow loomed too ominous. Kyrdthin shifted his position but said nothing.

She must have drifted. The star patterns had turned in the sky when he woke her. They left camp taking only a light knapsack with them. Hand in mittened hand they headed toward the summit. Breakfast would be after the battle if at all. They kept to the shadows until they reached a ledge just beneath the highest point. Kyrdthin unrolled his thin silver blanket, flipping its dark underside up this time. Then they waited, huddled against a cold worse than winter. Janille felt the topaz amulet against her chest. It pulsed a restless rhythm under her cloak.

"One more battle, Janie," said Kyrdthin. His frozen breath made his beard look white in the moonlight.

"One more battle and then what," said Janille, too exhausted and scared to share his enthusiasm.

"Then we plan a wedding and a coronation."

She did not answer. Her eyes searched the opposite peak for a sign of Will but saw nothing. A faint glow was beginning to spread across the horizon.

Kyrdthin saw it too. "Are you ready?" he said giving her a reassuring squeeze.

"But what if...?"

"Don't say it, Janie. The power is ours. Your topaz here and Will's skill on the other side."

"But I'm scared."

The sky brightened. Their nerves were wound tight, ready to snap. "Janie, this is it," said Kyrdthin. They stood up, faces turned to the east. A golden streak of sun crept across the plain below inching it's way up the mountain toward them. The dyke of ice the Dark had made lay like a sore across the virgin purity of the snow. The finger of light groped for the heights unaware of the dam built to thwart it. A small dark figure on the opposite peak held a mirror to the moonlight just once but that was enough. It was the signal. Will was ready.

"Now, Janie!"

Electricity surged from their outstretched hands. The mountainside jolted alive with golden fire. Sizzling from across the gap Will's power merged with theirs above the Dark-forged dyke.

"Again, Janie. More!" Kyrdthin shouted.

Her hands throbbed. The topaz burned at her throat.

"Aim! Aim!"

The dawn light raced toward the heaving barricade. Kyrdthin stood strong behind her, supporting her hands with his own. Fused in purpose their forces leaped again matching the bolts Will hurled from the opposite side. Blood red blasts thrust up at them from the pass. They would not win easily. Will changed position. His blue fire zigzagged to strike again at the dyke then stopped.

"What the...?" Kyrdthin stopped, momentarily confused.

"Is he...?" She dare not complete to question lest her worst fears be realized.

"The moon, Janie," Kyrdthin yelled.

"What?'

"Shoot the moon! Now!"

She obeyed without understanding. The topaz power surged with blinding force, this time toward the swollen moon. Will's shot met theirs. For one brief eternity the moon tottered on a fragile tripod of light, then seemed to explode. The shattered light rained back to earth. The stone leaped from her throat, snapping its chain. With a lightening blast it hurled into the depths.

At that precise moment golden dawnlight arrived at the dark dam. Flames leaped heavenward then dissolved into a boiling fury. The mountains shook. Avalanches thundered sizzling into the flames. The pass was a seething cauldron, reverberating with hideous screams and exploding debris. The mountains shook again and again.

Finally the steaming clouds thinned and the view cleared. Had they won? The light rose pale at first then tenuous pink, then golden strong and triumphant. It arched once, twice, three times across the valley then a fourth. Weaker but still bright it angled home. Five times. Complete.

Will stepped out on a ledge. His armor caught the homing ray. The star sign blazed victorious over the valley. The blue jewel in its core rose and expanded to greet it. Allarion opened.

They descended into its welcoming embrace. Will came to them, his sword still glowing at his side. Janille rushed toward him then stopped. Was this truly her little Willy? The young man who approached them with a light but confident stride was tall and thin and darkly handsome. He arrived flushed and breathless heady with pride of his first victory.

"Hi, mom," he said breaking into the grin she knew.

Chapter 15

Gil, Kyrdthin and Marielle met in the tower study to undertake the serious task of forging the end of the age and the beginning of the next. The people had to be told that Willarinth would come to take King Arinth's place. There was also a wedding and a coronation to choreograph and one last confrontation between Light and Dark to meet.

Kyrdthin was adamant that Janille be sent back to the world where they had fostered the children so that an avenue of escape lay open if their plans went awry.

"You can't confront Belar alone, little brother," said Marielle.

"You and Gil will be helping me," said Kyrdthin.

"Marielle is not strong enough," said Gil. "Even with my help we can not do it. We need a Five."

"What about the line of prophecy, "Then shall the Three be Five?" said Kyrdthin. "You're always ready to quote the prophecy to me. Now it's my turn. With you two together, with your love..."

"Kyrdthin, you know our powers have diminished since we left Allarion. We need Janille here, not off in some other world."

"What about Jareth?" suggested Marielle.

"Jareth doesn't know who he really is or what he can do," Kyrdthin objected.

"But he will help without question."

"Alright but that still leaves us with four not five unless we have Janille," Gil still argued

Kyrdthin tamped his pipe with a jab of his thumb. He plucked a straw from the half-naked broom and held it to the fire. "How many times must we go through this?" he said holding the flaming broom straw to his pipe. He puffed and drew. Great clouds of gray smoke arose.

Marielle wrinkled her nose but Kyrdthin did not notice. She sighed and returned her attention to the issue at hand. "Three or four will not work," she said. "Even with a Five we are a poor match for Belar. We are all too old and weak. It's the end of the game. We have lost."

"Marielle, my love, don't say that!" said Gil.

"It's just the beginning," Kyrdthin insisted. "This is what we all set out to do, you and Gil and Arinth, and Jane and I. We have the kids ready and waiting. They are powers not pawns. We have set the pieces on the board. Now we must play them. The game is not done. It's just begun."

Marielle sank down into her chair like a small, blue shadow.

"I will stay by your side, my love, my queen," said Gil. "What we have sacrificed to achieve our goal will not have been in vain."

"Do you think I know nothing of love put aside in the cause of the Light?" said Kyrdthin.

"Let's summon Jareth and Janille," said Marielle. "We cannot make our final plans without them."

They brewed tea and when the pot was empty they brewed it again. This time they did not argue. Each one contributed freely with their diverse knowledge and skills. They agreed the ceremonies would take place at noon on the summer solstice, with the wedding party arriving by the main road and progressing through the town to the castle gate. There April and Will would exchange their vows with all Arindon as witness. Then they would move inside to hold court. That procession had to be planned precisely. Each player had to be in the right position for the final hour.

Kyrdthin lined up the empty teacups on the table. "OK this is April and Will." He put a cup and saucer at the head of the line. "I will be right behind them." He laid his smoldering pipe on the table. Marielle wrinkled her nose again and rolled up her eyes.

"We will have to observe protocol as well as set up our plan. Frevaria will be watching," said Janille.

"Then next must be Marielle, escorted by Gil." Kyrdthin lined up the sugar and creamer behind his pipe.

"What about the girls?" said Gil

"Ann and Mari should be next but without escorts," said Marielle. "We can't have Tobar enter too soon and Jareth, well…"

She smiled at him then at Gil. "Your time will come but not now."

"OK let the girls escort each other," said Kyrdthin. He lined up two more cups.

Janille looked at the line of objects paraded across the table. "Frevaria must follow so let Elanille walk with Frebar. Then Tobar last and alone."

"That puts the Frevarian succession out of order," noted Gil. "Tobar succeeds Frebar then Elanille."

"But a widowed princess unescorted, when her father is present?" Janille objected.

"Janie's right," Kyrdthin agreed. "That puts Tobar last just where we want him." He put one more cup and saucer in line then looked around the room for something to represent Tobar. Gil handed him a book.

When the procession plan was complete they concentrated on the ceremonies that were to follow. Even with the game pieces in place they still had only four sources of power. To compensate they strategically placed Gil and Marielle to the left of the thrones with Kyrdthin and Jareth to the right. It was hard to keep their minds on the task at hand. All of them were worried about Tobar. He had arrived unexpectedly at the castle that morning just before breakfast. He was finely groomed and dressed. His demeanor was warm and light-hearted. His speech was courteous. He brought gifts for his wife and son. Analinne received him lovingly. Would her resolve hold strong enough to carry out their plan? There were too many questions, too many weak links in the chain of events that had to take place.

"What about the little ones? Will Kylie and Lizzie be safe?" Janille worried aloud.

"We will put them, and Jasenth too, with their royal aunties." Kyrdthin chuckled then added. "I just dare Belar cross Cellina. That tongue of hers would scorch even our wayward brother."

Marielle's smiled her agreement.

Jareth entered the conversation. "Be assured, Janille my bowmen will back them up on that side and Rogarth's castle guard on the opposite side."

"There is one more card we could play," said Gil looking first at Jareth then at the others.

Kyrdthin raised his eyebrows. "Who?"

"Dell."

"Of course Dell and his musicians will be there but how will that help?" said Jareth.

Gil's eyes darted again from Kyrdthin to Marielle. "That harp of his is also a powerful tongue for the Light. Let's put him near Jareth and the children."

Marielle nodded.

The table was now a clutter of teacups and books and silverware but the pattern was clear.

"What if the Dark is too strong? What if something goes wrong?" said Janille. "There is too much risk involved."

"There is risk in all we do, Janie. Yes, if things go wrong we could all die. The Light would fail and our world would end. If we don't try, if we don't take the risk, failure is a given. We will try and we will win." Kyrdthin laid a heavy hand on the table. The teacup procession jumped.

"What about Lizzie?" said Marielle with sudden inspiration. "Could we train her somehow to help?"

"Absolutely no!" said Kyrdthin. "We need a power we can control."

"Even if she thought it a game?"

"No! End of discussion."

"Marielle does have a point," said Gil. "If we could tap her power…"

"Then so could Belar."

"So be it then," said Gil. "Our plan is imperfect but it is all we have."

With that decided the meeting adjourned. Jareth left and Marielle soon followed with Gil soon. Janille sat beside Kyrdthin in silence. Tears welled in her eyes. She bit her lips to keep them from trembling. Finally she could no longer stay the flood. Tears spilled down her cheeks.

"What is it Little Bird?" Kyrdthin said tenderly dabbing her eyes with the hem of his sleeve.

"I will go to my daughter's wedding, Hawke. You can't deny me," she sobbed.

"And leave the gate unguarded?"

"Hawke, please."

"It is the only way, Janie dearest. You said yourself the plan has risk. Any one of us could fail at any point. Only you can pull the children through if there is a need. You would endanger them and all the world we know if you were anywhere else."

She sniffled and looked at the floor.

"Janie, love."

"Alright," she said without looking up. "What must I do?"

"Just what you have always done for me, Janie. Wait until the time comes."

"And when it does?" she asked turning up her pleading, tear streaked face.

"Your home spell is strong enough to draw anyone you love through. That is one spell you are much practiced in using." He teased her with a kiss. "It must be the children, not me if I have to make a choice. Do you understand?"

"Yes, but what will happen to you?"

"Janie, if I must send them I will have to seal the gate."

"Don't say that, Hawke. I'd never see you again!" She pulled away from him. Desperation warred with terror in her eyes. "We have faced so much danger, so often together but this time I know, this time I feel is horribly different. Belar is too strong for us. Can't we just take the children through now, seal the gate behind us and live there, just the four of us, like we always wanted to?'

"And lose everything we worked for? Janie some choices are already made for us. We are but tools to set the balance of Light and Dark in this age. You and I are not free to live and love as others do."

"After it's all over, then what?" Janille's eyes still pleaded.

"After it's over, Janie, after the battles and the crowning, after the Light has no more need of us…"

"Yes, Hawke, then what?"

"Then , my dearest Little Bird, then I will fly home to you."

She reached up to embrace him.

"Not yet," he said catching her hands. "There is still much to be done before our lives are our own."

She pulled away, hurt and angry. Her arms dropped to her side.

"Sleep lightly if you sleep at all that night. The moon will be full in your world. It will balance the noon sun here and that is good. Wait for me, Janie. Wait as you always have."

"Yes. Hawke," she said sullenly.

"Not, yes Hawke. Say yes for yourself this time. You are a powerful woman Jane. I need your strength. Now say it right."

"Yes, Hawke…I mean yes…for whatever."

"If I need you I will call."

He held her longer than usual. Then he was gone.

"Take one last look, kids," said Kyrdthin as their little party climbed to the pass. They dismounted to let their horses rest. Allarion lay beneath them, a pristine sea of beauty in a chalice of snowy peaks. Blue mist ebbed across the valley. They stood silent, each with his own thoughts. Gil wept. Kyrdthin reached out to comfort him but Gil drew away. "Are you ready?" Kyrdthin said as gently as he could.

"I can't do it, said Gil. "You have to do it for me. Please, friend."

In a voice filled with both joy and sadness Kyrdthin began the chant.

"Bright as the Moon, blue as the sky,
On the wings of the morning, away you fly...

He opened his arms. The sapphire mists moved.

"Fly away sapphire, jewel of the night,
Fly away north in the morning light...

Slowly the mists swirled, circling contracting.

"Rest in the depths of the icy sea.
Till the Stars fall and set you free."

The mists lifted, floating upward carrying with it the glittering jewel that was Allarion. Colors swam on its surface, colors of flowers and trees and all living things. Music tinkled as the sapphire rose trailing songs of birds and rushing streams. It floated higher and higher. Like a giant, blue soap bubble it rode the wind northward out of sight.

"Come on kids. There is one more thing we must do so your hearts will be free of Allarion."

"Why Uncle Hawke?" said April.

"After all this time you still call me that?"

"OK then Kyrdthin."

"Correct your Highness Princess Avrille." He affected a bow.

"Don't be silly, I will always be your April."

"Not after today. Perhaps not ever again," Kyrdthin replied with deep sadness. "Come here both of you. The memories you two have of Allarion will interfere with the life that lies before you."

"Won't we remember anything?" asked Will.

"You will remember," said Gil as he tried to put his own memories and regrets aside. Things will just seem faraway, less important."

"Like a dream?" said April

"Let's stop talking and just do it," said Will. "Then tell me how soon I will be king."

Kyrdthin began the song. Gil lifted his flute-like tenor to join him.

"All that was before be gone
Lost in blue Allarion.
Now is all you need to know…"

Gil's weeping drowned out the closing words. Kyrdthin took him by the shoulders and turned him away. They rode down the other side of the pass. They spoke very little making the trip seem long. April and Will were both anxious and frightened of what lay ahead for them. Gil kept to himself, wrapped in his own grief. Kyrdthin tried to lighten their spirits with humor without much success. The trail wound down the mountainside and across the river at High Bridge. At last they arrived in Frevaria.

Janille paced the ornately appointed room in the Frevarian women's quarters. Sixteen years! It had been sixteen long eventful years since she had fled this place with infant April. She was queen then, wife to a rigid, superstitious but basically good man. King Frebar tried to protect himself and his people from magic because he feared what he did not understand. The castle held many memories, some joyful, some filled with regrets but mostly drab, uneventful days marked her five years as Frebar's queen. She drew her dark shawl tighter over her peasant's dress.

She was grateful that no one had recognized her. Kyrdthin told everyone that she was a serving woman from the house where Princess Avrille was fostered, and that her majesty wanted her childhood nurse to be honored with dressing her on her wedding day. Janille's heart beat through the entire gamut of emotions. She felt fear of recognition, nostalgia for her former life and what might have been, and fear of losing her children today, perhaps forever. She was angry, no bitter was the word, that she would have to miss the festivities, waiting in an alien world not knowing the outcome of their plans, not being able to help until it was too late. Why? Why did Hawke...? But she knew why and that was what she feared the most.

She looked at April's wedding dress spread out on the divan. The under dress was a delicate, blue Allarian silk, Marielle's gift to her new daughter-in-law. The bodice and over skirts were heavy, gilt Frevarian brocade. She ran her fingers along the shoulders of the bodice. Little clasps were discreetly sewn inside. The star flowers to be attached to the dress were in a vase on the table. Tears welled in her eyes. She had insisted on the star flowers. She let her thoughts drift back to her own wedding day. She again felt the fear and loneliness and confusion of her childhood being severed from her before she knew what adulthood meant. She remembered standing helpless as the dour matrons dressed her in gold and blue satin. Then the bouquet of star flowers arrived, a gift from Kyrdthin, her treasured, secret friend.

Trumpets! She rushed to the window. Four horses approached the gate. She recognized Kyrdthin's gray cloak fluttering behind him as he took the lead. Gil rode behind him and then April and Will nodding and waving to the crowd lining the streets. Will rode straight and tall with regal pride. And April, was this beautiful young woman with dark loosely flowing hair really her daughter?

The next hour raced by. Janille helped April bathe and dress and arrange her hair. She braided the thick tresses with strands of pearls and wound them about April's head like a crown. When she finished she took the star flowers one by one from the vase and clipped them to the dress. With a final pull at the bodice laces she stepped back so April could see herself in the mirror. April stood speechless, not recognizing the woman she had become.

"You look like a queen," Janille said with a mother's pride.

Too soon the knock came to the door. "All is ready and waiting for Your Highness."

"In a moment," called April with a new ring of authority in her tone.

Footsteps moved away from the door.

"Can I really do this, mother?" said April her voice changing to a thin quiver.

"You can, daughter. This is what you were born for." Janille gave April a fierce hug, almost crushing the delicate star flowers on her dress. Then she pulled back. "Now go before I start crying again."

She brushed a quick kiss on April's cheek and opened the door. Princess Avrille was whisked away into a fanfare of trumpets and thundering cheers. Janille could not bring herself to watch out the window as the procession started on its way to Arindon. Sadly she took five candles from the box beneath the wall sconce. She placed them in a circle on the floor and lit them one by one, stepped inside the star sign and held her breath.

The people lined the road the entire ten miles from Frevaria to Arindon. The young king and queen rode side by side. Sometimes they waved and smiled at the crowd. Sometimes they reached between their mounts to hold hands. Kyrdthin and Gil rode unobtrusively on guard behind them. When they neared Arindon the noise of the crowd was almost deafening. Every building was draped with ribbons and banners. The streets were literally paved with flowers. The people pressed into the square in front of the castle gate as the royal wedding party dismounted and ascended the gate house stairs.

When they emerged on top of the wall the cheers swelled in a joyous crescendo. Kyrdthin raised his arms for silence. When the ocean of people quieted to an excited murmur he began to chant the prophecy.

"When the Sun and Moon,
Shine double in the sky.
Then shall the cask be opened..."

He lay back the lid of an ancient leather box and took out the crowns. He held them high then placed Frevaria's gold on April's head and Arindon's silver on Will. The twin diadems blazed bright in the noonday sun.

The new king and queen looked into each other's eyes. Will took April's hands.

"Be my queen, April," he said.

"My kingdom is yours, Willy," she answered.

Will blushed as he kissed her amid the thunder of well wishes and cheers. Together with Kyrdthin they turned to enter the castle to hold their first court.

The trumpets heralded their arrival in the great hall. King Willarinth and Queen Avrille entered in unabashed splendor. She was radiant, like an exotic Allarian blossom. He was straight and strong like a newly-forged sword. They walked hand in hand, moving with the elegant precision the solemnity of the occasion required but their youthful excitement could not be hidden. Their faces beamed triumphant with a mix of newly-gained maturity and childish delight. The assembled court bowed in rippling waves as their new sovereigns passed.

The balconies and stairs were garlanded with flowers. The crystal chandelier blazed with lights. Two thrones were set side by side on the dais. Above each, carved into the rich wood, rose half a rainbow arch. The king and queen took their seats. The royal guard stood at attention, ready. The center of the room was open, waiting. The star mosaic on the polished floor mirrored the light above.

Dell nodded to the musicians then took up his harp. His clear tenor floated above the excited buzz of voices in the hall.

> "Banished children of the Light,
> United here their troth to plight,
> On snow white steeds they pass the throngs,
> Wreathed with flowers and joyous songs…"

The room hushed. The air vibrated with the magic of harp strings and flute. The chandelier sparkled in a rainbow duet of flame and sunlight.

> "One crown of silver, one of gold,
> One star risen to behold.

Come bend a knee and homage declare,
To the Children of Light
Our Majestic Pair."

Queen Marielle escorted by Gil was the first to kneel. Willarinth received her with a kiss and called her "Mother" before all. To Gil he said, "Be ever at my side as counselor and friend."

The Princesses Analinne and Maralinne came next. Their speeches were eloquent but simple. Willarinth recognized them as sisters and Avrille bid them attend her as ladies in waiting then added, "To sit with me as my equals and friends." The princesses bowed then turned to the side where the Ladies Cellina and Liella waited with the royal children.

The heralds announced, "King Frebar of Frevaria." With unprecedented humility Frebar walked toward the dais with Princess Elanille on his arm. He wore gold ceremonial mail and a blue velvet cloak, dashing in any other setting but today his demeanor was subdued. He nodded his head to Willarinth then knelt at Avrille's feet. "I pray Your Majesty grant me but one favor," he said.

"Speak it," said Avrille with a note of surprise.

"That I may call you daughter."

Avrille reached out her hands. "Rise father. Our kingdoms are one," she said. Then to Elanille, "Dearest sister, finally I may call you so, share my joy today and always."

The trumpets sounded one more time and the herald announced. "Prince Tobar of Frevaria, consort to the Princess Analinne of Arindon."

Tobar swaggered in. The court stood gaping as he made his way toward the dais twirling his dagger and singing a bawdy tune. He stopped just short of the star mosaic on the floor. His eyes swept the room until they lighted on Analinne. "Hey Annie." He gestured with the dagger. "Aren't you going to say hello to your husband?"

Princess Analinne rose from her chair. Jasenth squirmed in her arms. Her hair and her eyes raged with the same fire. She advanced just to the opposite edge of the star mosaic from Tobar then stopped. "Tobar, you have gone too far." Her voice was low and steady. "I have stood by you as a wife. I have loved you and bore you this son. Though I knew you were wrong I have defended you loyally. I closed my eyes when you plotted to murder innocent children and wage holy war in the name of our son, but no more. Tobar, this time you have gone too far."

Analinne advanced. Tobar stood like a blackened stump buttressed against a raging forest fire. He held his ground but his eyes darted warily about the room. His hand flexed on the hilt of his dagger. He took a step forward onto the star pattern on the floor. Analinne shifted the child to her hip. She took a step, joining him in the arena. She drew in a quick breath and lunged, drawing a dagger from beneath her gown.

"Die Tobar! I release you. I love you. I love you!"

The child screamed. Clasped in one last human embrace Analinne and Tobar fell dead, each impaled on the other's blade. Darkness and Light cancelled each other's power once again.

The room was paralyzed with shock. Only Maralinne thought to rush out to untangle baby Jasenth from the bodies of his parents. Cradling his head against her breast she hushed his sobs and returned to her place beside Jareth.

Kyrdthin watched and waited from his place beside the thrones. Loosed from Tobar's corpse the formless Darkness seethed within the confines of the star sign on the floor. It slithered over the bodies of its victims searching for a weak spot. Kyrdthin stepped down from the dais and raised his hands. He hurled the first electric bolt. The Darkness reared up taking shape, half dragon, half human, a blackness veined with bloody red. Kyrdthin hurled a second bolt and a third. "Not this time, vengeful brother. Today is not the day to redress old wrongs."

The Darkness retaliated. The center of the star sign burst into flame. All that had been Tobar and Analinne was seared to ash. The Black Dragon roared inside the star sign barrier, breathing flame. His man-like body swelled. Ruby fire danced inside his transparent skin.

"You have lost, Belar," Kyrdthin shouted hurling another electric bolt. The closest star on the mosaic floor burst into flame. "The Children of Light are wed and crowned." A white column leaped up from the burning star. The chandelier rocked dangerously above.

That was the signal. Marielle and Gil aimed their combined strength at two more stars on the floor. Fragile pillars, one blue and one red, rose toward the light. Marielle's arms trembled but Gil held her steady. The blue veins in her moon-pale skin bulged with the strain. The Black Dragon writhed and fumed. The jewelled pillars wavered momentarily then held.

Dell's harp came alive. The strings vibrated with the thunder of the angry sea. The sound roared and rolled toward the weakening star sign. Behind him Jareth stood with drawn bow. His bowstring sang in sympathy with Dell's throbbing harp, weaving above and below the powerful drone. Another star ignited on the floor. A wave of emerald splashed up. Pale green droplets swirled then solidified. The flaming Black Dragon regarded the column briefly then darted for the fifth still unignited star.

"No you don't Belar!" Kyrdthin shouted.

The Dragon roared, belching flame.

Kyrdthin redoubled his efforts. The white column rose higher. The chandelier came alive. Flames jetted from the candlesticks fueling the three lesser columns rising beneath it. The fifth star shimmered faintly then began to glow. Time stopped. Kyrdthin's body expanded. White flame coursed through his veins and danced over his skin. Belar's body convulsed. His enormous wings flailed. He butted against the weaker columns like a caged beast. The ruby column flickered wildly. The sound of the bow and harp strings changed pitch and the emerald column sang. The color of the sky pillar deepened to midnight blue. Belar hurled himself, talons unsheathed and clawing at the weak glow of the fifth star.

From somewhere a child's voice screamed. "Bad, bad dragon. Go home." Lizelle's little arms reached toward the flaming chandelier. The room exploded with golden light. The fifth column rose triumphant. The star sign blazed complete in the center of the time stilled room. "Lookee, lookee, Mommy. Look at the pretty Lizzie made," she cried. The room echoed with childish laughter as a thousand rainbows sprang from the rocking chandelier and skittered across the walls

The enraged Dragon thrashed inside its flaming cage with malevolent fury. The earth shook and cracked. The chandelier swung like a pendulum. The jeweled columns danced. Kyrdthin fought desperately to hold the pattern. The floor buckled and bulged then split. Belar tried to rise but his gigantic wings dissolved into smoke. His form writhed and changed into a grotesque not-quite-human shape. "Vengence! I will have vengence!" he bellowed. A swirling vortex opened beneath him sucking Belar back to the depths of his prison.

Kyrdthin's outstretched arms gave one last surge of lightening to seal the gate but his strength gave way. The dazzling columns collapsed. The chandelier crashed to the floor. Kyrdthin toppled and fell headlong into the gaping abyss after Belar. "Janie! Janie!" he screamed, his arms flailing in spurts of flame. "Janie, pull me through!"

"Janie! Janie!"

Janille woke with a start. Had she really heard him or was it just the dream she feared?

"Janie!" So faint, so weak, but it was Kyrdthin. What had gone wrong?

Her bare feet hit the floor. She ran outside, grabbed the broom from the porch and swept a quick star sign in the stones of the driveway. The marks glowed feebly in the moonlight. She knelt at the edge groping, trying to embrace the flickering gray mist inside. "Hawke, Hawke where are you? Home, my love home," she frantically called. She reached farther into the cold, churning mist. Frail hands touched hers. She grabbed and pulled with all her might, chanting the home spell. "Five for One. One for Five." Gasping for breath she fought the dark maelstrom. "Hie thee home. Hawke come to me. Hawke!"

The hands slipped away. She plunged in after them. "Home to Love," she concluded the spell. She felt the hands again and grabbed tight. This time they held. With one final pull Kyrdthin's gaunt form wrenched free. He toppled over her shoulder, tumbling them both to the sharp stones of the driveway.

Heedless of her own pain Janille slid out from under him. She cradled him gently in her lap. She kissed his pale hollow cheeks. She stroked his forehead. His eyes were clouded with pain and tears. "You're burning with fever!" she cried.

"I'm so cold inside."

"Let me help you to the house."

"No let me finish it here," he said. His wild hair was whitened. His voice was parched. His breath came in rattling gasps. "Janie, Janie dearest, forgive what I did to you...I hoped...for what could never be..."

"Don't talk, Hawke. Save your strength."

"No matter now. I've spent it all...for you Janie...and for our April. Dearest Little Bird, how I have loved you, loved you always..."

He reached up to her. The lover's kiss so long awaited was weak and full of pain. She laid him back into her lap. His eyes closed then fluttered open again, bright blue jewels set in a waxen face. They were no longer saddened. A faint but glowing triumph reflected in them. "This time," he rasped just above a whisper. "This time, Janie love, I am home to stay."

With calm acceptance she held him until the moon set and the awful cold separated them once again.

Appendix I

Characters

Kyrdthin (Kurd thin), Hawke
: Magician

Janille (Jan eel), Janie, Aunt Jane
: Former wife and queen of Frebar. Mother of April and Elanille. Foster mother of Will.

Avrille (Av reel), April
: Princess of Frevaria. Daughter of Janille

Willarinth (Will ar inth), Will, Willy
: Prince of Arindon. Son of Arinth and Marielle.

Analinne (An a lin), Ann, Annie
: Princess of Arindon. Wife of Tobar. Twin sister of Maralinne. Daughter of Arinth and the late queen Veralinne

Maralinne (Mar a lin), Mari
: Princess of Arindon. Twin sister of Analinne. Daughter of Arinth and Veralinne.

Elanille (El an eel), Elani
: Princess of Frevaria. Daughter of Janille and Frebar.

Marielle (Mar ee el)
: Queen of Arindon and Allarion. Mother of Will.

Arinth (Ar inth)
: King of Arindon. Father of Analinne, Maralinne and Will.

Gil (Gil)
: Consort of Marielle in Allarion. Advisor to Arinth in Arindon.

Lady Cellina (Sel in ah), Celli
: Spinster sister of the late queen Veralinne of Arindon. Twin to Liella.

Lady Liella (Lee el ah)
: Spinster sister of the late queen Veralinne of Arindon. Twin to Cellina.

Belar (Bay lar)
: Dark Lord of Bellarion.

Borat (Bor at)
: Servant to Belar

Frebar (Fray bar)
: King of Frevaria. Former husband of Janille. Twin brother of Tobar.

Tobar (Toe bar)
: Prince of Frevaria. Husband of Analinne. Twin brother of Frebar.

Jareth (Jar eth)
: Gamekeeper of Arindon wood. Advisor to Arinth.

Rogarth (Roe garth)
: Captain of the king's guard in Arindon. Betrothed to Maralinne.

Keilen..(Ki len)
: Chief bowman of Arindon. Husband of Elanille.

Kylie (Ki lee), Young Keilen
: Son of Keilen and Elanille.

Lizelle (Liz el), Lizzie
: Daughter of Keilen and Elanille.

Jasenth (Jay senth), Jayjay
: Son of Tobar and Analinne.

Mabry (Mab ree)
: Miller of Arindon.

Darilla (Dar il ah)
: Daughter of Mabry

Armon Beck (Ar mon)
: Innkeeper of Arindon

Dell (Del)
: Bard.

The Watcher
: Guardian of the caves

Spida (Spy dah)
: Man-beast inhabitant of the caves

Appendix I

The Cards

The House of Light
    White King, White Queen, White Dragon, White Knight, White Fortress

The House of Darkness
    Black King, Black Queen, Black Dragon, Black Knight, Black Fortress

The Gifts of the Gods
    Beauty, Wisdom, Strength, Honor, Compassion

The Abodes of the Gods
    Sun, Moon, Star, Rainbow, Fountain

The Elements of Creation
    Fire, Water, Air, Earth, Time